Come to the War

Leslie Thomas was born in South Wales in 1931 and when his parents died he and his younger brother were brought up in an orphanage. His first book, *This Time Next Week*, is the autobiography of a happy orphan. Aged sixteen, he became a reporter on a weekly newspaper in Essex and then did his National Service in Malaya during the Communist bandit war. *The Virgin Soldiers* tells of these days; it was an immediate bestseller and has been made into a film with Lynn Redgrave and Hywel Bennett.

Returning to civilian life, Leslie Thomas joined the staff of the *Evening News*, becoming a top feature writer and travelling a great deal. His second novel, *Orange Wednesday*, was published in 1967. For nine months during 1967 he travelled around ten islands off the coast of Britain, the result of which was a lyrical travelogue, *Some Lovely Islands*, from which the BBC did a television series. Now a director of a London publishing house, he has continued to travel a great deal and has also written several television plays. His hobbies include golf, antiques and Queen's Park Rangers Football Club.

His other books include *Bare Nell*, *His Lordship*, *Onward Virgin Soldiers*, *Arthur McCann and All His Women*, *The Man with the Power*, *Tropic of Ruislip* and *Stand Up Virgin Soldiers*, all available in Pan.

Also by Leslie Thomas
in Pan Books

The Virgin Soldiers
Onward Virgin Soldiers
Stand Up Virgin Soldiers
Orange Wednesday
The Love Beach
His Lordship
Arthur McCann and All His Women
The Man with the Power
Dangerous Davies: The Last Detective
Tropic of Ruislip
Ormerod's Landing
That Old Gang of Mine

This Time Next Week
Some Lovely Islands

Leslie Thomas

Come to the War

Pan Books London and Sydney

First published 1969 by Michael Joseph Ltd
This edition published 1971 by Pan Books Ltd,
Cavaye Place, London SW10 9PG
10th printing 1982
© Leslie Thomas 1969
ISBN 0 330 02741 7

Printed and bound in Great Britain by
Hazell Watson & Viney Ltd, Aylesbury, Bucks

For Diana

Jerusalem sits on its hills, its houses the colour of old sunlight, its television aerials reaching up like ten thousand thin arms.

The city raises its head so high that you would think it looked over the entire world instead of a few bald hills. That is how it always was. That is why they *all* think it is so special.

1

It can get cold in Jerusalem in mid-winter. Much colder than you would think. It is a high city and it has sleet and heavy snowfalls at times. I have watched the Judean Hills vanish behind a flying storm and seen the Mount of Olives choked with snow. In the morning there would be bitter mounds of slush in Jaffa Road where Shoshana and I lived that winter.

At that season the brown of her body would fade to fawn and her breasts and small backside would not seem so white against the rest of her. She was a summer woman. The winter and the cold seemed to diminish her.

I remember when she first came to London to see me. I found her, on one February midday, at the middle of a small crowd of worried people in Waterloo Road. They were hunched around her and she was crying with the cold. I came out of the Festival Hall, where I had gone to retrieve some of my music, and I saw the people and spotted Shoshana's bright Israeli shopping basket on the pavement. I thought there had been an accident and ran, only to find London housewives clucking over her and an energetic middle-aged man actually rubbing her with his hands; to restore the circulation, he said.

She had a gift for releasing sympathy in people. The women bitterly blamed me for permitting her to be cold, just as though she were working the streets for me. 'Poor little thing,' they muttered as I took her towards a taxi with my arm around her small, lovely waist. They should have seen her throw a hand grenade.

In those first days in London when she was writing articles for her newspaper in Tel Aviv, including an uncomfortably truthful one about me, I don't think we did more than exchange two or three friendly kisses.

9

It was when I was sleeping with her in Jerusalem after the short war, and the summer and autumn went, that I realized the effect that the cold and winter had upon her. In the summer heat she was like a wet animal in bed, slithering and sliding as she sweated in lovemaking, and the city would be full of dry, night dust drifting into the room, clogging eyes and nostrils and adhering to sweat. She would stop loving me, at last, at about three in the morning and I would lie and let myself cool, watching the dim ceiling of the room which was like the curving, inside roof of a tomb. Then, when I was drifting into sleep, cooled and aching, she would put her hands down into my groin, work them under, and around as though she were washing them. Then we would start again. I had to sleep half the day while she was out. My performance went entirely to pieces that summer.

Not that I was playing at all. My concert programme in Europe that autumn had to be abandoned. There was a rumour that I had been killed or badly injured in the war in Jerusalem and something to this effect appeared in the papers. My agent denied it but I didn't care anyway. Philip John, my agent, and my manager, Eric Forth, sent me letters and cables, threats and promises, eventually both flying out to Israel. They went back and told people in Europe that their famous pianist was ill. I was not. I was in bed with Shoshana.

Philip and Eric actually arrived at our house in Jaffa Road in late September and stood at the bottom of the big knobbly bed while Shoshana and I sat in it, naked, with the damp sheet primly pulled up around us. They observed the hero, the idol, of the Festival Hall, the Lincoln Centre and the European concert circuit squatting nude in a dust-hung, stone bedroom in Jerusalem. They told me I was mad, which I was, and that they would sue me if they didn't kill me first. But I told them to go back to London and because they are reasonable men, friends too, and because they could see I was not going to get out of bed anyway, they went. They actually wanted to have me examined by a psychiatrist because they had some strange theory that getting my

10

kidneys full of sand from the Negev had somehow loosened my brain. A year later I went to a psychiatrist in Boston and he told me that he thought this could be true. Having sand in your kidneys could make you a trifle strange. I think it was merely being in bed with Shoshana.

In the winter she was different. She seemed to shrink and would have our bed piled with blankets and coats and dressing-gowns and even some curtains her mother had given her. She hibernated beneath this pile, hardly getting up even to make any food. When I wanted her for love I used to have to burrow down and find her. She seemed smaller in my arms in winter and she didn't fight and want to get her mouth to me or anything. I had to take her and do it gently while she lay and then leave her to sleep in the great piled bed. I only realized that spring was coming because she abruptly bit me on the leg one Sunday morning.

Today, long after, here in London, I thought about Jerusalem because I think about it almost every day. I remembered the cold of the winter there especially this morning because as I was walking through Cannon Street at seven o'clock there was a cutting edge of snow on the wind. Early people were moving with that low, doubled-up trudge of the dawn risers, yellow oblongs of light were in office buildings where cleaning women worked and the streets belonged to the crouching bicycle pedallers.

I leave Faith's flat early because her landlady does not like anyone being there all night. God knows why Faith has to live in the City. But she's always been there and she makes a good breakfast even though it's so early. She's very wifely. Her place is in Upper Thames Street which I like because from her bed you can hear the grunting of the ships on the hollow river. Faith is a nice, short, unusual girl, a librarian at the John Colne Music Library. We met about six months ago. When I stay at her flat she gets up with the alarm clock at five-thirty and does the breakfast; then I go up to Cannon Street and get the bus.

Nowadays I invariably get the bus because it's more private than a taxi. People waiting to go over the road at traffic lights and crossings always stare or glare into the back

11

of a taxi. On a bus nobody cares about you even if they're sitting immediately next to you. Quite a lot of people recognize me because they've seen my face in the papers or on the television, and some of them from the concerts. I've had a scrap of paper thrust through a taxi window at a December daybreak and scribbled my autograph while the half-hostile, frozen face was wondering what the hell I was doing out at that hour. Perhaps he thought I had a spare-time job at the docks.

Modesty has not been one of my noticeable features although I've been better recently (one critic said only last week that Christopher Hollings 'i smaturing') but in the early morning I don't want people. I sit downstairs on the left hand of the bus, so that if I'm due to do a concert at the Albert Hall I can see how many posters they've displayed outside and how big they've made 'Christopher Hollings'. They always make it very big but you need to watch these things. I'm doing the Rachmaninov Number Three there next week with the London Symphony. Even if I'm not performing I like to see who they've got working that week.

I really would get this bloody hair cut off if I could. But Philip and Eric agree that I'd be finished in a year without the image. It is as important as technique. When the fighting in Jerusalem was going on and when we were coming up through the Negev and the Egyptian jets caught us, my hair was about the only thing Shoshana, Zoo Baby and the others could laugh about. I remember on that blind corner, just by the Garden of Gethsemane, when the five Jewish boys were killed in about two square yards, how Zoo Baby kept yelling to me to keep my hair down. Not my head, my hair.

What a man, that Zoo Baby. Six feet three, and bulging all over with great puddings of fat. Right in the middle of it all, when it was at its dustiest and bloodiest, with dead men suspended across the walls of Jerusalem and children howling in the alleys, he got very sweaty and blamed the tightness of the Army trousers up his crutch. His name was Zacharia Berensohn, and he was the timpanist with the Israel Sym-

12

phony Orchestra. In the Sinai Campaign at the time of Suez he was a tank section leader – he was thinner then – and his radio call name was ZB or Zoo Baby. It was right for him. He had a big squashed face, marvellous eyes and was great and gentle. If you had seen him in the zoo you would have given him a bun.

Then there was Dov, the quiet Dov with the fine moustache and the dark face. Walking studiously through the war and the close death, compassionate and wise, one of the few who did not hate. When they took the Wailing Wall that morning he said a short prayer then went to look at the big mosque and the Via Dolorosa.

And O'Sullivan, who, like me, should never have been there at all. Only an Irishman could explain how an Irishman became an Israeli border guard. He was as thin and dry as a Negev river bed, going through the days of battle with charm and an Uzzi sub-machine-gun.

Yes, I'd have all this hair off if I could. I'm thirty-six now and it gets heavy. But Eric babbles about the damage it would do me professionally and he consoles himself artistically by saying that Chopin had long hair. In his heart, I don't think he embraces this pop-idol charade very closely because he has seen some of the finest in his time. Philip too. But we are successful. So the hair stays. Let it get in my eyes.

I got off the bus at Robin Hood Vale this morning and walked away from the roads and the people going to work. I made across the open common towards my place. The snow became more definite, I tugged up my collar and pushed against the wind. It was very solitary, although I did see a girl on a horse as I got towards the block of flats where I now live. The ponds on the common were blank and grey, gathering in the snowflakes and quietly destroying them. But the rough grass and the poor winter trees were taking the snow and keeping it.

You become more aware of animals in the snow, I suppose, because it neutralizes the background and shows them up more. If you are walking across a short desolate place like the common and you see cats or dogs, or even something wild like a rabbit, they seem like companion travellers on a journey, and you gladly leave your tracks beside theirs.

There did not seem to be much going on among the birds, but I could hear them making occasional remarks in the black bones of trees. It was a good walk because I woke up after almost dozing off on the bus, and I wanted to keep awake today because I thought I would start writing this.

When I came in out of the snow, into the foyer of the flats, there were two men waiting by the lift holding up a big mirror, full-length and the same width, done around with some curved carving. They were delivering it to somebody and I thought it surprising how early some people get things delivered. As I walked in the men were both the opposite side of the mirror, holding it up, waiting for the lift, and only their thick delivery men's fingers were showing around the edges. I saw myself come through the door, shake off some of the snow, and walk towards my reflection. The men didn't see me. They were talking and hidden behind their burden.

I strode up to the mirror and stopped in front of myself. As I said I'm thirty-six, but Eric has always told the papers and magazines, and it's written into my biographical handout, that I am thirty-one and nobody has argued. Under this hair you can lose five years without trouble.

It is not easy to examine yourself as you might examine a stranger. But I stood looking over myself. The men were still muttering around the far side of the mirror, holding it upright, waiting for the lift. Standing a yard away I fitted comfortably into the gilt frame and it was a six-foot mirror.

I'm a trifle thick from the shoulders to the waist, but it doesn't show in tails. My face is a bit square. People used to write that it showed my sense of humour, but I don't think it does now.

There is no doubt that I have more young fans than anyone playing on the concert circuit today. They are loyal and noisy, but I need them more than they need me. The critics have described me as a child of the moment and the longer the childhood, the better.

14

There were still small slopes of snow on my suède coat and I was brushing them away before the mirror when one of the mirror attendants peeped around the side and said:

'You 'ad a good look, then, mate?'

'Sorry,' I said. The lift was there now. 'Was I wearing it out?'

He sniffed but did not retaliate.

The other man said: 'Right Will, let's get it in.'

I got in after them, and in the confined cubicle of the lift found myself segregated from them once again by the broad face of the mirror.

'Which one?' one of the invisible men called to me from the other side of the glass. The button panel was on their side.

'Five,' I answered. 'Thank you.'

We stopped at five but I could not get out. The mirror was at an angle in the doorway and I could not squeeze by. I did not call over to them because I can be very reasonable at times and I thought it was best to wait until they had taken the mirror out at their required floor and then I would go back down to five. The doors slid together and we began to ascend again.

'Queer,' said a voice from the other side of the mirror.

'Long 'aired queer,' agreed the other. 'Tragic.'

'Tragic,' repeated the first heavily. 'Fancy 'aving 'im cuddling up to you, George?'

'I *don't*,' said his friend. 'I *don't* fancy it at all. Right mate, this is ten.'

I helped them out with the mirror. They must have been shocked to see my hands appear around the edge because their momentum ceased and there was a serious silence. Then they moved again, hurriedly, and between us we got the mirror on to the tenth-floor landing. I stepped back into the lift.

'Thank you, sir,' said George, glaring at Will.

'Yes,' agreed Will miserably. 'Thank you very much.'

'That's all right,' I said. 'Come down for a cuddle when you've done.'

It is a year today that I last saw Shoshana. That is why I

15

thought I would begin to write. I'm going to leave the piano to itself at the other end of the room, at least until it gets dark this afternoon. It is very warm and enclosed in this apartment now, elevated, five floors above the frozen ground, with all of London, gone off to work, leaving me perched here in the suburbs.

Now the snow has grown all over my window. Before, I could see it raiding through the sky, across the common, but now it has blocked itself out. I don't want the phone to ring all day, I hope nobody calls. I hope the mirror man doesn't decide to come in for a cuddle.

2

They say it is a small country. But it's big enough. Any country with a desert like the Negev tucked into its trousers is big enough. With the war they added another desert, the great brown gut of Sinai which belonged to the Egyptians. Dov Haran said when we saw our friends buried after the six days: 'Where's this country going to? Collecting deserts.'

I arrived there a week before the battle began. The true summer heat was moving over the southern Mediterranean countries, the heavy brown heat that arrives at the conclusion of May, disturbing the sky, distorting the sea and drying the land. The plane from Athens for Lod moved irritably in the hot air across Tel Aviv. Even from the air you could sense and see its heaviness. The habitual sea pushed against it and the yellow baked buildings seemed to be tiredly pushing it back. The cars in the streets moved like furtive woodlice from the shadows of trees and houses out into the hard sunlight and seemed then to hurry for the shade.

Lod Airport is the place they talk about in the Bible as Lydda. So Dov told me that day when the Arabs were trying to get us with machine-gun fire and mortars and he was giving me one of his historical-geography lessons about the country.

There were jet fighters lying like hunting dogs in the enclosed heat under the trees on the farther reaches of the airport. I could see their soft snouts sniffing out of the shadows from the oval pond of the Boeing window. There were some shabby old fighters too, resting around the perimeter with beards of grass growing about them. They had little glass cabins like tomato frames. I remember them from the days of the war – our war – I mean, the one against the Germans. They were called Blackburn Skuas. They were among my collection of model warplanes made from balsa wood and displayed on top of our piano in those days. I was a very patriotic boy and I would build only models of British and American fighting aeroplanes.

I had never been in Israel before. I was going to play three concerts with the Israel Symphony Orchestra, but I knew nothing of those people. I thought they were just Jews, like Maurice Greenbaum, the librarian at the Philharmonia Library in London or Joe Kaye, my barber. I didn't know. Beneath the canopy of the arrival building there was a nervousness so distinct that I was immediately aware of it. The fluid panic of most airports was not there. Men and women in desert khaki uniforms moved seriously about, the passengers were quiet, filing through the customs channels in dumb show, porters propelled luggage trolleys with hard expressions as though they were pushing fieldguns.

Abraham Metzer and three other men from the Israel Symphony Society met me. Metzer had previously come to London to arrange the tour. He was a squashed, small man; middle-aged, untidy, and with clothes too big for him. He kept tugging at his shirt sleeves and adjusting his uncomfortable shoulders as though he feared they might shiver and fall from him at any moment.

'I hope your tour will be safe,' he muttered when we were in the car going towards Tel Aviv. It was getting on towards the short evening and the land was lying low, relieved after the heat, under a sky going pale. I watched it from the window. Some young girl soldiers tried to thumb a lift.

17

'Why safe?' I said without anxiety. 'The contracts are all fixed, aren't they? Everything has been agreed.'

He shrugged inside his great blue shirt. 'That's all good,' he said looking straight ahead over the driver's shoulder as though expecting an ambush. 'But maybe we have a war in a few days.'

I waited a few minutes because I was annoyed. Then I laughed insincerely and said: 'You're always having a war in a few days.' I should have insisted on Philip or Eric coming with me. Philip was having trouble with a Brazilian soprano and Eric was ill. I had never toured without one or both of them before. And there was going to be a war.

'Wars and stories. Rumours,' he mumbled. The other three men all nodded at once, and so did the driver. 'But we think that this time the pot has come too near to overflowing. In a few days it may all take place, Mr Hollings, and we will be fighting, killing for our lives.'

Well I won't, I thought. They had better keep a seat on a plane for London.

'Sleep tonight and perhaps tomorrow you would like to think about events,' said Metzer. 'We will keep you to nothing in the contract. We would like very much for you to stay for many people here have been waiting to hear you play. They have waited a long time.'

They'll have to wait a bit longer, I thought. My God, I kept out of the way of bullets and bombs when I was frogmarched into our own bloody Army. To hell with getting caught here. In any case one of the best audiences I have ever known was in Cairo.

I said: I'll have to telephone my manager. If he says I must return then I will. Tomorrow is the Tel Aviv concert?'

'Tomorrow,' he confirmed. He shrugged his shirt straight again.

'Can they hold up the war until then?' I asked.

'For you, maybe they can,' he answered dryly. He was still looking directly ahead and so were the others. I had an idea they didn't like me very much.

18

The orchestra did *Scheherazade*, the *Pathétique*, and mine was Beethoven's Number One in C. It was a tremendous concert, one of those occasions when it is full and thrilling. It was the first time I had felt like that for a long time. In the early days I always experienced an onrush of emotion, because of newness and nervousness, and knowing how much the audience wanted from me – even ordered from me. But with professionalism some of that goes, worn off by the cunning and the craft that the soloist gathers and needs. You regulate yourself, pace yourself, use yourself and the orchestra to every good and mean advantage. But you lose that first pointed realization, the initial joy, and only rarely does it touch you again.

I don't know why it should recapture me that night. It was the people, I think. It was steamy and there were hundreds jammed in everywhere. When I was in the wings looking out I could feel them breathing. They were mixed people, all sorts of faces and tints of colour, not like Jews as you think of Jews, rag-traders, bookmakers or violinists. This was a dark people. They could have been Lebanese or Spanish. The hall was wide and magnificent and they were banked in hundreds right up to the darkest caves of the place. I had watched them coming in and thought at first how young they were. But then I realized that they were not altogether so, that I had mistaken vigour for youth, for there was in the concert hall that evening shortly before the war began, an energy coming from them that seemed itself to generate the close heat of that engulfing experience.

Many were soldiers in saggy uniforms, with sub-machineguns strangely prim across their knees as they settled untidily in the seats. There were girls in uniform too, brown girls with splendid hair and tight busts, striding into the auditorium with their military shoulder-bags. There were many people in opened shirts; people with brown necks and moving faces. And among all these a few men and women in fine, formal evening dress. They made a collective noise like all the hens of hell. From behind the curtains their voices came at me; hundreds all talking at the same time, shaking hands and recognizing friends and calling to them, settling themselves down and then theatrically getting up to attract somebody else. It looked more like a market than a concert hall.

When the orchestra went out the people applauded; they cheered and jumped like children. Igor Baraneski, whom we call the Russian engine driver, was the conductor, steaming up to the rostrum and pulling his familiar invisible valves and levers when he got there. Small hands clenched and then undone, making short nervous movements close to his chest. It is his trademark. It was strange that he should be a Russian because they weren't feeling well about the Russians that night, thinking that they were oiling the guns for the Egyptians beyond Gaza and the Syrians behind the Golan Heights. But it made no difference to the people. They shouted and hooted encouragement and Igor, a fussy little bugger but a worthwhile act as a conductor, turned and bowed and busily worked his hands as though he were in the cab of a locomotive.

Metzer shifted suddenly, uncomfortably at my arm. He was one of those padded men and when he moved he was quiet and smooth. It was only when he stood or sat that he began to fidget with his shirt or his zip fly or his plastic belt. He looked out with me on to the dark field of people, nodding his head at them as though bestowing some blessing.

'They're going to enjoy it,' I said.

He sniffed at the baking air around the curling curtains. 'They're alive and happy tonight,' he agreed. 'Tonight will be a good night in Tel Aviv. Tomorrow, next week, it could be concluded, you understand, Mr Hollings. All this. All our lives. The State and the people could be dead.'

'No one will kill you like that,' I argued. I did not turn to him. I kept looking at the people settling into the hot darkness as the orchestra tuned. His words had been untheatrical and convincing. I wondered, for the first time, then, if it were possible they might all die.

He continued looking through the fold in the curtains. Igor had brought the orchestra to heel now and the first slim theme of *Scheherazade* was moving like lazy smoke through the close air. Metzer whispered: 'Today Shukiary of the Palestine Liberation Army said that when the Arabs overtake the Jews the Jewish survivors will be helped to return to their original countries.' He paused and the music drifted like an aroma to us. He continued in the same voice: 'But he said that he did not believe there would be any survivors.'

Scheherazade, the first soliloquy anyway, sounds better on a mouth organ I think. I once heard a man play it like that at Plymouth when some sailors were doing a concert, the thin, erotic theme of the lonely girl and the thousand and one nights.

'There's the United Nations,' I suggested unconvincingly, half turning to Metzer.

He gave a little spit. 'The United Nations Force,' he said, making the final word an irony. 'This force was removed from the Strait of Tiran because the Egyptians wanted it moved.'

'Where's that?' The violins had really taken hold of it now and were folding the story in their thick sweetness. The musky dope that Rimsky-Korsakov planted, secreted, in his little suite was escaping into the heavy air.

'The strait?' Metzer said. 'It guards the entrance to the Gulf of Eilat in the south. The Egyptians have pushed the cork into the bottle, Mr Hollings, and we are in the bottle.'

We left it there. I went back to my dressing-room and exercised my fingers on the glass table. I wondered where Shoshana was. That day I had telephoned the newspaper office but they said briskly that she was away on an assignment and they did not know when she was likely to return. I thought of her face and her eyes and I heard Metzer saying again that there would be no survivors. Survivors. In the way that some races have hill-people, and plainsmen, and other categories of inhabitants, the Jews always seem to have survivors.

I went on to the platform, into the lights, and the applause was like a fury. Never had I known such a reception. Igor, on the stand, raised his Russian eyebrows at me and I grinned at him.

21

We took Beethoven's First Piano Concerto with a great verve; a beautiful enthusiasm, that came from the guts of the orchestra, caught me, and left engine driver Igor, at its conclusion, limp with sweat and round-eyed with exhaustion and elation. His locomotive had almost run away. He had only just held it. It had needed all his power and he could not understand.

Nor did I at the beginning. Playing with an orchestra is like riding a horse. Sometimes it is sluggish, constipated; it wallows and rolls. You drag along with it, glad when the last note is touched and the whole exercise is finished. I have known even something like *The Emperor* crawl along like a cartload of shit. But at other times the stallion gallops, goes joyously so that it runs above the ground, carrying the soloist like a breathless rider.

This is how it was. We plunged into it, my heart caught with its lyric bravery, my fingers making it a fine thing. The orchestra flew, Igor hanging on to his driver's cab, and I went, too, laughing with excitement, resting and then leaping upon its back again like some mad cowboy jumping from horse to runaway railroad train. I felt more like Roy Rogers than Christopher Hollings. My God it was hot. Falls of sweat rolled all over me, getting into my ears and my eyes, turning my hands to dishmops and yet not for a moment preventing or impeding the unstoppable running of the thing.

At the first pause I kept my head directly over the keys looking down at their smooth smile. I was panting with the effort and the realization, feeling the bursting of the emotional people who were listening in the hot dark. At the second break I allowed myself to look up and saw how much the musicians had been taken by it too.

Their wet faces under the lights worked over strings and brass with the dedication of men using guns.

Then it was finished. Done. I thought they were going to rush the stage. Igor clutched the brass rail on the podium, head bent forward, baton limp in hanging fingers, colour like pulp, face like running fat. I had almost collapsed across the piano, knowing that I had reached for something high

22

and caught it. Christ, I thought, that was so bloody marvellous.

The people exploded in the auditorium, their shouts, their noisy stamping like all the sounds of a marauding army. I could feel them rising. Igor glanced my way as we took our bows with an expression that told me I had played far above anything he had considered possible from an English soloist. To me he was the celestial engine driver. The violins were standing, dumb and wet, some blankly grinning, others shakily looking down, examining their bows. The brass and the woodwind puffed out their cheeks as though eager to play it again, and the timpani player, the great fat exuberant Zoo Baby, bent across his drums like a man who has lost something invaluable down a well.

There was a party after the concert at a house on the beach at Herzliya, a long-spined villa, its rooms spread out like padded feet each side of its main body. It belonged to a man called Nicolas Tobin, a patron of the arts in Israel. Igor and I travelled from Tel Aviv in the same car, both relaxed now. His English is good, but we talked only a little. We went from the concert hall along the wide, white street called Dezingov, all lights and traffic and people in the hot, bright night. The people were thick at the pavement tables and promenading, processing each way before the fringes of cafés. In the car we had the windows down and we felt the heavy summer air coming in to us with the strong lights of the street and the broken voices of the people.

They moved like a long reel of fragmented film passing us as the car went slowly among the traffic along Dezingov. There were hundreds of Jews there, drinking at those arranged tables, greeting friends, and prodigiously shaking hands. There was overwhelming talking and some laughter. We stopped at traffic lights. A woman was howling in argument with a taxi driver. People at the café tables watched and laughed and called raucous advice. The taxi driver climbed from his seat and began disputing with the woman. He was a mound of a man: fat and white, his sleeves rolled, his forearms like large fish. His face sweated and he glared in exasperation at the scolding woman, and then threw out his thick arms to the spectators appealing for help or judgement. They laughed. Some girls in fawn uniforms, their shoulder-bags slung like guns, were wrangling lightly with young, green soldiers, cockily sitting at a corner table, faces up-turned, grinning, sub-machine-guns lying like pets across their legs. A man was scraping at a dead violin at one corner and a juke box cried from a hamburger bar. Everyone was out in the bright lights of that street.

'You were excellent tonight,' said Igor looking out of the window, away from me.

I returned: 'You were also.'

'A gregarious people, the Israelis,' said Igor nodding his head benignly as though acknowledging a salute from the street.

'Anything for a night out,' I replied quietly. 'Perhaps there won't be many more.'

'It is nothing,' he shrugged. 'Nobody is happy unless they have something to fear.'

I did not talk to him about it because just then I did not want to. In any case I was fascinated by that silver ribbon of street. It was like all avenues of the world, all the warm streets I had ever known; Paris, Rome, Budapest, Rio, brim-ming with sounds and moving people.

Eventually, as we drove, the lights dimmed and decreased, almost as they do in an auditorium, and then it was quieter and the tepid air that came into us turned dark; we left the resounding street behind and drove away from the city. We made a turn into a subdued road and then approached a wooden bridge across a creek. There were soldiers guard-ing both ends of the bridge. They stopped each vehicle and examined it. Our driver told them who we were, but im-mediately a young dark, damp face was at the window staring at us in our tailed suits and white bows. The soldier had brown eyes, wide and cautious like an animal at night. But his boy's voice was firm and calm and he looked us over carefully before moving our driver away with the snub of his rifle.

The car bumped woodenly across the bridge which must

have been a strategic strongpoint because on the farther flank of the river a pair of armoured cars crouched like moles in the night, beside the skeletal shape of a settled helicopter. The guards looked in at us again, this time a small-faced soldier and a fat girl with chocolate eyes and a rifle. They let us go on. We could hear the sea ruffling the night beyond the road and the camel-backed sand dunes. It was very dark and the car rattled irritably. Then we were on a good road again, well lit and moving behind two medium tanks which coughed, roared and squealed along the tarmac surface until ponderously swinging into a gap in the dunes and sniffing away towards the sea.

'It is nothing,' repeated Igor defensively from his darkness. 'They make loud noises, and the Arabs also. It is just as the Russians and the Americans. Noise, noise, bang, bang, squeak, and then silence. Some day I maybe would write a Cold War Symphony, only I think that the theme would become too monotonous. Always the same sounds.'

'There will be more than noises between this bunch and the Arabs,' I said. 'This time.'

'Just noise,' he grunted. 'Symbols and cymbals.'

He obviously thought that was good because he went to some trouble to separate the two words for me. I muttered an acknowledgement. We were travelling very fast now along the black coast, away from the lights, with a small wind stirring in the sand dunes. The road bent and we emerged on to a clear horizon with Tel Aviv lying luminously on the sea to our left. There were some isolated houses at this place, bulky houses with terrace windows open to the Mediterranean and the lights at their windows and porches making rich ovals on the beach. The driver turned up a drive cut through the hilly sand and we arrived under a stone arch and turned into a courtyard.

All the people at the party were full of congratulations over the concert. Tobin, the host, a slight man with a surprising cushion of tight-curled black hair supported by a stick of a face, talked to me by a door opening out to the beach. The sea was breathing without fuss and the city lay like a pile of diamonds on the distant cape. Behind us the room was crowded, but subdued so that some music which should have been in the background became much louder and played above the people. I did not recognize it.

'Yarom Nathan,' Tobin said. 'A young Israeli. This is his *Ruth and Boaz in the Fields*. I think he has much promise.'

Tobin held his glass at a slope and moved his head at about the same angle. His hair was extraordinary. Slim grey hair would have suited him for he was spare and neat. The black bush was a worry because he continually pressed it back and a sigh clouded his face as inevitably each time it sprang forward again. He was listening to the music. There was a vivacious little bridge piece which folded over on itself a few times towards the middle of the work, and unrolled sweetly to the conclusion.

'He says that he felt unhappy about the conclusion, you know,' said Tobin moving his head towards the music in a manner which suggested that Yarom Nathan was drinking in the lighted room.

'He goes out on his own,' I said. 'It is most original.' There was an aeroplane moping about in the night, high but insistent. The strings dropped quietly and the plane's engines were heavy. But then it went out over the dulled ocean and the sound whittled away.

Tobin said: 'He was unhappy about many things when he wrote it, but they were usually less to worry about than he thought.'

'We all do that,' I said.

'Do you think we will be fighting soon?' he said anxiously turning from the sea.

'So everybody tells me,' I answered cautiously. 'I am the one least likely to know. I am a stranger, remember.'

He shook his head across the top of his glass as though testing the drink by smell. I thought again how his hair was odd and unfortunate.

'A stranger maybe can see such things better than us,' he said. 'Sometimes it is better to look into an unfamiliar room from a window.'

'Well I would say there will be no war,' I answered. I said

it firmly, not because I believed it firmly but in some way to reassure him when he needed reassurance. 'Symbols and cymbals. Signs and noises.'

He smiled gratefully. I did not know whether it was for the reassurance or the pun at first, but then he said: 'Very graceful. Symbols and cymbals.'

I wanted to return to the room. But he touched then tugged my sleeve and said: 'Do you think America or England would come to help us?'

I began to feel annoyed at his insistence. 'You won't need it,' I smiled firmly. 'There will be nothing. No trouble, no war. You see.'

He shook his curious brush head. 'I cannot see how it can be avoided,' he said. He looked at me, tilting his chin. 'Everyone in the world thinks we are so brave,' he smiled. 'Israel will take on the earth! And then take the afternoon off! Ha, I wish it were so. Some are brave, my friend, and some are not. I am not. I fear it so much. I have sent my two sons to Rome. They went two weeks ago and I miss them. But I do not want them here. My wife, she will get out tomorrow. I would like to go too. The truth is I do not *want* to fight, to die, probably. Not for anything. Not even for Israel.'

This time I made a determined turn into the room and the party again. 'Patriotism has become devalued,' I assured him. 'It is not what it was. With the Bomb and one thing and another we've given war a bad name.'

We walked into the room. It was like entering a new layer of warmth. A tall, tanned woman in a long red dress leaned towards me and said, 'It was brilliant. So beautiful.' I would have liked to have stopped near her but Tobin was still worrying at my side.

'Patriotism, you say, may be old-fashioned. But not for the Israelis, unfortunately,' he went on. 'To be a person of this country you must fight. It is part of being a citizen. And I don't like it.'

I was introduced to a stony-looking archaeologist who took me to meet a seedy horticulturist who knew the woman in the red dress and introduced me to her. Her name was Selma

27

Haydn. She was in her forties but good, taller than me, leisurely; a woman who was used to having time to care for herself, to dress herself with concern and finesse. Her tan was a sunbathing tan, gentle layers of it, not the harsh sun-brown of the outdoor working woman of Israel. She had careful make-up and veneered nails. Her fingers were slim and soft and she had a well-tended smile. This one had never worked on any kibbutz.

'Our friend Tobin has been worrying you about the war,' she suggested at the outset. She had a firm English accent.

'A trifle,' I agreed. 'But he is one of millions.'

She was drinking a Martini. She sighed. 'The war, the war. Everyone talks about it as though it were an accomplished fact, as though it were all definite and done. By one side or the other. I find it very tiring.'

'You're English,' I said. I grinned at her. 'Let me see – perhaps a girl ambulance driver in the war. Singing while the bombs fell.'

She looked at me quietly. Then she smiled: 'I'm a bit disappointed that you pinned down my age so quickly.'

'I am sorry,' I said.

'Oh, it's fair if it shows,' she protested holding her hands forward. 'I'm "White Cliffs of Dover" vintage, all right. But you got the other thing wrong. The bombs. Jesus Christ, you wouldn't have got me in that business. I spent the whole time in Bermuda. Every last day of it. I remember watching the Duke of Windsor playing golf in August 1940. I was having a lesson at the Mid-Ocean Club from the professional. In those days I was something of a golfing girl wonder. And that was while brave old Britain was standing alone. She was standing without the duke and without me, just to name two.'

'He couldn't help it,' I said. 'As I remember.' She wasn't being loud about it, talking quietly and not rattling it off like someone who has told it many times as a joke.

'No, it was none of his fault,' she agreed reasonably. 'It must have been nasty for him to be playing golf in Bermuda while all that bombing and suchlike was going on. He holed out from a bunker at Riddells Bay I remember. There was a picture in the paper.

'But I *could* help it. And I wasn't going to budge. My father had gone scurrying back to the old country to do his bit, whatever his bit was. He was put on cutting up ration books and he got killed by a fire engine one perfectly peaceful lunchtime in Birmingham. I suppose that's counted as a war death, isn't it?'

I laughed. Her dress was low, over one shoulder and her right breast was swollen out half clear of the downward slope of the material.

'My father was something like that,' I admitted. 'He deserted from the Army two weeks after war was declared. He simply cleared out, and then dropped dead from a heart attack in our front parlour. The War Office, through some strange process, sent my mother a telegram informing her of his death, just as if she didn't know. In a way we were quite proud of him. He was one of the first British soldiers to go.'

She laughed like a girl. Then she became quiet and said: 'It was splendid tonight. Quite superb.'

I nodded my thanks. 'Something happened to everyone,' I said. 'It was like going for a ride.'

'If you had been a Jew I would have thought it was the emotion of this immediate time,' she said. She spoke now very correctly, not lightly as she had done while talking about Bermuda. 'The audience was full of it. Just exploding. And it caught the orchestra too.'

I smiled my agreement. 'There was a feeling,' I said. 'And I don't have to be a Jew to know it. Are you Jewish?'

'Christ no!' she said quite loudly. 'I'm an Israeli, I suppose. I married one of the buggers. He's a reserve officer, a colonel this week, I think, and tonight he's out on the Golan Heights waiting for the Syrians. He's a soil engineer, always picking up bits of dirt and running his fingers through it treating it like gold. He's very nice really. A bit Jewish though. Not that he can help that. He can't wait to get into Syria just so that he can start stealing the earth from their back gardens. He says it's unique around Damascus.'

29

'People want to fight for odd reasons,' I observed.

'Ah, he wants to fight for the fighting too,' she said. 'They all do'. Her fingers took in the room. 'They're all so bloody effervescent. They're like the damned sixth form. All in love with somebody, and then somebody else. Can't wait to get out of school to have a battle with the kids next door.'

'And the kids next door also want a fight,' I pointed out.

'That's the damn pity. Typical too. That's another lousy school.'

'What will you do if it starts?'

She pouted. 'I'll tell you what I'll be doing,' she said determinedly. 'Playing golf.'

'Like nineteen forty,' I said.

'Right. I shall go up to Caesarea and I'll play golf through until either the Jews win or the Arabs arrive to rape me or whatever.'

I laughed but then I thought she was serious. 'Why don't you go home to England then?'

'Home? England? God, I couldn't stand it. Not Haywards Heath in June. I'd rather stay. If the Arabs have me then they have me.'

'You concentrate on your golf,' I advised. 'There's nothing like holing a few long putts to help the war effort.'

'How long will you be in Tel Aviv?' she asked.

'Always excepting Acts of War, Acts of God, and that sort of thing, I shall be here for three more days. When the tour was arranged I had some idea of making it part-holiday. Then, of course, I didn't know everybody would be sharpening swords. After that I go down to Eilat with the orchestra and then to Jerusalem and to Haifa. And then home to England in June.'

From the edge of her eye she saw the worried Tobin coming towards us. 'Please come to my house for lunch tomorrow,' she said. 'At twelve. I will send a car to the hotel for you. Which is it?'

'The Dan,' I said. 'Let's hope they don't start shooting before then.'

'It's the Sabbath,' she assured me. 'It won't be on the Sabbath.'

Tobin had heard. He, as host, had ostensibly abandoned his depression in the company and now said to Mrs Haydn, 'War! Which war is this?' He laughed, his smile splitting unconvincingly under the ugly mop. Igor, who was sharing the car back to the city, stood by. Tobin laughed again, even less reassuringly. 'It is all just noise and propaganda,' he said. 'Symbols and cymbals.'

Igor raised his Russian eyebrows at me. I shrugged.

3

It was one in the morning when we reached the Dan Hotel but the city was still brimming with light and people. Igor went to his room, but I changed my clothes and went out again walking in the cool air up through some streets of trees until I came once more to the Dezingov.

The clamour and the activity were not slowed. Now I was no longer in the car I knew there was music everywhere along the broad channel of the street, threaded between the people's voices and the coughing and blowing of the cars jammed under the blatant white street lights.

Newspapers flapping like birds around the café tables went from hand to eager hand, were pointed at and discussed. The man bowed over the terrible old fiddle was still there, scraping at it tenderly, as though trying to nurse some sweetness, some life, into it. The boyish soldiers in their uniforms of green and brown, or splashed with camouflage like an animal skin, still lounged at the tables laughing with dark girls. One table was littered with sub-machine-guns. The soldiers wore ungainly long boots, laced high, and shapeless little hats. They did not look smart or alert. They looked tired, untidy, and not very tough.

I sat with a cognac for twenty minutes, watching it all. No

one recognized me and I was, for once, grateful. They were too occupied with their arguments and discussions, their plans, their newspapers. They seemed like massed swimmers jumping in and out of a pool. Two young, brown women with cherubic faces leaned back in their chairs, their strong, long legs bridging to the table before them, singing quietly in fine unison. The soldiers were examining marked out battle maps on the stained cloth with the interest and enthusiasm of hikers. On the other side of me six deaf and dumb people talked excitedly with whirling fingers.

There was a flashing sign in red Hebrew and blue English across the road, a hundred yards up the vibrant thoroughfare. I realized that I had come out of the streets with the trees to within a short distance of the newspaper office where Shoshana worked.

I finished the cognac and walked among the promenaders to the corner building. From open windows on the first floor the office lights flew into the street. People were standing thickly about the ground-floor windows reading news bulletins. I went by them and up the stairs to the first floor. The rooms there were full of yellow hazy lights, and men in white shirts, sweating in the night heat, were hung over desks and typewriters, or moving about carrying wet printers' proofs delicately between fingers and thumbs as though they were fly-papers. The building began to shake, a long noise above the claustrophobic din of the people in the office. The presses in the basement were moving.

I walked through the activity, unquestioned but hesitant, unwilling to speak to anyone in case I intruded on something momentous. There was a sharp bend in the big room and I went around it like a stray cat. Immediately I saw Shoshana wearing khaki shirt and trousers, which made her look small. She was with some white-shirted men around a coffee machine, left hand on her hip, right hand lifting a paper cup. She had her back to me, but two of her companions looked up at me and she turned and saw me. The men looked pale against her. Her skin was deep and dark, far more than I remembered it, and her hair was much fairer, and tied behind her neck with a small band.

32

The coffee was near her mouth. She stopped it there and put it down, then laughed and turned towards me, glad to see me. Her face was strong and striking, but she looked hung with tiredness. Christopher she smiled. Then, 'Mister Hollings! Ha! How strange to see you here. So far from England's cold.'

'It's not cold there now,' I said. She had a sheen of oil on one side of her face. 'Have they turned you into a mechanic?' I smiled at her, thinking how weary her eyes looked.

She let out a half-laugh, her teeth showing quickly against the dark of her skin. 'Not yet. But there is time. I have been away.' She took my arm. 'Let us go and have a drink, if you have time. I am so tired.'

We went down to the street again. In the few minutes I had been in the newspaper office the people and the cars had thinned. She took me along the pavement, holding my arm still, almost dragging herself, not saying anything, until we came to some steps dropping to an open basement door. The door was almost round, like the end of a big pipe, and from the hollow came some indefinite jazz and a sulky light.

'It won't be too bad,' she said. 'I would like to get somewhere *inside*. It will make me feel better. I have been in the open too long these days and nights.'

The cellar was crowded but quiet, the people listening to a man playing the vibes, leaning over the instrument lovingly, curiously like a carpenter making something intricate at a bench. There were two somnolent guitarists and a drummer like a shadow in the smoke at the extreme of the room. We found a table at the back near a whitewashed wall. The musicians were putting together something of their own, wandering about with the music, trying things, fitting bits together, unhurried, lost in it.

'I knew, of course, that you were coming to Israel,' she said watching the vibes player intently. 'But so many things are taking place . . .' She spread her hands and looked at me smiling. She was a Sabra, a third generation Israeli, the people they call after the prickly thorn of the desert, as she once told me. Her nose always looked to me as though it was spoiling her. It was not an ugly nose, but it seemed that it belonged to someone else, with a different face to hers. She had truly magnificent eyes, but that night the rings beneath them looked like the imprinted heels of two shoes.

'Who have you been fighting today?' I asked gently. 'You personally, I mean.'

She giggled quietly. 'I fight no one today,' she said. 'Maybe I look that way, but no fighting. Travel, travel, travel. They say this is a little country. Do not believe them. It is plenty.'

The waiter came through the haze with our drinks. It was close and sticky in the little place. 'What have you been doing?' I asked.

She drank. 'No, you first,' she insisted. 'Your concert was a magnificent success. Already I hear that in the office.'

'It went well,' I said seriously. 'Everyone wanted it to go especially well. The people, the audience, were unbelievable. And the orchestra – *boom*!' I made an explosion with my hands.

'And the soloist?' she smiled.

'Never played better. *Magnifique*!'

She laughed now and ran her fingers across her cheek leaving tracks in the thin oil. 'That is better,' she said. 'That is more like you. This modesty is not becoming.' She looked closely at her hands and screwed up her nose in annoyance. 'Oil,' she said. 'Oil on my face. Like you say, maybe I am a mechanic.'

The musicians came to the end of their journey and stopped, I applauded with the others but Shoshana lit a cigarette. They began again, slipping easily into the subdued music, the vibes thinking and hesitating as they sounded, the drums moving the piece along, but very slowly.

'You like this music?' she inquired as though surprised.

'Yes. I enjoy hearing them put it together. It is a luxury I would like myself.'

'I like that one,' she said pointing to the vibes. 'So much like a slow musical box.'

'Where have you been?' I asked again.

'Everywhere,' she said wearily. 'I am tired so to cry. I have

34

been in Gaza and along the borders of Sinai, and last week in the Golan Heights, where the bastard Syrians have been shelling the people gathering the crops and also in the villages. My driver was killed there on Friday. He was an old friend. There was a land mine and he was driving the jeep back to Tiberias to send something I had written for the newspaper. I had only left him a few moments before and he had gone two hundred metres along the road and the road exploded and the car was thrown off and he was killed in a moment.'

The vibes player was leaning close, nose over his keys as though seeking some small fault in them. His soft touches resounded deftly through the room. The drummer seemed to have fallen across his drums, the guitarist nodded at his fingers finding the strings and the bass player held the neck of his instrument like a man loving an ostrich.

'That must have been terrible,' I said inadequately.

She pushed the root of her hand across her cheek as though to push the surface oil away. 'My God this is going to be such a war,' she said. 'I have seen them all these days and nights lying in the hills and among the sand dunes. Lying there like dogs. Our side and their side. Waiting to get to each other.'

Her voice was slow. But she took a decisive drink. 'We cannot lose,' she said. 'We will not lose. That is not possible. They think they can come in and take us, but they will never do that. We will give them a war to remember.'

Inadequately again I said: 'Perhaps nothing will happen. There have been plenty of times when things have become as hot as this.'

She shook her head. 'If you had seen it all you would know that you don't speak any sense,' she argued. She did not say it roughly. It was her way of framing the words. 'You see, if they do not attack us we *must* attack them. We cannot have them sniffing beneath our doors and windows all the time. In Israel we cannot afford to have the battle on our own ground. There is not enough of it. One sweep across the Negev and we are cut. Then we have only two halves of a country. That is no good. The battles must be outside our

doors – in the Sinai, on the far bank of Galilee, around Bethlehem and Jericho.'

There was a hardness in her voice now. She was gazing
into the misty smoke, towards the veiled jazz players. Her
dark face, with her Sabra-fair hair pulled so sternly back to
her neck, looked as set and lined as a man's. She spoke as
though I were not there. 'Then there is Jerusalem,' she
muttered. 'The matter of the City of Jerusalem.'

She turned to me, as though recalling my presence, and a
wry smile softened the unaccustomed set of her face. 'I'm
sorry,' she said shrugging. 'Propaganda. And to a neutral.'
She pulled away and regarded me from a new distance.
'Maybe I have been writing too much about it for my
newspaper. I am too much part of it.'

We got up and went out. The night was much cooler now
and almost empty. Many of the lights in the street had
gone out and the cafés were closed. Some taxi drivers stood
by their cabs at a corner, still arguing over a newspaper
spread open on one of the bonnets. I thought, if they don't
get a war they'll talk themselves into one. A group of young
Jews were still around a table at one of the cafés that remained lit. Some dogs walked the pavements and a lately
arrived moon was now dangling over the metallic inland hills.

We walked by the group at the café. Two of them were
soldiers. Their chairs were pushed back from the tables and
tilted as they pushed their boots against the café walls. There
were some beer bottles on the table and two sub-machine-
guns. One of the soldiers had his arms around the waists of
two girls. The other laughed in argument, wagging his
finger at another youth. One of the girls turned to look at us,
but not the others.

'Your young people should not be up so late,' I said.
'They'll be too tired to fight.'

For a moment I thought she was going to pull away from
me, but abruptly she relaxed and shrugged her shoulders.
'Everyone will fight,' she assured me. 'You see.'

'I won't be here to see,' I said decisively. 'I have things to
do all over the place.'

She looked at me, then hooked her arm comfortably in

36

mine. 'Of course you have,' she said reasonably. 'And you must go on and do them. It is important.'

We had reached the corner of one of the short tree-crowded roads that runs to Dezingov. Shoshana stopped. She fumbled in her trouser pocket like a man. She took something from the pocket, something small. She had it between her finger and her thumb. I realized it was a ring. She worked it on to the third finger of her left hand.

'My wedding ring,' she said. She gave a tight smile. 'I wear it tonight because I go now to my husband. Just a few houses down this place.'

'I did not know you were married,' I said quietly.

'There is very little to it,' she shrugged. 'This country is a bad place for marriage. Too much falling in and out. Divorce is very big. We marry too young and for not long enough. Soon, after the war has come and gone, Uri and I will divorce. That is if we are still here and such things matter.'

I said: 'But you are going to him now?'

'Yes,' she said simply. 'It is the right thing tonight. We have an apartment along here and we were very happy once. Sometimes we still find something in each other. We meet only sometimes because of my work and because he is also away. He is one of the Israeli Air Force. But tonight we are meeting because we are still in marriage. *Erav tov*, goodnight Christopher. I hope you play well in the concerts.'

She walked under the deep black of the lined trees. There were no lights in the little street. I remained at the corner and watched her walk, calling, 'Goodnight Shoshana,' after her. She answered only by waving her hand in the deep-cut shadows and without turning about. Then I could not see her at all, only a slice of light suddenly thrusting from a door and then vanishing again.

I walked back along the Dezingov. I was almost alone now, although I could hear the taxi men laughing farther down the wide street. At the café the two girls were with the third young man and the two soldiers had gone. It was five days before the war.

*   *   *

Mrs Haydn sent her chauffeur and her Mercedes for me at noon. It is surprising how many Mercedes and Volkswagen cars there are in Israel. We went along the sea road again, over the bridge guarded by the young soldiers and along the flowing hem of the sand dunes. It was a brilliantly hot day, still and stainless, petrified beneath the sun; the only moving things the languid sea and Mrs Haydn's car.

We ran quickly past Herzliya and to Natanya, a small town with a beach. The house was a mile outside the town, on the sea's fringe, set on a small cape of green land where, from somewhere, came a light touch of breeze. It touched the cedars in the garden giving them some refreshment from the bronze sun.

'My own private zephyr,' said Mrs Haydn waving her hand at the breeze. 'This is the only place from Haifa to Ashkelon which has a breath of air today.'

'All modern conveniences,' I said walking up the white steps of the house towards her. She was wearing a blue and white towelling jacket over a two-piece swimsuit. It was almost open at the front, held loosely by the tied belt, and when she moved towards me the tanned stomach underneath pressed against the narrow aperture, her navel peering out at me like a lone spying eye.

'This little piece of land sticks out just far enough to catch a whiff of whatever breezes are blowing on the sea. There is nearly always something and we can commandeer it.'

The walls within the house were cool green and there was a creamy marble floor, wooden furniture, softened with big bright cushions in traditional Eastern patterns. She walked with me, her sandals clapping lightly against the floor, her arms moving to and fro together as though she were pushing the air away. We walked into a slim and elegant room with white chairs, light rugs, and french windows embracing a square of fierce sun lying across a profuse flower garden and a blue swimming-pool. The water in the pool rubbed fondly against its tiles.

'A drink, Christopher,' Mrs Haydn suggested. She moved towards a cocktail cabinet.

38

'A Martini. Dry, please.'

Along the wall was a parade of twisted ornaments in what appeared to be dark metals, red, black and brown each with a subdued shining surface. I walked to them and saw they were glass tubes and bowls and bulbs, turned and stretched imaginatively. They were filled tightly with the red, brown and black.

'Earth,' explained Selma from the cabinet. 'Earth from all parts of the world. I told you about my husband, didn't I? He's a soil scientist and they're his. You might say he collects dirt.' She smiled thinly. 'Actually that's his joke not mine.

'They're different,' I said. She brought a Martini over and sat down.

'The place is full of them,' she said. 'Red dirt from this desert and black dirt from that mountain. We've even got some green dirt upstairs. It's in one of the bathrooms. My husband thought it was suitable for a bathroom. None of them are labelled, so no one but he knows what the hell they are or where they've come from. He knows them by heart. Which bit of the planet, when dug up, when bottled, and all that sort of thing. He treats the bloody stuff like some people treat a stock of wine. To me it's just dirt.'

She laughed. She looked more her age today without her evening make-up. 'Here's to the rest of your concert tour,' she said tipping her glass.

'Your health and happiness,' I responded.

'It's a very quiet day,' she said. 'When it gets too hot the day, especially at this time, becomes almost ghostly.'

I stood and looked out beyond the emblazoned garden and the pool to the sea climbing indolently up the legs of the beach. There was a white flagpole at the end of the garden, standing out like a seam of the sky. Its blue and white pennant moved with the unconscious stirring of a curled animal. There were no other people.

'I don't even have any house help today,' she said. 'The two men have gone off to be soldiers in the Negev and the two women are down in Natanya learning how to be bloody

air-raid wardens. Now the chauffeur has gone to fill sand-
bags. It was all I could do to persuade him to fetch
you.'

'This could be the day before the war,' I said.

'It has a certain feeling about it, I admit,' she shrugged.
She pulled her naked legs up underneath her using her left
hand to tuck them in and cover them with her towel coat.
'It's an empty feeling. Usually from here you can hear the
people shouting from the beach down below.'

'That's just it,' I said. 'Empty. Days-before-wars must have
always been like this. When our war broke out . . .'

She smiled at my pause. 'You mean the one *I* missed?
Of course I know about it. I may not have contributed, but I
heard.'

'I'm sorry, I didn't mean that,' I protested knowing that I
had meant it. She laughed silently. I continued: 'Anyway I
remember the Saturday before the Sunday. We lived in a
village in the West Country and it was deserted that day. I
was about six years old and I walked along the road wondering where everybody had gone. It was like a place struck by
the plague. It was a hot day too and the village was full of the
smell of dandelions and grass and the cows were out grazing.'

She shifted and got up, walking gracefully to the french
windows and looking out at the weary sea. 'There was some
sort of regatta in Bermuda that day,' she said. 'I remember
going down Front Street, alongside Hamilton Harbour, with
my old man to see the start of one of the races. I was wearing
my first American bra. My father stopped to talk to an old
boy who was sprawled in one of the wicker chairs outside
one of the stores. They do that there, you know. They have
chairs under the shop awnings. It's a nice idea.'

'Revolutionary,' I said. She pivoted on the marble floor.
'This old man telling my father that the storm clouds were
gathering, or some such thing, and in my teenage uncaring
way I thought, "Jesus Christ, this will bugger up the regatta".'

I laughed and walked towards her at the window. 'In our
village that afternoon,' I said, 'I met one other boy. He was a
bit older than me and he was dragging along in the dust at

the side of the road. He had a hell of a stutter, this kid. I remember we used to call him Tut-Tut and at school the teacher made him *sing* everything because he couldn't get started by merely saying it.

'He was coming towards me, at a shuffling run, his mouth opening and shutting like a haddock. When he reached me his eyes were bulging and he put his hand out to me to tell me what was so momentous. I remember he started off saying, "W ... w ... w ... war," and I stood there, arms folded, and waited for him to get the next bit out. We stood facing each other in the middle of this deserted village street, me six, him about ten, and he couldn't say the next syllable.'

Selma laughed. 'It sounds like the politicians of the world,' she said. 'Trying to say things and nothing being said.' We walked down towards the pool and I could see a table set out under a blue and white beach umbrella. 'Everything is blue and white,' she sighed. 'My husband is intensely patriotic. Then what?'

'I couldn't stand the suspense,' I said. 'So I told him to sing it, just as he did at school.'

We had reached the table. Her eyes widened with amusement. 'And he did? He sang it?'

'Exactly. I remember him looking defiantly at me for a while and then he began to tap out the time with his foot – that was another thing he had to do. That was the way he got the rhythm. Bang, bang, bang, went his foot and he started to sing it:

> ' "There's goin' t'be a war termorrer.
> All the German bombs will come down
> and kill everybody.
> My dad says ..." '

Selma was laughing into her brown fingers. 'My God,' she said. 'What a scene! That's really awful.'

We had walked into a vivid band of sun now. You could never call it sunshine in Israel for it never had any gentleness, no mild well-being about it. It seared across my back and burned my neck and ears.

41

Selma said: 'Perhaps you would like to swim before lunch?'

'I think I would,' I said. She pointed out a pair of blue and white changing cubicles far back beyond some vines. I changed into a pair of Yacob's bathing trunks there and returned across the hot stones to the pool. There were bulb-eyed lizards squatting on the stones, stony themselves. My feet sent them running.

She was already in the pool moving delicately on her back, the underside of her bra, the topside of her breasts and her pelvis clear of the lucid water, her face staring at the lurid sky, her toes propelling her. The sun poured over my white skin, running like a liquid streak along my back-bone and flowing over the backs of my thighs.

I dropped into the water quietly and swam the length of the pool and back again. The water had a velvet warmth, it was thick and rich, there were no sharp edges to it. It pumped away from my arms and legs, from beneath my arm-pits and from the channel of my crotch. Selma paid no atten-tion to me, but floated regally still looking up, pushed by the merest action of her toes. From my new level her breasts in their white satin cups looked like islands on the water.

I paddled towards her and floated alongside. Our feet col-lided and I wheeled clumsily away. She said: 'I would like to show you Jerusalem before they destroy it. We have a house there.'

I said: 'I would enjoy that.'

'You are free tomorrow?' she asked.

'Yes.'

'Then I shall call at the hotel for you and we can drive there.'

'Good. Then I go down to Eilat. On the following day.'

'At Eilat you will play in the desert, then. Or on the beach, which is really the same thing. The beach and the desert are one,' she said.

I stood on the floor tiles of the pool. 'No concert hall? No one mentioned that.'

'The beach is a good concert hall, Christopher,' she said. She stood on the bottom tiles now, facing me, her face three

42

feet away across the surface. I knew if I put my hands out I would touch her body. 'The acoustics are perhaps not what you would like, but it will be an unique experience for you, won't it?'

'I'm full of the pioneer spirit,' I said. 'I'll be wearing an open-necked shirt like Ben Gurion next.'

She splashed towards the side. 'They would like that,' she said. 'This lot, I mean. My God that would impress them! Not that I can see you doing it.'

I followed her to the side and caught hold of the rail. 'The open neck doesn't go very well with the tails,' I said.

'Perhaps the white tie and tails will seem odd in the desert too,' she said. We were standing very close now, side by side, like two people in a queue. I intended to touch her then, to put my hands to her. But she began speaking again.

'Actually I have two houses in Jerusalem,' she said. 'The one I like best is quite small, but white and very beautiful, with a small walled garden and a terrace with a well. It's at the foot of Mount Zion. But I haven't been in it for a couple of years. It's all shut up.'

'Why is that?' I asked.

She stared straight across the glassy, low-bumped surface of the pool, her eyes just above water level. She said: 'It's in the Arab sector.'

I whistled and blew a furrow across the water. 'Only someone like you could say that,' I said.

'Of course no one here knows, least of all my husband. He would kill me on the spot. When I went two years ago – I just wanted to see the house because I was very happy there – I had to go to Cyprus and then fly to Beirut and go to Amman from there and then Jerusalem. I have a British passport and a separate one for Israel and there was no bother. When I returned I came back the same way. It seemed very strange because the other Jerusalem house, my husband's house, is only a few hundred yards away in the Israeli sector, in the New City. I can see each house from the other. But they are a long journey apart.'

'How did you get the house?'

'My mother married a second time, a Greek, just after the

war,' said Selma. 'He was a jeweller and he spent a long time in Jordan, mostly in Jerusalem, and the house was his. When he died he left it to my mother and when she died it came to me. It has some fine furniture and other things and an old man who was a friend of my stepfather's has a key and goes into it sometimes to look around. It's all shut up and quite safe. The people over there are very good.'

She swam out towards the centre of the pool leaving me by the wall. She turned gracefully, with a kick of her legs, and faced me. Then her smile dropped. A voice came from the house and she looked up guiltily, then looked at me.

'My husband,' she said across the water.

'Selma!' I heard him call. His Army boots struck heavily across the marble and out on to the terrace. He stopped just above my head. He must have been a couple of feet back from the edge because he did not see me close against the tiles at the side.

'Yacob,' said Selma uncertainly. 'Have you finished the war?'

'That's *not* funny,' I heard him say. 'It does not seem to disturb *your* life very much. I am going into Tel Aviv so I came in. I have only half an hour. There is some lunch?'

'There is,' she said pushing out her arm towards the laden table at the end of the pool. I heard him go over there.

'A big lunch!' he called back. 'You have guests coming?'

'My guest is here,' Selma said. I had thought of trying to escape and she must have thought of the possibility too, but rejected it. I heard him turn about on the concrete.

'Where?' he called to her.

I peeped out. Hell, I thought, I'm only in his swimming-pool, not in his bed. 'Here I am,' I said with unconvincing cheerfulness. 'Just here.'

Now I could see him, a tall warrior, with Jaffa-coloured hair, a ginger moustache and heavy brown freckles plastered all over his burned face; a fighter in a shapeless uniform, an officer's cap pushed casually back from staring blue eyes. He had an automatic rifle slung like an usherette's tray about

44

his neck and a string of casual grenades over his shoulder.

We stood without moving, two in the pool, one on the side, a trio in the rough sunlight.

His forearms were like pieces of husky wood, layered with shining red hairs. From the table he had taken a great slab of potato salad. Now he began to eat it from his hand, and some of the raw pieces stuck to his extravagant moustache.

He marched with an exaggerated military stride towards me and looked down at my pale face and shoulders in the pool. Then he squatted as a visitor squats by the seal tank at the zoo.

'This,' said Selma thinly, 'is Mr Christopher Hollings, the English concert pianist. He has come to lunch.'

Yacob pushed some more potato salad from his hand into his face. '*Shalom*, Mr Hollings,' he said deeply, offering me the cream-stuck palm in which he had held the food. I made to put my hand up to shake it when Selma said stiffly, 'Yacob. Your hand. For God's sake!'

'Oh, I am so sorry,' he laughed withdrawing it. '*Shalom. Shalom* anyway. Are you coming out of my pool? Let us have some lunch. All of us.'

'Oh yes, of course,' I said. I could have waded to the steps but because he was watching me I heaved myself up on the swimming-pool rail and got my knee on to the wet concrete just at his feet. Then I slipped ignominiously and rolled back into the water. Furious with myself at the stupidity, I tried again, became fixed halfway, and eventually had to accept the assisting hand offered to me by Yacob. The hand in which he had held the potato salad.

4

She telephoned me in the night when I was asleep at the hotel. She said: 'He's cleared off now, thank Christ.'

'Who has?' I asked stupidly because I had been sleeping.

'Yacob,' she said. 'You've been sleeping.'

I looked at my watch. 'That's reasonable,' I said. 'It's ten past three.'

'Yes,' she said. 'And I've just got rid of him. He hung on here for hours. I think he expected that you would be back.'

'I thought he was on military duty,' I said pulling myself up in the bed. 'He only dropped in for lunch, didn't he?'

'That's what I argued, but apparently the Army can wait for proof of adultery. So he waited. He mooned about all the evening, looking at his bloody samples of dirt. Then we went to bed – he wanted to – and after that was all finished he cleared off. I suppose he thought that once he had been to bed with me that would lock up the shop for the night. So he felt safe to go.'

Drowsily I said: 'I don't seem to remember us behaving in any way improperly. Unless swimming in your pool is improper.'

'It must have looked strange,' she said.

'To the man from the front line,' I nodded at the phone.

She said: 'With the lunch all laid out and everything.'

'I know that. My back is just starting to burn. He made me sit in the sun all the time, the bastard.'

She said: 'That's my husband you speak of.'

'Indeed,' I agreed. 'Why did you ring?'

'I don't know,' she replied. 'What are you doing?'

'Sleeping,' I said. 'What else? I was dreaming I was riding a dromedary to a desert of ice-cream.'

'That's Freudian,' she said. 'Very nasty. Particularly on a dromedary.'

'Probably, but I'm going back right now.'

'To the dromedary?'

'Of course.'

'I'll bow out then. I'll pick you up at ten to take you to Jerusalem.'

'The Golden,' I said. 'All right. At ten. Goodnight, Selma.'

'*Erav tov*, Christopher. Happy dromedaries.'

She arrived at ten with her Mercedes. She was driving and we went off together out of Tel Aviv towards the jumped-up hills, first through the Vale of Sharon and then on to the gradually rising country to Jerusalem. All the hills were brown and strewn with white boulders as though some primitive battle had been joined and finished and all the ammunition left lying around.

She looked very young again that morning. She wore a multi-patterned shirt and white slacks, flared at the bottom which was an advanced fashion then for a woman in Israel. Her shirt was silk and her breasts stuck out like prim pyramids under the material. All the time she drove she smiled to herself as though she had some specially good secret, but when I asked her about it she replied that she enjoyed driving before noon and the prospect of going to Jerusalem always pleased her.

'Do you know many women in Israel?' she asked as we were going through Ramla, by the prison where they kept Eichmann before they executed him. She half-turned, moving the car expertly around the backside of a donkey in the street. 'Or is that a rude question?'

'It's a rude question,' I said. 'But I'll tell you. I know two women here – to talk to that is. You and a young lady called Shoshana Levy who works for a newspaper in Tel Aviv.'

She said: 'She writes a column in one of the morning papers. It's usually rubbish. It's in Hebrew, but I get someone to read the papers for me.'

'Well, I know her,' I said. 'She came over to England to

47

write some articles about me. I had a drink with her the other evening, after going to the party.'

'She works late,' Selma said.

I said: 'That's correct, she works late.'

'I remember the articles,' she said. She did not drive like most women, having to look at the person with whom she talked. Her eyes were on the road. 'I got someone to read them to me because I was interested in your visit here. They were pretty shitty.'

The road was sunlit, then clouded with shade in parts by the piled hills of rock on either side. It ran at one place around the lip of a gradual crater and beyond, on the opposite rise, were the square-eyed houses of a village.

'Abu Gosh,' she said. I had made no reply to what she had said about the articles.

'Who lives there?' I asked.

'It's an Arab village. Integrated Arabs. The Jews are very proud of their integrated Arabs, you know. They show them off like we show off the Tower of London.' When she chose, I noticed, she would suddenly claim her Britishness. Especially when she talked about the Jews. 'It's a sop to their conscience for driving all the others out,' she said. 'They point to this lot and a few thousand subjected others and ask you to realize how democratic Israel is, at the same time thanking God under their breaths that there are no more of the rotten bastards about. I hate to think what will happen to Abu Gosh and the other places when the real Arabs come up this road.'

'You think they will come up this road?' I asked.

'Certainly,' she replied. 'As soon as the Jordanians get on the move they'll cut straight through here and join up with Nasser's army coming the other way.'

'The Israelis don't believe that,' I said.

'No,' she admitted. 'It keeps them happy not to believe it, I suppose. You wait and see.'

'Are you still going to play golf throughout the war?' I smiled.

'Of course. Caesarea golf course will be the safest place to be. I shall wear a bright red shirt so that everyone can see

I'm not one of the military and I shall have my British passport in my golf bag along with my scorecard. I always keep a scorecard, you know. It's good discipline, even when you're going around by yourself.'

'And when the Arabs arrive?'

'I shall wave my putter and my passport to the nearest officer. I think it's better to wave a putter than, say, a five iron. A putter doesn't look so aggressive.'

'Where are we now?' I asked. We had run down through a steep valley with the road in its gully, the sides crowded with rocks and pines. It was cool and enclosed.

'This is the Corridor,' she replied. 'The Jerusalem Corridor. Where they made all the fuss in 1948. The Jews got convoys through to the city and the other lot were shooting from up there on the hills. See along here. They left some of the casualties as mementoes.'

On the flank of the road, blind, dead, hollow, were some armoured trucks, wheel-less, rust-red, garlanded with flowers, some alive some dead, lying peacefully beneath the pine branches. They were struck at grotesque angles like small shipwrecked vessels, strewn out at intervals along two miles of the Corridor road.

'They left them where they were hit,' she explained. 'It was very unhealthy down here, as you can see. But they hung on to Jerusalem, or half of it anyway.'

She drove the Mercedes elegantly around the painful bends of the road, now rising all the time. We passed struggling buses and huge gasping lorries, and were passed ourselves by frantic cars.

Eventually she said quietly: 'There it is. The city.'

It lay like a lion across the stony hills, tawny in the sunlight, a fine amber, brightening to gold, its towers and walls beautiful, assured, with all the calmness of four thousand years.

'The prettier part is theirs,' she said. 'That is, the Jordanians. This side, the New City, is dowdy to say the least and not even very ancient. The Jews on this side sit out in the evenings and watch the wall and the roofs of the other side and think how much they would like to be there.'

'You're very anti-Jewish,' I said. 'For someone who lives in Israel.'

'Perhaps that is the reason,' she said. 'Sometimes they're okay. Yacob is okay at times. But they make you a bit sick, too. They're like kids playing with a pile of building bricks.'

The road widened and eased as though encouraged by the nearing end of its journey. We ran into the first streets, humped across the bending of the hills, lined with gritty open shops, hung blinds, people squatting in the dust, and animals in the road. 'That is the YMCA,' she pointed. 'That tower. I always thought how funny it was to have that stuck in the middle of a place like this. And this is the King David. Shall we have lunch.'

It was a firm statement. She took the car into the curved gravelled drive and we lunched in the cool dining-room. 'They blew this place up, of course,' she said.

'I remember.'

'Bloody fools the British. They even had a telephone call to warn them but they pooh-poohed it, and went on drinking their gin and tons. And then bang. Half the place fell down. They were lucky too, it was only half, because it's not often the Jews short change themselves.'

Her house was not far from the Jerusalem Railway Station looking towards Pentecost and Mount Zion. There were cars parked at meters in the main street. We went through them and down an overhung alley and then beneath an arch into a little walled garden, the sunlight dulled by vines and figs. There was a formed hole like a grave under the figs, lined with stones, which she said was an ancient wine press. In this, its neck sticking up like a curious bird, was a clay jar. Selma felt into the neck and produced a Yale key. We went up the white steps towards the fine wooden door, held by brass hinges and ecclesiastically arched at its top.

'There's a housekeeper here normally,' she said pushing the key and turning. 'But she's gone off to the Navy or some other worthy cause. What with my husband and all my servants, it seems I'm providing the bulk of the bloody armed forces for this country.'

Inside the house was dim. She began moving about, elegantly, raising shutters and opening doors. One door overlooked another garden with a running view of the Old City Wall, the capped heads of its towers peeping over like people overwhelmed with curiosity, and the shelving land of the Jewish sector on our side, and the wire-tangled frontier. There was a terrace outside and then a drop into the green branches spread like the arms of dancers in the garden. Sunlight came strong and white into the house and Selma walked about drawing light, cloudy curtains to filter it.

I was on the terrace and she came out and stood beside me. She was only a few inches away and I knew that it would not be long. I realized that with her height she would lie almost exactly alongside me in the bed, like one ship moored against another.

'There is some lime juice,' she said. 'Would you like a glass, Christopher?'

I said I would. She went and returned with the pale drinks. 'That is my house,' she said pointing across the garden, across the untidy wire of no-man's-land. 'My other house, you remember.'

I followed her eyes to the Jordanian houses piled in the other sector. 'The one with the two cypresses and the little round tower. It is no distance, is it?'

'Just like living next door to yourself,' I said. 'Does it make you unhappy to see it?'

'Sometimes,' she admitted. 'There is a short flagstaff on the little tower. You see it? My mother and my stepfather used to make a great joke about flying flags from there. On St George's Day we always had the Union Jack run up and on the Greek Independence Day the old man used to have his flag flying.

'But I'm not a sentimental person. I am happy enough to watch the house. I used to purloin Yacob's military binoculars and sit here spying on the house and the people who live round about it. Most of them I remember well. Abdullah the postman with his red racing bike. He must be eighty now. Then there's Hassan the watchmaker who owns the house across the way. That bugger lets his goats graze in my garden. I've stood here and watched him open the gate and push them in there. So I wrote to him via a friend in London and told him not to do it. That must have given him a hell of a shock. He's probably been sniffing around trying to find out who shopped him.'

I laughed with her. 'What's the golden egg?' I asked pointing beyond the castellated wall, over the crammed roofs of the Old City.

'The Dome of the Rock, in the Temple area,' she said. 'Beautiful isn't it. It's dazzling in the sun, but in the evening when the light is richer, it is so magnificent.'

She turned back into the room. 'But the Wailing Wall is just a wall full of old birds' nests, and the Church of the Holy Sepulchre is such an ugly damn place, and a lousy package deal at that . . .'

'How is that?' I asked. I had remained on the terrace viewing the lion-coloured city, dusty under the bitter afternoon sun.

'Oh,' she said from within the room, 'it's all buttressed up with bits of wood, for a start. It's a bit unsteady after an earthquake. But it's full of touts and nasty Greeks with beards.' She laughed. I could hear her moving about in the room so I turned and went in to her. It would not be long now. She was standing in the filtered sunlight by one of the curtained windows.

'They show you quite blatantly where the Cross was stuck into the ground, and they obligingly push aside a floorboard to show where the earth cracked on Good Friday, and then they trot you across a few yards of the place and ask you to have a squint at the Tomb. It's all nicely parcelled up. Quite laughable really.'

She had been talking hurriedly, as though she were nervous. Now she stopped and we stood, half a room apart, me with the empty lime glass in my hand, her looking half away from me through the fine curtain. I put the glass down on a side table.

'Are we going to bed, Christopher?' she asked. I heard

some birds quarrel suddenly in the vines in the garden.

'Yes,' I said to her. 'I think it would be worth doing.'

'So do I,' she said. 'I've been looking forward to it.'

I walked to her and we kissed, almost formally, without passion, as though sealing some bargain which we had negotiated and understood. It was then I became aware of her smell. It was an English sort of smell. My mother smelt like it, fresh and unsubtle. It wasn't a young odour. It was strange to find it there in a city of spices and hot aromas.

Until then I had not touched her. I drew away a little when I smelled her and she now turned towards me and we smiled knowingly at each other. I had never before made love to a woman older than myself. My hands went to her breasts, but she quietly encircled my wrists and brought them down.

'I want us to undress separately,' she said. 'The bedroom is down that little flight of stairs and immediately through the doors. You can see Pentecost from the window. Wait for me for a few moments.'

She went up a companion flight of stairs to the set which went down to the bedroom. I watched her go, tall, good carriage, slim backside, and then walked down through a white door and into a fine bedroom with white furniture and a lime-green bedcover. It had a french window letting out on to another, lower terrace, and I stood and watched Arab soldiers moving along the great crusted walls of the Holy City, and a windmill sitting in the middle of the low buildings on the Jewish side.

It was brimmed with mid-afternoon heat out there, but cool where I stood. I pulled the light curtains and undressed, casually, easily, full of anticipation for the next hour. I dropped on to the bed and felt it give. Then I lay there, watching the egg and dart moulding around the ceiling, until I heard her bare feet coming down the short run of steps and into the room.

When she had gone off I had thought that she wanted to put on something conventionally glamorous, some silk or filmy thing that would hide some of the imperfections of her approaching middle age. But she came into the room naked. She stood by the bed.

There was no sagginess about her. She was tall and brown and composed. She smiled at me lying across her bed and put out the extremes of her right-hand fingers to me. I touched them then held them lightly. It was the first romantic thing we had achieved. I am always held by a woman's breasts. These were medium and quite firm with only a little hammocking. They were white against the brown of her trunk like some fruits deprived of the sun. Her nipples were small and pinched and redcurrant-red.

'Does your back hurt?' she asked kneeling forward on the lime counterpane. 'The sunburn?'

'It's all right when I remain still,' I said looking at her steadily. 'It feels very raw when I move against something.'

She laughed and lowered herself towards me, kneeling like an animal on the bed, her breasts hanging down. When I see a woman in this position it always reminds me of the statue of the female wolf in Rome, her dugs dangling, standing over Romulus and Remus. I pushed my entire arm out, my hand like the head of a snake, thrusting it in the soft channel between her legs. She remained on all fours and I pushed my fingers along the warmth of the crease and held her backside in my hand so that my wrist was against her tender parts. I could feel her place pounding like a beating heart. There was a fly on the egg and dart moulding. Selma moved over me. I removed my hand and with both sets of fingers began tugging gently at her nipples like an apprentice bell-ringer. I watched the tight red nipples soften and flower with my touching.

'Put it back, please,' she said.

'What back?'

'Your hand, and your arm, for God's sake.'

'I forget where it was now,' I said.

'You're a bastard, Christopher. You're playing about with me. Put it back. Here.' She caught my hand and threaded it like a cable through the tunnel of her legs again pushing the end of my fingers into the culmination of her backside. 'Like that,' she said. 'Under and through . . . and then up.'

'I remember,' I said.

'I'm so glad you do.'

She moved on to me now, careful though not to press her weight into me because of my sunburned back. Her tongue went to my forehead and touched it as though in some sort of benediction. She began to run it down towards the centre of my eyebrows.

I said to her: 'What's that windmill doing in the middle of Jerusalem?' She was right. I'm a bastard.

Her tongue stopped at the bridge of my nose.

'Do you want to know *now*?'

'Well I saw it from the window and it seemed a bit strange having a windmill in the middle of Jerusalem. I could understand it in Amsterdam.'

She brought her tongue down my nose, let it spread itself across my nostrils for a while and continued to my mouth. We kissed very passionately then, for a long time. Her hand had gone down to me and she had hold of me like an Arab holding a donkey. I was feeling explosive.

'Why is it there?' I asked.

'Because I chose to put it there.'

'The windmill, I meant.'

'Oh, it was built to ...'

'Yes?'

'To grind corn for the people around here. Years ago.'

'Who built it?'

'You bastard. Sir Moses Montefiore. I know because I've read it all up. Eighteen fifty-eight. Turn over and lie on top of me now. Please.'

I did. As I thought, we were exactly the same size. My eyes were an inch away from hers. I was complete with her now. She closed her eyes and when she opened them again a minute later mine were still an inch away and still looking at her.

'Who was he?'

'Christopher, I feel terrible.'

'So do I. Think of something else. Like the windmill. Who was this Sir Moses Monty ...'

'All right,' she muttered. 'Montefiore. An Englishman. A

55

philanthropist. Oh, my Christ. Gently baby. He built a settlement for Jews . . .'

'Called?'

'Christopher,' she pleaded. '. . . Christopher . . .'

'Called?'

'Bastard. You really are. I've met some, but you are the
biggest. . . It was called . . . oh, what the hell. History at a
time like this. It was called Yemin Moshe. . .'

I said: 'What's *that*?' I couldn't go on much longer. Not
the first time.

Her eyes were screwed up. 'That's me,' she whispered.
'That's all I can let you have. I can't tell you the anatomical
name, but it's *me*, darling. It's my very end. You can't go any
farther.'

'I meant Yemin Moshe. What's it mean?'

'The Right Hand of . . . Christ . . .'

'That's poetic.'

'No,' she said. 'It wasn't *Christ*. I just said "Christ" as a
sort of exclamation. It's to do with what we're doing, you
see.'

'Oh.'

'Yemin Moshe means the Right Hand of Moses, meaning
Moses Montefiore, not the better known one.'

'I think I'm coming,' I said.

'Me too. So shut up.'

I slept for about five minutes afterwards and when I woke
up I was lying in her arms and my sweat was cooling, and I
could smell my mother's smell.

'There was quite a battle about it once,' said Selma.

'What?' I asked.

'The windmill.'

'Oh yes. The one that Moses built.'

'Yes,' she said. She was looking at the egg and dart orna-
ment on the ceiling. The fly was up there too. I watched him.
'That was in 1948. The Jews and the Arabs had a battle
over it.'

'It's a natural strongpoint,' I said like a general.

'Exactly. It was an extremely bloody battle. The Jews
called it Operation Don Quixote.'

'Don Quixote – windmill. Very apt,' I said. I turned and kissed her gently and she kissed me in return.

'I'll tell you something about that windmill, love,' I said.

'What's that?'

'It's the second-best grind in Jerusalem.'

5

Eilat lies under the sun in the south, at the pouting lip of the blue gulf that issues from the Strait of Tiran and the Red Sea. The Israelis call the sea the Gulf of Eilat; the Jordanians, whose port of Akaba squats across the bay, call it the Gulf of Akaba. From the hotel at Eilat you can look over the sea to Akaba, white under the red mountains and see the traffic moving in the streets. Ships for Israel and Jordan steam up the Gulf and sometimes a captain will negligently take them into the wrong port, turning left for right or right for left at the cul-de-sac of the Gulf and have to be politely re-directed either by the Arabs or the Jews.

Metzer had come to the hotel in Tel Aviv to pick me up and take me to the little Sede Dov Airport which was near the river bridge where the guards had stopped the car three nights before. He was fussy but cheerful.

'This week,' he announced, 'I think that maybe there will not be any war.'

'What makes you change your mind?' I asked. We had walked out to the car and immediately out of the shadow and the air conditioning of the hotel the sun leaped on my back like a cat. My shoulders were pink and smarting under my shirt.

Metzer and I got into the car. He smiled fondly out at the people hurrying in the sun of Hayarkon Street, and at the tired blue waves coming into the land from the belly of the sea.

'It will be all right, all nice and peaceful, I know,' he re-assured. 'Now everyone is talking, all the politicians and the United Nations and everybody. Eshkol is having Government trouble here and Nasser is having the same trouble in Cairo. Nobody feels secure enough to fight. Everybody's talking and that's good. Maybe you have a good concert tour after all.'

'When the first bomb, shell or bullet goes off, I go off too,' I said conversationally.

He looked around at me. His head dropped in acknow-ledgement and he smiled a bit. 'I suppose that is reasonable, Mr Hollings,' he said. 'In any case I do not think there would be a lot of opportunity for music. We would make sure that we got you out. You are a neutral.'

'Most neutral,' I said.

'Would you think it rude of me if I said that you are a strange man. . . No that is incorrect. . . An unusual young man for a concert performer.'

He laughed but was obviously uncertain about going on. 'I mean it in the most kind way, you understand. But you are strange for your profession, and I have known many, as you will appreciate. You are so ordinary.'

Sometimes I get nasty and I almost let go then. But he corrected himself. 'No, that is a bad word. Excuse me, my English is sometimes limited. . .'

'Yes,' I agreed. He gave a little pout of embarrassment. I said: 'You mean that I don't seem to fit the part?'

'No, not exactly, Mr Hollings. You play like the hell. I never remember a solo like yours the other night. No, it is in everyday things that you are different.'

'Ah, you mean my image. Well I am a roughshod lad, you know, Mr Metzer. I'm not one of your eighteenth-century-candelabra, drawing-room boys, touching each note with a moonlit smile. And I'm not one of your dedicated bores who live every moment of the part. They have long hair because they practise so much they don't have time to get it cut. Mine's long because I want it long.'

He nodded agreeably. 'Ah yes. I understand well. It is El Cordobes and the Beatles and that manner of presentation. It is very modern, of course. Very modern...' His voice slackened off pensively. We had turned off a dusty road into the mouth of the small airfield. At the end of the runway there were some toy-like jet planes looking uncomfortable with a clutch of rockets under each wing. The planes looked like little men carrying too many parcels.

'Fouga Magister trainers,' said Metzer seeing me looking at them. 'They are baby planes for new pilots, but we will use them in the battle, if there is a battle.'

'Every little helps,' I said. 'Somebody obviously doesn't share your confidence in the talking power of politicians.'

He shrugged miserably and kicked at a lizard on the concrete apron. 'It's just a little readiness,' he said. 'A little readiness is a good thing, Mr Hollings.'

The airport building was not much more than a wooden shed. I walked towards it and saw two Dakotas sitting like old grey geese at the end of the runway.

'I didn't know there were any of those things still flying,' I said.

Apologies flooded into Metzer's face. 'They are very good,' he said. 'The same two have been flying down the Negev for years, to Beersheba, to Masada, and up to Rosh Pina in Galilee.'

I continued walking towards the airport building. I could feel the sun seeping through my shirt and on to the sore pink of my back. Cursing Yacob Haydn I went gratefully into the cool interior.

'Well, I can't say I'd like to trust my precious hide in those grandfather things,' I said to Metzer. He went to get me a drink. He was obviously upset when he returned.

'Those grandfather things, as you so-call them,' he said nodding heavily and unhappily out of the window. 'The two Dakotas, renovated only a year ago, and flying very well. Those two are for us... For you and me, and the rest of the orchestra for our journey to Eilat.'

'I thought you might tell me that,' I told him. Taking the

59

drink from him I looked miserably from the wooden room first at the Fouga Magister trainers with their ungainly rocket claws and then at the Dakotas. 'It's a great country for making-do,' I said.

He did not look as though he fully understood, but he was ready to agree with anything I said. 'Yes,' he said. 'For that it is surely a great country.'

On the Thursday Moshe Dayan became Defence Minister in Jerusalem. They were setting up the orchestra on the beach when Metzer came in by jeep from the town and shouted it in Hebrew. The musicians and the others who were out there working in the late afternoon began cheering and clamouring around Metzer. The two grey Dakotas rested on the airstrip across from the beach unperturbed by the bumpy flight over the hot air rising from the bad teeth of the Negev Desert.

I was on the balcony of the little hotel drinking tea and going through the score. There was no piano available for practising and they had only just unloaded the one to be used in the concert from the aeroplane.

Metzer ran heavily along the beach and puffed under the balcony. I leaned over. Two motor torpedo boats had just set out from Eilat harbour and were chewing their way truculently across the bay towards Akaba. I watched them.

'What's the cheering about?' I called down to Metzer. 'Have the Arabs surrendered?'

His face dropped heavily. 'No, no,' he said childishly. Then decided to make a joke of it. 'Not yet. Maybe tomorrow. By then they will hear that our new Defence Minister is Moshe Dayan; you know him, him with one eye.' He closed his right eye and put his hand across it. Then he flustered. 'No. Sorry, it is the wrong eye. Our Minister has no eye *this* side.' He changed to the left.

'I know the man,' I said amiably. 'He looks like Richard Widmark.'

'Who is that?' Metzer called up.

Instead of answering I pointed to the twin torpedo boats going like dolphins for the Arab shore. 'Where is the Jewish

Navy going?' I called to him. He looked at them and returned face-up to me.

'Just for a look,' he said. 'Every day they go to look at the Arabs and then they come back. There is no trouble. They always do it. It is a habit.'

'Provocation,' I shouted down at him. He took me seriously and wobbled his big head. 'Just habit,' he replied. 'Will you come down to the beach when you are prepared, Mr Hollings. The piano is just being taken there.'

I nodded that I would be down. The afternoon was well gone now, the water in the bay was dulled and a faint rouge touch was on the table of hills behind Akaba. The desert between Israel and Jordan was still and empty, but at sea the two silver boats drove on wickedly through the outlying waves.

There was an Italian fisherman on the beach with two Abyssinians who had travelled up from Africa to work in the gulf. Time brings some strange people together. At the finish of that afternoon, as the orchestra was setting up its instruments by the sea, a tribe of fish was spotted out in the flat water.

The Italian was a miserable man with a browned and sour face, shouting in a rough tone that made his own melodic language sound bad. The Abyssinians had journeyed to Eilat in a small boat rowing the course that the Queen of Sheba had travelled. They were childish men, giggling and gesticulating, running seawards towards their boats, carrying the seine net like a dead serpent, hurt clouding their black faces when the Italian shouted at them.

Some men had carried my piano on to the beach and settled it in front of the orchestra stands. It looked illogical there, like a clever advertising picture, sitting on the shelving sand with the sea behind it, with the men rushing to trap the fish, and the two motor torpedo boats a long way out and turning back from Jordan.

Metzer was standing on the beach, exploring the notes of the piano as though testing the acoustics of that widespread place. On one side, the dull hills of the Egyptian Sinai were burned with the setting of the sun, with bloody streaks cutting through their chasms. On the other, the quick sunset caught the Jordan hills making them like livid coals. I walked across the cooling sand and stood by him. The musicians had stopped carrying things now and were grouped together like children watching the working of the fishermen.

Zoo Baby, the biggest of all the orchestra players, and the only one I knew by name, turned and shouted back to Metzer in Hebrew. Metzer laughed and returned the shout as though he were directing the fishing operation. Zoo Baby acknowledged the remark and called to the fishermen who were bending their boats in a pincer movement around the backs of the populous fish.

Metzer said to me: 'It's a fine catch of tuna. They have been waiting for three days for them. Now they are caught. Everybody down here will eat tuna.' He shook his head in admiration: 'We Israelis are good fishermen,' he said.

He was the same as all of them. Full of themselves. Any Israeli is better than ten others, from anywhere. I don't know how they got this arrogance. Perhaps in the Warsaw Ghetto when they first learned to fight and kill. They boast and they mean every word they say about themselves.

'The fishermen are not Jews,' I pointed out. I used the word Jews purposely, instead of Israelis, because I had some idea it might irritate him, but it did not. Metzer considered the correction. 'True,' he said squeezing his eyes to look out to sea, as though the next order had to come from him. 'But the methods we use down here, my friend, are our own. The Italian and the black men have come to learn them. Ah, they have the fish.'

Across the purple water the Abyssinian boys began hooting with excitement and from the other boat the Italian steadied them hoarsely. But they had the tuna, trapped and trembling, a great horde of rotund fish in the arms and fingers of the net, panicked and thrashing the water. The musicians on the beach, all in bright shirts, some with trousers rolled up like seaside fathers, were chorusing encouragement, and ran into the water when the boats returned to help tug at the aching net. They scampered and splashed and heaved with the exaggerated effort of men of a soft occupation suddenly encountering a physical task. Finding that one ear of the net was more heavily manned than the other some of them ran across, through the shallows, to reinforce the other side. Then there were too many on that side and some scampered back to their original places. At the centre Zoo Baby, the huge back heaving under a bright yellow shirt, urged them on like the captain of twin tug-of-war teams. His trousers were rolled up and the broad hairy trunks of his legs were planted apart in the sand.

'The Jews,' said Metzer turning to me, although with no noticeable emphasis on the second word, 'have always been great fishermen. Peter and James and John, all that gang, you remember were fishers. Didn't their boss call them fishers of men?' He spread his hands. 'I don't know. I only hear about these incidents.'

'I remember the story,' I said. 'Those fish are bleeding, they are kicking about so much.'

'Yes,' he said with interest. 'See, the water is turning to pink. And fish have little blood you know. They are killing each other trying to get out.'

The whole mess of tuna was now sprawled in the shallows about the feet of the excited musicians. They were writhing trying to find salt water with their mouths, gasping as the air drowned them. They were sturdy fish, none of them less than two feet in length and very fat about the middle. Some were very big, perhaps twenty pounds. The musicians danced with the excitement of the conquest. Then the Italian came from his boat and with a wide wave of his arms that immediately demonstrated his native nature, he silenced the musicians with all the authority of a notable maestro. They became quiet and quickly organized, catching on to the fisherman's simple Hebrew, spliced with Italian, taking the fish one by one in their hands and carrying them up the beach to a mud-coloured truck.

The Italian was smiling now he had his fish, and he made jokes with them by calling instructions in musical terms – *presto, pianissimo, profundo* – when they sorted a particularly big, limp fish from the net. They transported the tuna, one by one, about three hundred of them I suppose, carrying the smaller fish by the tails and the bigger ones across their arms, hugged to their bellies as though they were rescuing children. When the net was clear except for oddments of fish flesh and debris, the Italian gave each of the orchestra a fish to himself, and they walked towards Metzer and myself carrying their prizes, smiling with achievement and pleasure and reeking with an engulfing stink.

They gathered around to show off their fish, as though seeking credit and admiration. Metzer seemed as pleased as they were and stuck his thumb and forefinger into the moribund creatures as if to test their fibre and quality.

I felt I was seeing them for the first time. At the rehearsals and at the Tel Aviv concert they had only been an orchestra, laying a carpet for my individualism, rolling it out royally so that I could march, run, dance or dawdle upon it. To me, until then, they were sounds; brass sounds, and string sounds, thin breezy sounds, and wide windy sounds. Only Zoo Baby I had noticed. You always notice the man at the back sitting over his drums like a chef fussing over his cauldrons. And you would see Zoo Baby anyway, because he was big and laughing, and was always shaking hands and making jokes, and because of his nickname which everyone called him.

The Italian had, in a joke, given him a small fish, but he regarded it with friendliness, as though he had saved its life. With his yellow shirt, his damp rolling face and his spread hips he stood out in front of the sweating group. His hands were fat, but with fine muscled fingers. He looked at me and laughed, but a little shamefaced as if he were embarrassed about their antics with the fish.

Metzer said to me with some formality: 'Everything has been conducted in the wrong fashion on this tour. It is unfortunate, but it is the war business and the worry. It is my fault.' One of the musicians had given him a specially large tuna to inspect and he looked into its surrendered eyes and sadly agape throat with the professional manner of a doctor diagnosing a head cold. He returned the fish heavily to the man.

Turning to me again, he said: 'This perhaps is a good opportunity to introduce you to the members of the Israel Symphony Orchestra. They all know you, Mr Hollings, but you do not know them. Only by their music.'

I met them all then. Each one coming forward and bowing politely with the fish held possessively. I shook each smelly hand and felt the small scales and pieces of silver skin sticking to mine. Some of them tucked their ogling prizes under their arms like walking sticks, some hung them by the tail, some laid them on the sand and afterwards had to brush the grains off the flesh; some handed their fish to neighbours before shaking hands with me, and two on reclaiming theirs fell to quarrelling, disputing the fattest.

What men they were. I thought it then and in the frightening days and nights that followed after I thought it many times. On that first afternoon, I know now, that my inward attitude was patronizing, watching them come forward with their personal fish to shake hands. My right hand was getting wetter and more scaly with each introduction, I got the extra wave of smell as our hands moved up and down. Metzer was watching me. It was like being an explorer meeting a coy tribe in some jungle place.

Zoo Baby had a big olive laugh that squeezed then spread generously across his wide face. He came from Budapest originally but he spoke good, if heavy, English.

'You want to look at the Arabs, maybe,' he suggested politely at the front of the hotel. Metzer glanced at me. 'There is little to see,' he put in, 'but there is time enough if you like. Some of the others maybe will go too.' He moved closer to me. 'It makes them feel that perhaps they are living dangerously also, going to the frontier.' He looked at me appraisingly. 'But, no worry, there is no risk. There is hardly a frontier, just an amusing string of barbed wire.'

There was a Volkswagen van from the airstrip outside the hotel, a bright German-blue, and Metzer pulled himself into the driving seat and called me in beside him. Zoo Baby lumbered into the back of the vehicle and called out in Hebrew from there. Some of the musicians waved him away and laughed. One called in English: 'When the war begins we see all the Arabs we want, Zoo Baby!'

But half a dozen moved towards the van, two of them still clutching their fish as though they would not trust anyone else with them. They hunched into the back and Metzer set off across the road that went like stitching between the Negev desert and the sea.

We were pointing directly at Jordan and the evening grew redder across the powerful mountains. A small high-winged aeroplane, its landing lights spearing the uncertain evening in front of it, did the obligatory banana turn over the gulf and floated into the airstrip. I watched it cross us, its silver turned orange by the sunset. Then the road turned for a short distance at right angles along the peninsula and I was able to watch the plane run in across the sea, down the beach and touch with a playful bounce on to the airstrip.

'Our conductor for tonight has arrived,' said Metzer. 'The noted Herr Scheerer of Munich.'

'And no Wagner on the bill?' I said.

'An accident,' said Metzer unconvincingly. 'We Israelis, of course, are great lovers of Wagner. I am glad Herr Scheerer's plane was on time at Lod. The pilot of the little aeroplane is not very good at night.'

'Herr Scheerer is very brave to risk his neck,' I said.

'He did not know.' Metzer gave his round-shouldered shrug, turned the Volkswagen off the peninsula road again and pointed it towards the growing lights of Akaba. The headlights of the cars moved in the distant streets like fire-flies and there were yellow haloes about the masts of the ships in the port.

'I didn't know either,' I pointed out. I still did not know whether I liked him. 'I never expected to be transported down here in a clapped-out grandfather of a plane and then have to perform on the beach like a seaside concert party.'

He laughed over the almost horizontal steering wheel. 'They all say that,' he admitted. 'That is why we never tell them. We just say we are making all arrangements.'

'And you do,' I nodded.

66

'You are not enjoying it, this tour?' he asked as though he was worried.

'Let's say I would bring my own camel next time.'

He laughed to himself again as though that was a cliché too. Then he butted his head at the gloomy sand to our left and said: 'They've brought your camel.'

'Arabs?' I whispered. I realized how low my voice had become so I said more firmly: 'Are they Arabs?'

'Bedouin,' he nodded. A short caravan was coming across the low broken hills of the hem of the desert, dark and riding, coming towards us slowly but then veering away and moving out of our view. Metzer said: 'They come, they go. Camels, humans and goats, moving from Jordan to Israel and Israel into Egypt, as they have always done.'

'What about the frontiers, the defences?' I said.

'Defences!' he snorted. 'You cannot guard a desert. We know that and so do the other side. The Bedouin go from one watering place to the next, from one patch for their goats to another. They smuggle drugs from Amman to Port Said, but it is too difficult to stop them. They are neither for us or the Arabs, they are for themselves.'

'So you leave them alone.'

'Everybody does. There is no other way. They cut the telephone lines between Eilat and Beersheba and used the wire to make copper bracelets to sell in Damascus. We went after them and some got shot, so they waited a month and then ambushed a bus coming across the Negev. Six people were killed. So now we don't fight them any more. It's too much difficulty. Our trouble is all around us without it is right in our belly too. So we just tell them to not cut the telephone lines and we let them take their camels across the country, out of Jordan into Egypt without trouble.'

Zoo Baby grunted from the back of the wagon. He said heavily: 'When they cut the telephone cables they said they thought it was okay because they only cut five of the six. They left the other one for us.'

It was rougher going now, with the van throwing stones and grit from its wheels. We slowed and stopped and Metzer said: 'Here we are. This is the border.'

67

I climbed down. I could hear the sea washing close by, but it was over a low parapet of dark amber rock and out of sight. The musicians were climbing from the back door, and came around to the front, one still holding his personal tuna fish, to look at the pathetic single strand of barbed wire which bisected the barren place. Most of Akaba was shut out by the surrounding rock, but now it was getting close to dark its lights were thrown up into the sky. The blood red of the mountains had diminished like a dying coal and some stars, early and cool, were showing.

Dov Haran, who was the leading oboe, stood by me and pointed to a tree, alone and unkempt as an urchin, standing on a flat of the desert to the north. He was a quiet, informed man, as I learned, and he liked telling things. 'That tree,' he said in slightly American English. 'You see it? It is the final tree of Asia, so they say. It is a palm of a species that grows only in Asia and that is the last one. The story is that the place where the tree has its roots is the dividing place between Africa and the Orient.'

'And you have your foot in the Hashemite Kingdom of Jordan.' It was, astonishingly, an Irish voice. It came across the dull dunes and after it came a stumbling man in a police-blue uniform, shorts, and a peaked cap like a park keeper.

'United Nations?' I guessed.

'Wrong,' said Dov. He had a graceful moustache and he pulled at it. 'Israeli Border Police. We have many types, Arabs, Druzes even. And English.'

'Don't tell him he's English,' I whispered. 'He's Irish.'

Metzer had gone forward and was offering explanations. The border guard listened and then walked sharply towards us. 'A party of musicians, you might be,' he said. 'But this is no time of the night for strolling players.' Only Dov laughed. 'And that man . . .' he pointed directly at me, 'still has his right foot in the Hashemite Kingdom of Jordan. Will he please withdraw it. There could be what are called repercussions.'

Metzer became surprisingly pompous. 'This, officer,' he announced, 'is the very distinguished English concert pianist,

Christopher Hollings.' He and the frontier guard looked towards me, Metzer with his hand outstretched towards me like a conjurer after a trick. The guard walked forward. He had his hands around a little machine gun and he now slipped it by the sling across his shoulder.

'I'm glad to see you've moved your foot, anyway,' he said. 'I'm pleased to meet you.'

'I was glad I moved,' I said. 'I didn't know I was trespassing.'

'I'm Richard O'Sullivan, *Segan-Mefakeach*, Border Police, some time of Wexford and Liverpool. We speak the same language,' he smiled.

We shook hands. 'What is Segan? . . .' I fumbled.

'*Segan-Mefakeach*,' he repeated. 'Deputy-Inspector, that's all. Lowest rank in the force. I think *Segan-Mefakeach* sounds better. Deputy-Inspector sounds like someone who examines drains.' He was very thin, with hard-edged bones pushing at his face skin. It was difficult to see his eyes under the sinister peak of his cap, but he smiled with a disarray of teeth, and his hand was rigid with bones.

'The Irish in Israel,' I said. 'And in the frontier force.'

'They'll have anybody,' he retaliated amiably. 'It's steady too. I'm glad to meet you. I am off duty at seven and I'll be over to the concert. A lot of the lads will be across there to-night.' He looked about at the others and released a separate small smile for each. He also gave a nod to Zoo Baby, smiling at him, acknowledging his size as an Irishman does.

There was a movement from the top of a sand pile a hundred yards away and the lights of a motor vehicle were flashed. They were low and I could see it was a jeep. A voice shouted in Hebrew.

'Coming. I'm coming,' called O'Sullivan. He turned to us. 'See you all soon. But get back now because at this late time of the day there's liable to be misunderstandings along here. You could get shot and it makes a lot of paperwork for us and for the UN boys and the Arab border lads on the other side.'

When we returned to the hotel by the sea I saw Shoshana

standing in the tiled entrance hall with Herbert Scheerer, the conductor. Scheerer, a blancmange German, round and pink with hair apologetically combed forward over his fat forehead, was fussing over the aeroplane trip.

'She go bump, bump, bump,' he was complaining to Haim Mendel, the leader of the orchestra, who had waited to meet him. Metzer walked in and Mendel gratefully introduced him to Scheerer. Metzer in turn introduced me, but he knew that we had already met. I remember doing the Tchaikovsky Number One in Hamburg once and Scheerer conducting, fatly and fussily, and bowing all over the place with a big white cloud of talcum powder on his trouser fly where he had powdered himself, been to the urinal and had forgotten to brush himself off.

'The plane go bump, bump, bump,' he told the impassive Metzer. 'Up and down, all der time. Also it was very small. This I did not expect.'

'It's the heat that goes to the sky from the desert,' explained Metzer. 'It makes the aircraft bump, bump, bump. But you are here, Herr Scheerer, and we are very glad.'

Shoshana was looking at me across the people and I smiled towards her. She was more feminine now wearing a blue skirt and white sweater. Her neck looked very tanned against the roll of the sweater neck and her arms and legs slender and brown. I walked towards her and said: 'Where did the war go?'

She looked at me seriously. 'It is hiding for a small while,' she said. 'Everybody in Tel Aviv thinks it has gone away for good. But I think it will be back.'

'Down here?' I said thinking of the Strait of Tiran down the gulf and the motor torpedo boats of that afternoon. 'Is that why you have come?'

Now she smiled. 'No,' she corrected. 'I am not here for any battles. Only to hear you play.'

'Your editor sent you?'

'I suggested it, since I came to England to write about you. How do you feel about playing in such a place? It is like the last piece of the world, is it not?'

I grinned. 'The end of the world.'

She seemed embarrassed. 'This is correct. The end of the world. Sometimes my English goes a little away from me.'

I thought I had offended her by my correction because she turned abruptly from me and began conversing with Zoo Baby. She obviously knew him well because she pushed her long index finger into his thick waist and he admonished her in quick laughing Hebrew. But then she turned and continued her conversation with me.

'Dayan,' she said putting a mimicking hand over one eye, 'has become the Minister for Defence. Not everybody would have that, Eshkol the Prime Minister for one example, but he is a leader and we need a leader. He is a fighting man, Dayan. This is why I could never understand how they once made him the Minister for Agriculture. A warrior has little to do with chickens.'

'But the situation has quietened,' I affirmed.

'Oh yes, there is a small quiet. But now that Dayan is one of the Cabinet I am certain that a war will follow. You don't put a man of war in a possibility – no – a position, like that and expect him to make peace. We will be fighting in a short time that is without doubt.'

'Perhaps the Arabs will not attack,' I argued. She wanted to fight, I could see that. There was something in her lovely eyes. She sniffed like a schoolgirl. 'It matters nothing if they do not attack,' she said quietly arrogant. 'I have told you that we cannot afford to have the battle on Israeli soil. We may have to make them fight. It is enough that they threaten us.'

'You are foolish,' I said with offhand anger. We had walked from the main group of the musicians and the fluffy protests still coming from the German. 'How can you hope to win in the long run?'

'Of course we shall,' she answered. 'And it will not be a long run, Mr Hollings. I do not wish to argue tactics with you, because you would not understand. I will discuss the war with you when it is over. Then I will have more time. What are you playing tonight?'

'Rachmaninov,' I said. I was surprised how she was able to

71

terminate a conversation, particularly with me, on her own terms. 'Prelude Number Three.'

She produced a tiny note book and wrote it down. 'In C Sharp Minor,' I added and she wrote again. Then I said, 'Opus Three,' and she wrote that too. 'What else?' she asked as though accumulating evidence.

'Grieg,' I said. 'The concerto.'

'Has it got a number?'

'Number One. He only wrote one.'

'I did not know,' she said, writing. 'Music I know little about.'

'But the newspaper sent you to England to do the interviews with me, and they sent you down here.'

She looked up. 'I had a free airline ticket to England,' she explained without spite. 'I was travelling there in any case. I had to do some work so I wrote about you because you were coming to Israel. I also did an article about a small bear that was being sent from London to the Tel Aviv Zoo.'

'You are very adaptable.'

'Of course. And they sent me down today not because I am full of the knowledge of Grieg or Rachmaninov, but because I have had much hard work and experiences recently, and everybody else is too busy.'

If that had been my final public performance as a concert artist, and it very nearly was, then there could have been no more dramatic a stage for it. An orchestra and a soloist and the works they fashion can occasionally be lifted and enhanced by their physical surroundings like a stone in the setting of a ring. In Tel Aviv the atmosphere and the emotion had brought the experience to fullness, but sometimes it is the landscape which lends character and fineness.

A year after all this happened I sat on a damp deckchair in Holland Park, London, with two thousand people under the evening trees, listening to the London Philharmonic. There was a pale, late sky, washed clear by rain in the afternoon, and the airliners going into the airport were dropping down every few minutes in the sky behind the orchestra. The breeze was blowing their sound away from the music and they were silver, silent and slow, cutting cleanly like scissors through blue satin. It was strange how, although their paths were direct and unfaltering, their descent was in time and sympathy with the feeling of the orchestra.

On the beach at Eilat that evening it was the same, the sky littered with loitering stars and the sea all black and silver avenues. The land on all sides had backed away and only the lights of the two ports, one each side of the bay, broke the night below the level of the stars.

People had come in from the town, walking in hundreds down the hunched road that topped the airstrip; rough quiet people in odd clothes, pulling black-eyed children with them, walking but hardly speaking. They were quite unlike the alert and lively audience of Tel Aviv, the urban Jews, for there was about them something of the desert, something formed, I suppose, by winds and harsh sun and the living in that lonely place.

Others looking like dusty gypsies came in from the desert villages and the *kibbutzim* aboard trucks and half-track vehicles, rough people again with hard expressions, carrying rifles and sub-machine-guns as casually as walking sticks. Their clothes looked as though they had come immediately from the fields and although they were noisy enough among themselves they appeared to have no contact, no communication with the other people from the town.

No one needed marshalling to their place. They formed about the orchestra in concentric circles growing out to the fidgeting edge of the sea, and then farther along the beach each way in a long oval. O'Sullivan, the border guard, told me afterwards that his friends who were on duty that night, together with some Swedish and Indian United Nations soldiers, and the Jordanian platoon from the other side all stood along the barbed wire half a mile away and tried to listen to the diminished concert in the subdued night.

Everyone seemed very quiet; either that or the sound of an indoor audience was completely dissipated in the open night. I looked down from the balcony while I was dressing. Metzer had said that the orchestra would dress with complete formality, so I was in a ruffled evening shirt and tails,

73

with the silver cuff-links that Malcolm Sargent had given to me. I stood feeling the freshness of the shirt and watched the audience gather about the orchestra.

It was like primitive tribesmen coming in from a desert for a meeting, sitting rough and quiet, waiting for the proceedings to commence. Power cables had been run from the hotel to the beach for the orchestra lights, but around the perimeter of the people were flaming brands fixed into metal horns. They threw sheets of orange light across the audience, sitting like a patient herd, contrasting with the steady white lights that held the low stage built for the orchestra.

The orchestra first performed *Till Eulenspiegel*. I stood on the hotel balcony, in a curtain of shadow, looking out over the beach and the sea and over that quiet, settled, powerful cloud of people squatting on the sand and listening to the music. This, again, was a different experience. The little fable of Richard Strauss rose up out of the close night and hovered over the place. The sky was choked with stars and from my place I could see the glow of the lights on the resting ships in the harbours, Eilat on the one hand and Akaba on the other. The dark air added a new sound to the music, as though an additional instrument had been added and from the hills across the desert came the mewing of the wind in the large mountains.

Metzer knocked and came into the room behind me, walking fatly through the yellow light and out on to the subdued balcony beside me. 'I think the news is *good*,' he whispered as though afraid to disturb the orchestra even at that distance. '*Kol Israel* has just broadcast a statement by Eshkol who is back from London and America, saying that there will be settlement in a peaceful way.'

'Good,' I said tapping my fingers on the balustrade of the balcony, working them through the exercises I had done since I was a child. 'I told you so. Everything will be fine.'

He grasped on to my encouragement like a man who fears he is incurably ill holds on to any words of hope, no matter how thin, from a surgeon. 'Yes, yes,' he answered, his big head nodding like a hammer. 'Many of the troops who were mobilized have been sent on leave. Tel Aviv is full of them.

The beaches were very crowded today, they say, and everybody is having a good time. Yes, it is all right. I think.'

All the week the radio station had been broadcasting sly little messages in between records by Ray Charles or Sandie Shaw, calling men to Army units throughout the land. In Tel Aviv Metzer had translated them from Hebrew for me. 'Green Dragon and Wishing Well report to border unit by twelve noon tomorrow. Benji the Yemenite is waiting in his grocer's shop. The Rose of Sharon is picked in the fields of Dan. . . Now, for your pleasure, the Number One record in America, Aretha Franklin and *Respect*.'

'The military messages have stopped,' said Metzer. 'They are giving weather reports too, even for the Galilee and Sinai. They would not do that if they were expecting a war.'

Till Eulenspiegel came to its jovial end and a momentary cloth of silence fell over the scene below to be flung wildly aside by the swelling applause of the Jews sitting all about the beach. It was not like the applause in Tel Aviv, not stamping, whooping acclaim, the enthusiasm of a city audience. It was the hard applause of a different people, desert people, with sand in its throat, unused to demonstration. I looked at Metzer and he smiled. 'It is not often they have a chance to hear anything,' he said. 'Tomorrow they'll be back at their work.'

I walked from the room into the corridor and down the resounding concrete steps. At the entrance to the hotel there were some young waitresses and other staff and when I walked through the foyer out towards the beach it was they who turned and began to applaud. I felt very good that night, strange, but very happy. Strange because of the way I was dressed in the fine dark blue tailed suit and the white ruffled shirt, going out to play to those Negev people, those steely Jews, waiting in their rough clothes. The applause ran ahead of me like a rapid fuse, spluttering through the people at the door and those outside it under the hotel lights, and then igniting the great crowd waiting on the sand under the flaming brands and the low stars.

I had the impression of walking through the shallows and then into the deeps of a powerful sea, the waves thrown up all around. The sound of the hands was extraordinary even to someone like me who has known acclaim for a long time. There were no raised voices, only the hands, clapping, clapping, seeming to reach out to me as I walked through them. Then I mounted the few wooden steps to the platform, under the brilliant square of light, and I had lost them.

It was like stepping into a boxing ring. The sound still rose, but the forms and the faces had gone, all but those immediately about the fringe of the platform; gone, submerged into that applauding ocean. I could sense them, even when I was on the stool and they were quiet; sense them encircling me, people and people and people, going out in a rippling pattern far across the beach and into the Jewish night.

6

Inland from the Gulf the road drags across the desert. It is a road only in the sense that it is a way, an access. It is bitter red, scarred, rutted and turned, littered with torn tyres and fractured wheels. The lorries that traverse it journey from Jerusalem and the northern towns to Beersheba and then to Eilat, carrying all the goods that life needs, for there is no railway. They make their own bonfires of dust as they work their way through the miles and the mountains. The telephone wires, the same that the Bedouin use to make copper bracelets and bangles, sag on poles forced into the hard desert. They straggle, each one alone yet attached to the pole in front and the one behind by their thin wires, some straight, some crooked, like a desolate chain gang or a party of men lost in the wilderness and strung together in case they stray.

Dov Haran was going to a kibbutz where his brother worked and lived. It was the day before the war began, a bright, hot forenoon at Eilat, and hotter inland. 'I will take you to King Solomon's Mines,' he offered. 'You have the whole day to fill.'

Shoshana came out into the white sunlight. She was wearing her khaki denims, clean but rough, with her hair tied back severely behind her neck. I thought then that people like her, particularly Jews like her, *have* to be soldiers all the time. If there *is* no war they will hope for one, and see in it an opportunity to fight and die for something they believe is bigger than the whole world. The Germans were like that.

She was wearing squat boots, dusty and wrinkled like tired hunting dogs, and her baggy trousers were tucked into the boots. Her shirt was wide at the neck like a navvy's collar, and the skin over her breastbone was hard and almost black with the sun. The only tenderness in her hard little frame came in the something she was unable to deny; the full circle of her breasts under the squared pockets of the shirt.

Dov had apparently already told her he was going up the desert road. She said to me: 'We will see the diggings of King Solomon,' and jerked her head with a man-like motion telling me to get into the jeep which Dov was about to drive away.

Starting a car on that surface of grit and dust was like opening a jet engine. The red clouds gushed from behind the jeep and trailed us as we took the track into the Negev, puffed and rising immediately behind the back wheels of the vehicle and then thinning and trailing out and finally dropping back, dust to dust.

Shoshana sat in the front with Dov, leaving me alone in the rear seat. She sat straight like a shotgun guard on an old Western stage coach, looking sometimes left or right but returning to straight ahead.

'It was very fine last night,' she called over her shoulder.

She was so unemphasizing about it that I was undecided if she meant the concert or the weather.

'Splendid,' I grunted covering both eventualities. I wondered why she always made me, Christopher Hollings, feel that I was riding back seat. The track was bumpy and the whirls and whorls of the violent desert rock were reaching

77

higher. Dov was driving quite fast, but he began to brake abruptly, and eventually brought the jeep to a halt slightly to one flank of the track. We sat while a tribe of Bedouin rode from the sandstone crevices, blanketed people, as disdainful as their camels; their goats and other animals were layered with rusty dust. They made no sign that they had noticed us but filed across the track, silently and without fuss like a group of mysterious but well-behaved nuns embarking on an exotic outing.

Neither Dov nor Shoshana moved or made any comment. The whole incident unfolded and passed as though it had been well rehearsed. When they had gone, slipping again into a crack in the rocks, Dov put the jeep into gear and we stuttered forward. A boy, a goat-herd, driving half a dozen skinny and wall-eyed animals before him, appeared three hundred yards farther on the road, heading in the same direction as the camels and humans. Dov stopped again and motioned him and his herd across the track in the suburban manner of a driver at a school crossing.

When we moved again I said: 'There's a lot of traffic this morning.'

Dov laughed deeply. 'They always have the right of way. At least they believe that, and it is as well to go along with them. They were here before us. That boy, he could have been Moses or Benjamin.'

Shoshana said coldly: 'They are a weight on Israel. They do no good, but make many incidents. They are diseased and smelling and all trouble.'

Dov laughed: 'They're Bedouin,' he said as though that explained it all.

'They are spies,' she alleged obstinately. 'And drug smugglers, and they have killed Israelis, even down here in the desert. And yet they walk from country to country as they please.'

'Perhaps they are setting a good example,' I suggested.

She became very angry, biting, but containing her voice. I could see her shoulders shaking under the shirt. I thought she was going to turn on me, but she remained looking to the front.

'Beasts,' she said. 'They treat their goats better than the women. The goats eat first, then the women.'

'Feminism!' exclaimed Dov turning to me for confirmation. 'Feminism, that's what it is called, correct?'

'Correct,' I laughed. 'And from Shoshana.'

Dov was laughing at her anger as he drove the jeep, now fast and kicking, along a straight stretch of the road.

'Nothing! That is nothing!' she shouted, then, unable to get enough meaning into her English, she attacked him in Hebrew. He still laughed, heaving the jeep around a bend in the road, almost scraping a hanging wall of rock, rising on one side and falling on the other. Shoshana returned to English and this time turned about to face me. Her eyes were magnificent. 'Because the women eat after the goats,' she shouted, 'when they come to bear children only half the children live.'

'It happens with all primitive people,' I said aloofly.

Shoshana let her annoyance escape. 'AND,' she screamed, 'AND, MISTER Hollings, the dyings of those children are used on the Israeli figures to the United Nations regarding infant mortality! These foul Bedouin are officially Israeli citizens!'

I faced her seriously. Dov was crouched over the wheel and watching a now straight road as though it were heavy of booby traps.

Shoshana reduced her voice but her back was hunched like a nasty-tempered cat. 'Arabs,' she grumbled. '*Israel* is full of *Arabs*. Jaffa, Nazareth, all Arabs. Why do we have them? Do they have Jews in Jordan?'

Dov shrugged at her childishness. He joked: 'We will build a kibbutz right outside King Hussein's palace.'

She whispered: 'One day perhaps we will.'

The sky was like a deep plate with the rising desert brilliantly red against it. The sun was getting towards its noon height. I could feel it burning through my hair. There was a khaki cap on the floor of the jeep, one of those tureen-shaped Jewish caps, and I put it on my head. From behind us, from the sun, at that moment issued three jet fighters, searing noisily across the wide chest of the desert, flying their low shadows over our vehicle and then arching spectacularly

79

into the sky with the surprised grace of birds shot in the belly. I had only time to squeeze my shoulders to my neck after the first sound and the planes were away and curving far off.

'Ours,' I laughed unconvincingly.

'Ours', confirmed Shoshana indicating with the same expression that she meant to add 'not *yours*'. She sniffed at the sky like a mongrel investigating a temporary smell. 'Mirages from the north,' she added. She turned to me, facing me with sudden enthusiasm. 'They are stronger and faster and have better pilots than any of the Arabs.'

'So there,' I joked. Her English was not adequate enough to appreciate it.

'Of course, the Arabs have more,' suggested Dov patiently. 'But we have what's good in little parcels, as you say.'

'It will seem like we have more,' asserted Shoshana.

Dov did not reply. He had turned the jeep off the choking road now and driven it, frisking like a goat, up a lesser track going towards the mountains that guarded Egypt and the Sinai. 'Did you see the stick the Bedouin boy carried?' he asked suddenly as though the goat-herd had just crossed the track and was not ten miles back. 'That is a hollow tube which he pushes down into the desert waterholes. The water of the Negev is so bitter with minerals that it is not possible for drinking. We had some soldiers in a camp here and all their hair fell out because they drank the water.'

Shoshana unexpectedly giggled. 'They are the oldest young men in Israel,' she said. Then quickly serious: 'But very good soldiers.'

'Of course!' I shouted.

Dov said: 'The shepherd boy pushes the hollow stick far down into the waterhole, beyond the water heavy with minerals, and he sucks through it the sweet water that is below that.'

'An old Bedouin trick,' I suggested.

He agreed: 'Very old, Mister Hollings. It is the same magic trick. . . How do you express it? . . . A con . . .'

'A conjuring trick,' I said.

'No, a word I know. Con . . .'

80

'Confidence trick, then.'

'That is true. My English grows every day don't you think?'

'It's excellent.'

'Yes, the same confidence trick that Moses did here in the Negev to impress the Children of Israel. You read in the Bible that he struck the rock and out came the fresh water. All he did was push his staff down through the bad water to the good spring underneath.'

'And so saved Israel from being a nation of bald heads,' I suggested.

Dov laughed but Shoshana did not react. She could never take a joke about Israel. Dov brought the jeep around, a dusty tail curling behind us, and stopped in the middle of a flat red area of desert where columns of sandstone heaved themselves vertically into the hard and brilliant sky. They were chiselled and carved by winds and age, fat fingers of rock spread wide, and then another, a hand clenched and fisted, the knuckles bulging out over the hot bare flat area below.

Shoshana had jumped from the jeep and was walking about, looking up, arms spread, with a sort of staged holy excitement, like someone walking in a beloved cathedral. She walked fifty yards away from the jeep, her tied hair touching the back of her khaki shirt, her trousers baggy where they were pushed into her boots and tight around the backside. It was like watching a film where the star wanders into some wondrous place, spreads her hands and begins to sing. Shoshana shouted: 'The mines of King Solomon. Is it not great!'

Dov and I remained at the jeep. He was going to drive five miles farther into the desert to the kibbutz where his brother lived. At one moment we both found ourselves staring at this girl in the uncompromising male clothes, standing gracefully on high toes, tiptoeing about like a dancer.

'King Solomon!' She turned and called the words to us. 'This is his place. Do you like it, Mr Hollings?'

Dov said to me: 'You had better say you like it, Mr Hollings. This girl is a patriot.'

'*I like it!*' I shouted back to her. '*I like it very much.*' The strength of my voice rustled rocks and segments on the crumbling sandstone ledges, dry from years without rain, and brought them chuting down to the foundations. Dov returned to his driver's seat and revved the engine bringing wider avalanches tipping from the crevices.

The jeep turned like a circus animal going around a ring and made for the narrow exit that led out to the desert and the road to Beersheba. Shoshana was still standing theatrically, her face bright in the sun and raised towards the tops of the cliffs. I walked to her.

'You like this place?' she repeated as though we were buying a house. 'You *do* with no doubt?'

'With no doubt,' I smiled. I did a complete slow circle, eyes straining up, running along the frayed hem of the rocks and the sky. Red and orange, brown, sliced and spliced, layered and latticed rock.

'We have further places,' she enthused with all the gush of a bad salesman. 'So many. Even outside the famous towns. Israel is full of history. It has been here such a long time.'

I almost said: 'Most countries have,' but I restrained it because of her obvious happiness. She caught my hand. Her palm was unexpectedly soft. I wondered why I thought it would be hard. 'In this area – over here –' she said leading the way, 'this is where the fires would burn. Here the slaves would ... how is it? ... boil the metals for the making of the bronze. See the ground is still black. It was not a good job for employment.'

'He was a hard man that Solomon,' I said. We had begun walking up the crumbling path that projected like a dry tongue from the straight column formations. 'Cutting children in half ...'

'Nonsense,' she interrupted seriously. 'It was only a suggestion.' We walked farther and higher. It was difficult under the sun and my shirt was sticky on my back. The heat was going through the material of the little Jewish cap I still had over the back of my head. 'Imagine,' she said with unconscious poetry, 'how it was when the Queen of Sheba in

82

her lovely ships came to Eilat and King Solomon there to welcome her. What a day that was for Israel.'

'A different Israel,' I pointed out.

'No. The same Israel,' she argued. 'But we were bigger then.'

I laughed and the sound started red nuts of stone tipping down from a great bulb of rock just above us. She walked a little behind me and we reached the top of the rock and sat on its flat cap. From there we looked out across the boiling desert to the steely sea showing in the far south. Egypt was almost at our shoulder, Jordan rose to the left and beyond the gulf the dusky mountains of Saudi Arabia.

'We are surrounded by enemies – the poor bastards,' Shoshana observed. Her hand remained quietly in mine.

There was tuna for dinner again that evening. The Italian fisherman's catch had to be eaten by as many people along the gulf as possible so that it should not waste. It was baked and light brown, like veal or venison. Some of the musicians of the orchestra had gone back to the north that night leaving about twenty of the party at dinner at one long table near the window that was by the sea.

It was a good evening, full of benevolence, because the threat of the war had, they said, now reduced. Metzer was saying jovially that everyone would forget it soon and that Dayan could go back to his archaeology or even to his former job of looking after the nation's chickens as Minister of Agriculture. It was strange how they wanted the hooded general as their saviour when they felt they needed a saviour, but how they wanted him eliminated because he was a man of war as soon as the danger had apparently died. Zoo Baby dominated one end of the table, his bulk hardly contained in his huge white shirt, his thick neck thrusting like a trunk from his open collar, his eyes screwed up against the light of the table candles, his firm but soft voice moving in and out of the conversation. I had watched him carefully the previous night at the concert on the beach. A pianist and the man behind the drums have a lot in common for their attitudes to music both physical and emotional are alike, the crouch over the instrument, the waiting and watching for the moment to move into the work, the solitary feeling among the ranks of pipes and strings. There is a sensation too of ministering to the instrument, of leaning over and working it. The others hold their instruments to themselves like babies, kissing them or stroking them, but the pianist and the timpanist are as separate from theirs as a doctor over an operating table or a housewife over her kitchen board.

All the men were in clean white, open-necked shirts that evening at the table. They have this attitude to collars and ties in Israel which believes that nothing constructive is ever accomplished by a constricted neck. They also roll their sleeves up, or have short sleeves, with the open-air readiness of Boy Scouts, but most of the musicians about the table had their shirt sleeves long and cuff-linked indicating some sort of refinement allowed for men of their artistic stature. Herbert Scheerer, the conductor, and I alone wore jackets, demonstrating that we were foreigners from more northern and less workmanlike parts of the world.

There were few other guests at the hotel for any tourists had flown with rumours of war. In the dining-room were four Israeli naval officers from the little motor torpedo boats I had watched putting out from Eilat. It was they who stopped their laughter and talk first when Shoshana entered the room and walked towards our table. There was an awkward coughing of chairs as we all stood up. There was a place waiting for her between myself and Dov and she smiled all around and made her apologies for being late in Hebrew and then in English. Then she sat down.

She had tried to do something about herself and had failed. She wore a white dress of some material like lace, but not lace, which was a size too small for her. The buttons across her breasts were dragging at the buttonholes, and when she moved as she ate the material stretched all over like a series of hawsers. She had nail varnish clumsily applied and uncomfortable make-up sitting on the natural smoothness of her face. Her lipstick was odd enough to make me remember that her lips were full and lovely when she was not wearing it. She sat hunched and complicated in the dress, trying to stretch and be at ease, blinking her eyes under the black geometry she had drawn over them. When she had walked into the room I had noticed her walk and the graceless open-toed white shoes she wore. She looked and moved better in denims.

She had washed the red desert dust from her hair. It was magnificent, full and falling naturally in fair runs over her shoulders, and the skin of her arms and shoulders was even and fine.

Zoo Baby smiling with fat from the deep end of the table said: 'Shoshana, tonight you look like the Queen of Sheba.' The others laughed and clapped in their Jewish way because they knew he meant it. I clapped too with only disguised politeness and was closest to the look of pleasure in her eyes and the heightening of the colour under the make-up. With intended grace, but with the buttons on her dress forcefully trying to escape their holds, she turned to Zoo Baby and thanked him. '*Toda raba*, dear Zoo Baby,' she said quietly. 'And you tonight are like King Solomon.'

There was extra laughter and clapping, with the naval officers from the other table joining in, and only Herr Scheerer and myself, although giving lip and hand service to the acknowledgement, catching each other's expressions of minor puzzlement over the huge acclaim for such a small joke.

Zoo Baby said: 'I am glad there is no war. My Army uniform is getting tight in many places. Today I tried it in front of the mirror. It was not a good experience.'

He stood at his end of the table and amused us by demonstrating the various soldierly poses which he had adopted before his mirror. He amused the others well, but immediately I realized again that I was on the outside of a private joke. Zoo Baby stood and pretended to throw a grenade, use a submachine-gun, and then gave a great murderous jab with an imagined rifle and bayonet. With each movement he made a rubbery comic face and examined the cloth beneath his armpits and across his chest portraying the man who finds he is splitting at the seams. I was looking towards him, away from Shoshana, but I sensed her pulling at her own tight

85

clothes. Dov and the others in the room laughed at the military mimicry, especially when Zoo Baby held the seams of his shirt together while he tossed another grenade towards the roaring naval officers.

Unfortunately I suddenly became aware of what it was all about. I think Scheerer did too. He glanced at me for the second time in a few minutes; he the product of a generation of invaders, and again with that puzzled, disturbed expression. Zoo Baby going through his battle drill, the others all laughing, suddenly looked very businesslike to me. Perhaps I missed the point because of my lack of Hebrew because occasionally he made exasperated remarks and was answered by the others. They all called at once on occasions, Shoshana immediately in my ear, and I had that sensation of swimming in the carrying current of an unknown language. It was the ungainly man's obvious proficiency in what he was about that was so startling. Despite the laughter and the voices he had in his movements a killer's intention, the decisive mobility of a trained and dedicated soldier. When he threw the supposed grenade you could see the fat fingers tugging the pin away expertly and know that the broad forearm had pitched it sixty yards away killing the crew of an Arab machine gun. His spraying fire with the sub-machine-gun was intense and determined and the 'glug' as the bayonet was forced home made me push away what remained of my dinner. Zoo Baby was an Israeli soldier.

He ended the act by throwing his hands in the air, with eyes rolled once more down to the shirt under the armpits, and surrendering in a loud Hebrew, and then fearful Arabic, tongue. All the musicians, the naval officers and Shoshana, collapsed laughing across their food on the table. There were shouts in Hebrew and applause. Scheerer and I, once more turning our loyal glance towards each other, strange aliens that we were, applauded the display also.

Then Zoo Baby, still surrendering, pretended that the Arabs had shot him. He collapsed to the table like a felled elephant and lay there, but with occasional, exaggerated examinations of his tight clothing. It was a splendid act, full of the rare expansive talent that only fat men seem to know and possess. When he had finished and raised himself, beaming, from the table, everyone applauded again. I turned to see Shoshana and Dov streaming with laughter tears. One of the violins was asking Scheerer what he thought of the performance and the puzzled stubby German was nodding seriously and saying: 'Goot, goot. I like very much. *Kamerad! Kamerad!*' He threw his hands in the air and imitated Zoo Baby's surrendering act. Once more all the Jews threw themselves upon the table and howled their laughter.

I prodded at my tuna fish.

7

The plane taking us back to the north was due to leave at eight the following morning. Most of the musicians, and Scheerer before anyone, decided to go to bed after dinner. The last one to go was Zoo Baby who stayed with Shoshana and me in the hotel lounge while we drank coffee with cream, which we couldn't do in the dining-room itself because it was kosher. Then Zoo Baby stood and stretched himself. It was like a hippo stretching.

When he had gone Shoshana and I, as though by some tacit agreement, stood and walked out of the hotel, turning along the dust road that cut between the sand and rock of the beach and the rock and sand of the desert. There were some eggs of light on the airstrip and another clutch at the port. There was a breeze now coming in airily from the gulf, a flat current that pushed its way unhurriedly through the thick hot daytime air lying over the land. Big unsubtle stars dangled over the reclining hills towards Egyptian Sinai. There was a complaint of wind in the mountains on the other horizon, in the desert hills behind, reaching north from Akaba.

For the second time that day I reached out for her hand and it responded to mine, curling within my palm like a small comfortable animal.

'Zoo Baby, he was very funny tonight,' she said.

'Hilarious.'

'That is a good English word,' she said. 'Say it again please.'

'Hilarious,' I said.

'Hilarious,' she repeated carefully and then again. 'Hilarious. Yes, it is a good word. It means laughing?'

'Yes.'

'It sounds laughing.'

I said: 'There is a lot of sand here. It's different from all the rock.'

'Yes, it is soft beneath the feet, is it not? And warm.' She kicked off her ugly shoes and pushed her feet into the sand. There was no moon but the low stars made it light. I watched her feet going into the comfortable sand. 'It is like putting on a different pair of shoes each step. Old easy shoes,' she said.

We stopped. I brought her near to me with both arms and she stood, wrapped in me, quietly, her chin on my shoulder, her face next to my neck, her breasts full against my chest. I was facing the port and the airstrip and the ghostly lights were suspended in the night, just a little above the earth. She would be able to look across the desert, shortened because of the night, towards the ships in the Arab harbour, and see the stiff backs of the hills in which the wind still sang. The lights and the sound gave us some measure of navigation, an assurance, some means of knowing that we were not lost. The hotel, some of its lights still yellow, was sitting by the sea only four hundred yards away. But the desert was complete immediately around us, the daytime heat still rising from the valley of gentle sand into which we had walked.

'I will take this dress away from myself,' she whispered without moving from me. 'It was borrowed from a friend and the friend is a size smaller than I am. All tonight it has been tight.'

'No one would have noticed that.' I said.

'I have felt like being in a trap with it,' she answered. She moved a pace from me and without shyness unbuttoned the white dress and dropped it from her. She stood looking at me, close enough for me to see details of her face. She pushed back her hair nervously. I moved towards her and took the other clothes off her, feeling her skin as I took them away from her body. It seemed then like no skin I had ever touched, delicate, fine, warm, alive. Her breasts were full and sleepy and as I bent forward to kiss them at their roots I felt her heart moving. As I lifted my head her lips were there and we kissed fully, her naked body soft and also hard against my clothes.

Her hands went to my crease and she closed them over the immediate swelling there, pressing against the material of my trousers. She kneaded at the swelling and then rubbed it with little movements of her palms. Then she ran the flat of her hands up my stomach and beginning at the bottom shirt button undid the measured row, not looking into my face, but murmuring like a child: 'Hilarious. Yes, very good. Hilarious. Zoo Baby was hilarious.'

My hands were under the fat of her breasts and my lips went from her face to her somnolent nipples, and then my tongue to them. Immediately her hands were back at my swelling and she rubbed it again still repeating. 'Hilarious. Oh, yes. Hilarious.' She seemed to be talking through sleep; through a dream or a trance. I dropped my fingers to my zip and released the hardness, pulling my trousers away and kicking them backwards in the sand.

She dropped in front of me, eyes almost closed, right hand now hooked on to my neck and pulling me down upon her. We collided on the sand, my hands going quickly out to each side so that I would not fall heavily and wind her.

The sand shifted as we shifted, hurrying in its million panicky parts to get out of our way, tumbling in little drifts from beneath us. It was very strange making love in the desert. There was about us a huge void, that somehow in itself was enclosing, covering, comforting. I entered her, the distant moaning of the mountain wind accompanied her own little moans. Her arms were working all around my neck and about my chest. Her breasts and the strip of flesh about her navel were tanned but more lightly than the rest of her body. Against her brown skin my white English carcass glowed strangely.

I moved at her carefully at first, watching the effect of the intrusion reflected in the reactions of her face. Her agony was as immediate and real as though it was the first time for her. Every advance, prepared though we both were, hurt her.

'You split me, Christopher,' she whispered. Her face turned away in the sand and her eyes and mouth screwed up. But her hands and arms pulled at me like hawsers demanding that I stay, and not merely stay but go into her farther. Then we were fully together, the last piece of me sunk into the final, deepest cavity of her. She relaxed her arms and her face and I went forward on top of her feeling the foundation of her remarkable body, feeling the sand about my knees and along the line of my forearms, wallowing in her hair and hard against her face and then her complacent breasts. My tongue ran up them like a puppy lapping spilt milk. Then something happened. We felt it at the same moment, a startling truth, an undeniable, uncomfortable fact. I stopped.

'Christopher,' she said sleepily. 'We have some little pieces of sand in there.'

'I know darling,' I said miserably. 'I can feel it too. Maybe it will go.'

'Where to can it go?' she asked logically. Her passion was immediately replaced by relaxed composure, but she did not seem discomforted or angry.

'It will go somewhere,' I assured. 'We will lose it.' I began to move into her again. But the grains remained there, big as boulders they seemed, biting into the smoothness of our love-making, annoying as fleas in a soft bed.

Embarrassed I withdrew from her and she ran her finger over me trying to find the grains of sand. I was kneeling in front of her and she was kneeling too, but lower. Her finger was running across my peninsula and her sombre eyes were upon my face.

90

'I cannot feel those little devils,' she said. Her finger was driving me mad.

'Perhaps it is still in you, Shoshana,' I suggested.

'That is possible,' she agreed her eyes steadily upon mine. 'No. Here it is! I have it!'

She was as delighted as a schoolgirl winning a prize. I looked down at myself projecting towards her. She used her fingers like delicate tweezers and nipped at me once, twice, half a dozen times, bringing her face very close to my loins like a scientist conducting an experiment.

'It is well,' she said sweetly. She held up her tweezer fingers, the tips tight together. 'I have the last small piece.'

She threw away the grain with great ceremony as though it were a great rock at the same moment shifting her weight so that accidentally I was momentarily pitched forward. I half-stopped myself with one hand, but the lower parts of me collided with the warm thick sand.

'My God,' I whispered. 'Now I am covered.'

She began to laugh, a sweet loud laugh, that bounced over the desert. Her hands went to her face and she shook her head from side to side, making her shoulders swing and her hair dance.

'Oh Christopher!' she said in a laughing whisper. 'Tonight in the desert it is not to be.'

I stood up and tried to brush some of the adhesive sand from myself. She kissed me fondly and then put her clothes on. I dressed too and we walked arms about each other, still laughing, back down the desert track towards the hotel.

'Our love,' she whispered her mouth almost under my armpit. 'Was it not hilarious?'

'Hilarious,' I agreed kissing her forehead. I looked at my watch. It was two-twenty. At seven forty-five the first Israeli aeroplanes were dropping bombs on the Egyptian airfields at El Arish, Bir Thamada, El Minya, Luxor, and other places.

She had been with me all night, wandering about with me in the great old-fashioned feathered mattress of my bed. It was very hot in the mattress and we sweated among its folds, not sleeping for a moment, until the day was an early red

91

outside the window. My eyes were sore with salt by then. My body was wet outside and drained within. I watched the daylight enlarging and I could hear shouts, single and spaced, from the beach. The Italian fisherman and his Abyssinians probably. Shoshana, who had been pretending to sleep, but kept moving her firm body regularly into the bends of mine, suddenly rose from the ruffled bed and stood naked and stretching.

The lower part of her trunk was smeared with the traces of our love, the thick part of her legs too. She slowly extended her arms, with that occasional elegance which, when revealed, was contrary to her other movements, then lowered them and now, without grace, wiped the inside planes of both legs with the flat of her right hand. It was the practical, unrefined movement of a soldier wiping oil from the butt of a weapon. She did it without embarrassment, looking away from me lying on the bed. Then she lifted her browned arms again raising the strong snouts of her breasts, which looked sharp and upturned like the noses of hedgehogs.

I put both hands out, lazily but demandingly, and caught her first at the round of her waist and, as she leaned and looked at me, at the sleepy lump of her breast. Her eyes came to me and she dropped on top of me. I did not want to make love to her again then and she did not want it either. Instead we lay thickly together.

'It is like we are cooking,' Shoshana whispered.

'Stewing,' I suggested.

'What is that?'

'Cooking, but a sort of wet cooking. Like soup would be.'

She giggled. 'You are not English sometimes. You are too low.'

'I think to say we are stewing here is very apt,' I claimed, 'even poetic.'

'What have we cooking?' She turned her potent, childish eyes to me to show me that she had caught on to the game and was pleased that her English understanding was enough to play it.

'Oh, let me see.' I kissed her ear. 'Little bits of cabbage.'

Then her hair. 'Some of those thin straggly onions.' I felt her laugh.

I rolled half clear of her, feeling our gathered sweat clinging as I did so, and kissed her down from her brown neck.

'And some turnips.'

I sensed her protest. 'Melons, then?'

'Yes,' she agreed. 'We will permit melons in our stew.'

I rolled down her, bending myself almost double like a dreaming cat.

'Here is some meat,' I said running my tongue over the firm area of her belly. 'And this . . . this is the spice and the seasoning.'

Games like this always pleased us, from then on. We used and amused each other.

'*You* must put something to the stew,' she said brightly, kneeling up and leaving me lying. 'Your nose, for a beginning. It is like something, some vegetable, but I do not know the name.'

'You're the sort who throws anything in a stew,' I said. She kissed my nose. Then my neck. 'That tastes good also. It will be a good stew,' she said.

She moved down my body, pushing her impudent tongue into my navel and decided it was some Hebrew vegetable, something I had never heard about, and then lower, muttering about egg-plant and carrot and finally lying with her face buried between my legs and laughing.

'It is no good,' I said. 'Not kosher.'

She raised herself on her hands. She looked magnificent like that, her face open towards me, which was the best way to see her, her shoulders and arms shaped and brown, her trunk arched away and her breasts hanging full.

'The game is finished,' she announced. 'I must go to my correct room. It is too early to make stew.' She raised herself to the side of the bed and then bent and kissed me primly. I touched her, one final contact, and then she dressed and went.

It was ten past five and I meant to sleep until breakfast, but I only drifted into uncomfortable shallows, and then was awakened by further noise from the beach. There was, finally, a round of excited shouting from below the window. At first I imagined that the Italian and his Abyssinians had gathered around another netful of fish and I thought that I was glad I was returning to the eating of the northern cities that day. I was still conscious of the smell and the feel of Shoshana, moving about the expansive and untidy bed feeling for her in half-sleep and then knowing that she had gone.

The noise outside did not diminish, but seemed to spread itself. I rose tiredly from the bed and rubbing at my sore eyes went to the window and looked out upon the exquisite morning. The land on either side was sitting calmly upon the warm sea, the air clear blue and settled, and the small currents of the gulf nudging waves upon the beach in front of the hotel.

There were rounds of people standing before the hotel and on the beach, everyone talking. I had a momentary thought that they were the musicians and others waiting for the bus for the airstrip and that I had overslept and would have to hurry. Then I saw Metzer and he saw me at the same moment, pulling himself away from the group in which he had been talking.

'War!' He called the word up to me, hoarsely, half whispering, as though he were giving news of someone's death. 'The war has commenced, Mr Hollings.'

I did the instinctive thing. I looked immediately across the radiant sea towards Jordan, towards Akaba, clear in the early sun. Perhaps I expected to see great guns protruding from it or to see black fires burning there. But it was not changed. I could see the cars moving in its streets. Then I turned to Eilat, on our side (I thought: 'our' side) and looked for the motor torpedo boats but I could not see them.

Instead, sitting in quiet brightness on the shingled edge of the sea was a blue and white amphibian, a lumbering water-vehicle which, Zoo Baby had told me, was used to give tourists a ride in the desert and then a trip in the bay. I was to see more of that.

Zoo Baby was standing with his meaty hands on his hips talking with Dov. I had a thought about Zoo Baby now having to get into his tight uniform.

Dov had said that usually the Israeli reserve troops were

94

only permitted to retain their boots in normal times, receiving their uniforms when they were called to service. But the musicians, who often travelled, kept their soldier uniforms with them.

The men gathered below began looking towards the Jordan border, where we had been at the wire the day before, and calling in Hebrew to each other. A moving bloom of dust was travelling towards us. From my place on the balcony I could see it was a single vehicle coming along the road between the shore and the desert. I went back into the room and got into the shower. I talked to myself.

'You've got to get out of here, son. And very smartly. Dinner in London tonight, I fancy.'

There was no point, of course, in me, a neutral, becoming involved in any shooting between two alien enemies. 'Yids versus Wogs,' I recited quietly as I towelled my legs. 'Wogs and Yids. Imagine being stuck here now. "Will you play for our troops, Mr Hollings?"'

Shoshana came to the door, arriving at the entrance to the bathroom briskly and with a stony face. All the softness was gone.

'Did you come back for some more stew?' I tried.

'We are at war.' She sounded very hard.

'So I gather. Serious?'

'Our Air Force has bombed many Egyptian bases,' she answered. 'We have had great success already.'

'Naturally,' I said. I was still naked. I walked into the bedroom and began to dress. 'Tomorrow you will be in Amman and in Cairo.'

'It is possible,' she nodded. 'Perhaps a day or so more.'

I laughed directly at her. I was nervous myself and her confidence seemed preposterous. 'What will you do for the rest of the week?' I asked.

'You make too many jokes, Christopher. The war is only an hour started. You will see.'

'Not if I can help it.'

'You will go?'

'Of course. It's not my war.' Then I added lightly: 'Some of my best friends are Arabs.'

'That is not true!' She screamed it angrily.

'How the hell do you know it's not true?' A sharp anger took over from my nervousness. 'I have played in Beirut and in Cairo. Why should I not have friends there?'

Her face had stiffened. 'I did not know this,' she said.

'Oh come, Shoshana. You cannot expect all my concerts to be kosher.'

'This is not hilarious!' she bawled at me. She used her new words whenever she could. I had noticed before, when we were playing at making stew and I said it was not kosher, how she had iced a little. 'Why do you make these jokes about Israel?'

I calmed her. I was dressed now. 'Who started it?' I asked her taking her arm. 'The war, I mean, not the jokes.' Even her arm seemed to have hardened. She was wearing the khaki denims she had worn the previous day, but her shirt was clean. I looked at the shirt's fullness at her bust and imagined her breasts lying enclosed there.

'The war?' she asked. 'Who started it?'

'Yes.'

'It was started many years ago, by the Arabs.'

I insisted: 'Who started it *today*?'

'Our aircraft are raiding the enemy because of provocation and threats. It was on *Kol Israel* – on the radio.'

'So *you* started it. You have struck the first blow.'

'It matters nothing.' She stopped on the stairs and, suddenly full and human again, pressed herself against me. 'Just think, Christopher. We could have all of Jerusalem again. I want to see it for my newspaper.' She sounded like a selfish child coveting a toy.

I kissed her. 'And you may have none of it.'

She remained very tender and close to me. 'That cannot happen,' she said. 'The city will be for Israel. You see, Christopher. I am going there today. I am going there for my newspaper. It will be something for history, my Englishman, something for history.'

Suddenly I felt very sorry for her. To me patriotism, when I had thought about it at all, had seemed like wearing underpants; a fact, but a properly concealed fact. I was on nodding

96

terms with my country's requirements of her sons, but reasonably sure that I would never be equal to these requirements or even desire to be equal to them.

But here was Shoshana, the warm, wet Shoshana of the night before, striding now eagerly down the stairs, her arse tight in her denim trousers, longing to be off to the war, desperate for her country, urgent to follow the call to bloodshed in the sacred city of Jerusalem. And she was going gladly as a child going to the fair.

A few steps behind her I followed. Her hand trailed seeking mine, but I kept mine away. Her brown face shone like a coin, her eyes were loaded with joy, her smile was wide and happy. I felt old myself. I wanted to get to Lod, or any other airport, and get on the nearest BOAC jet heading for London. I did not want any part of Jerusalem. They could keep it. Either of them could keep it.

O'Sullivan, the border guard we had met down at the barbed wire the day before the concert, had arrived in a big truck. He had made the mushrooms of dust I had watched from the balcony. The nine o'clock sun was making the first sweat run down the well-used channels of his face. The skin over his protuding cheekbones was white at the tightest spots. He was sitting crookedly at the wheel of the truck and looking out to sea as though he expected an enemy fleet or a shoal of fish.

"Morning, Mister Hollings," he said. When he said 'Mister' he said the whole word, elongated it, not making it into a polite abbreviation.

'Where's the war?' I asked. I tried to be breezy. Zoo Baby and Dov and some of the others were loading suitcases into the back of the truck.

'We're going in the general direction,' said O'Sullivan. He grinned and his awry teeth seemed to be hanging on to the very parapet of his gums.

'It's very peaceful,' I said turning a half-circle. Down there by the beach the gulf was spread out like a beautifully worked bib, the sand and the mountains looked firm and settled and Akaba and Eilat were crouched under the sun, waiting for its full heat. The Italian fisherman and the Abyssinian boys were moving along the beach carrying nets, slowly, as they would do any other, quiet, hot morning, as though the fish could wait or they knew there were no fish swimming in that part of the sea. The amphibian squatted like a bulky toy.

A skein of jet fighters, Israeli jets, suddenly exploded across the desert and then the sea, curling impudently over the Egyptian mountains far out to the west. They were low over the water when they first passed us standing before the hotel. Then they rose a little in the fine air as though they had sudden pains in their guts and then drove on until they became small as currants in the remote sky.

'*Sharm el-Sheikh*,' murmured O'Sullivan. The Irish voice was careful with the Eastern vowels. 'That's where they'll be having the action, Mister Hollings. And which side will you be playin' your piana for?' I caught his eye. He had said it purposely like that – 'piana' – and he looked at me with eyes as crooked as his teeth.

'I'm getting out,' I explained firmly, logically. 'I'm not playing the piana for any side, old friend. I'll be on the first seven-o-seven going towards peace and tranquillity. The first one out of Lod.'

'That's if there is any Lod,' he said. The sweat from his hands had smeared about the rim of the wheel and he wiped at it with the same hands, as though it would make the surface better. 'Maybe it will be bein' bombed at this very hour, Mister Hollings. Maybe you won't get an aeroplane to your peace and tranquillity.'

'I shall try,' I said. 'Is there nothing at all flying from here? From Eilat?'

He made as though to crane his neck to look across the mile of red rock and sand to the airstrip. 'Well, not unless they could get that ould lorry in the sky,' he said. 'There's nothing with wings though. I think maybe they cleared all the aeroplanes away so that the Arabs won't drop things on them and maybe to use it as an emergency landing place.'

'Nothing there?' I said.

'No. Not a thing to fly. Exceptin' a few birds of the desert.'

He leaned forward towards me. The remainder of the luggage was being humped into the rear of the truck. I could see my suitcases going in. 'They're very methodical, you know,' he said. 'These Jews. They like everything to be good and businesslike, even a war.

'In Ireland, now, if we'd gone about our little troubles with the British in the same way, we'd have been far better off. We went on in little dribs and drabs, a few bombs and a bit of an uprising, for years. But these boys! It's all or nothing, mister. Take it from me, it'll be all over by the end of the week. One way or another.'

Zoo Baby and Dov and some of the other musicians came into the sunlight from the deep shadows of the hotel. They were now in their Army uniforms, self-conscious and joking about them, and carrying sub-machine-guns. Zoo Baby had not exaggerated about the fit of his uniform. As he walked it tugged at him at every joint and cavity. The others had to pull him up to the back of the truck and he was muttering in Hebrew as they did so. 'My God,' he said to me when I went around to the back. 'If this war does nothing else it will get me something more big to wear.'

'If you had been on the other side,' I said. 'In the Arab Legion. Then they would have given you some nice flowing robes and things and you would have fitted.'

He laughed, but only a half-laugh – you had to be careful then about mixing Arabs and Jews even in jokes – and said: 'My father chose to be Jewish and he chose a Jewish wife. So we have the lousy clothes.' He spread his arms and laughed a full, real laugh now. 'Are you coming?' he asked.

Shoshana climbed about the truck and held down her hand to me. Dov and Zoo Baby helped me up like a child. 'I might as well come,' I said. O'Sullivan started the rattling engine. I said: 'The nearer I get to an international airport the better. My luggage is on board anyway. I don't feel like staying down here to be massacred by the Arab Legion. I'm a neutral, remember.'

In the truck with us now was Haim Mendel, the orchestra leader, a desperately quiet man, looking very old and comical in a scruffy uniform. I asked him what he was.

'For the bombing,' he answered hesitantly and glumly. 'In case.'

'He is an air-raid warden,' said Dov with a straight expression. Mendel's doomed face was apparently a joke in the orchestra.

'He stops air raids,' said Zoo Baby pretending he had misinterpreted.

'On Tel Aviv,' added Mendel sincerely. 'That is where I now go.'

Zoo Baby and Dov were going to report to their Army units in the north. 'Two weeks all the others have been taken into the Army,' said Zoo Baby holding up a fat pair of fingers. 'But the Government let us play the music for the people.'

'They thought the concert tour was important for morale,' explained Dov. 'But now we must get to the Army. My wife has joined her unit, already.'

'Mine is digging a bombing shelter. Also my children,' said Zoo Baby. 'Also I must get to the Army.'

Shoshana said: 'And I must get to somewhere where I can see the fighting for my newspaper.'

'Just drop me at the airport,' I said.

Metzer was also squatting in the truck, heavy with thought. Once he moved to the back to look out over the sweet and placid sea, as though seeking some comfort from it.

There were two other musicians whose names I cannot now recall, one was a french horn I remember; middle-aged men being tugged off from their lives to the violence of conflict.

The truck stopped abruptly after a few yards and crimson-faced, Herr Scheerer, carrying a pathetic little case, emerged from the hotel and puffed after us.

'Another neutral,' announced Dov as everyone helped the breathless German into the back of the truck. He reminded me of a puffer-fish I once saw in Brighton Aquarium.

'Neffer hav I know anything zo like this,' groaned Scheerer. His eyes seemed twice their normal size and he was cascading sweat. 'Neffer in all my conducting days.'

'Another neutral,' repeated Dov. He looked at me steadily. He held his sub-machine-gun like a seasoned soldier not like a musician. He smiled, a hard smile. 'We'll have to make sure those naughty wicked Arabs don't get hold of you,' he said.

8

Ten Israeli air strikes had that early morning attacked Egyptian airbases in Gaza, south into the Sinai Desert, along the Nile Delta, and even as far as Luxor. Israeli armoured columns and eager infantry were, within an hour, forcing their way into the Egyptian soldiers entrenched in the Gaza Strip and in the sand fortresses of the Sinai. In Jerusalem nothing had happened.

As our truck moved up along the desert road from Eilat, Dov was helped up on to the khaki canvas roof and lay up there under the clean sky with a transistor radio. *Kol Israel* was babbling its sweet Hebrew into the desert air. Sometimes they played a few minutes of music and Dov turned temporarily to Radio Amman.

'The bastards!' he called down over the edge of the truck canvas. 'They shelled our cornfields in Gaza today.'

The other Jews in the bouncing truck looked at each other and nodded their consciences clear. 'They shelled our cornfields,' repeated Shoshana to me as though I could not understand Dov's English. 'They started it.' I wondered why he had called out in English instead of Hebrew. Then I knew it was because even he, the liberal Dov, wanted to be sure that Scheerer and I, the neutrals, received the information.

I stood up and, catching on to the metal stanchion at the back of the truck, I looked on top of the canvas to Dov. He was lying relaxed as a sunbather, the small radio held high with one hand, like a prize, so that he could capture the best reception. 'Who is winning?' I called. The sun struck me in the face and the hot Negev wind blew at me. The canvas of the canopy smelled oily.

I went back into the interior and sat in the close air. The truck bounced and I could feel Shoshana's thigh move against mine. I could feel how hot her leg was under the trousers.

'Radio Amman says the Arabs are winning,' shouted Dov. His head was comically lowered below the top fringe of the truck and his upside-down face was lined with desert dust. '*Kol Israel* says there is no information at the moment. That means *we* are winning!'

The others half-laughed, half-cheered. That handful of Jews in the jolting back of the truck did not seem like yet another generation of their race facing extinction.

'Jerusalem,' called Shoshana up at the roof. 'What news of Jerusalem?'

Dov's inverted head magically appeared again. 'No news of the city. All fighting is in the south and the west.'

Zoo Baby made a large rubber face. 'Perhaps the Jordanians will not fight,' he said. They were all speaking in English now because of me and because of Scheerer. 'The other time, in 1956, they would not fight. They were still. It is a sad thing. If they do not fight we have no chance to fight them back and to take Jerusalem.'

Metzer, who had been silent, watching the desert road scurry beneath the lorry, turned and said something in Hebrew. Shoshana nodded and affirmed in English. 'This is correct. Hussein and Nasser have kissed at Cairo Airport.'

'May thirtieth,' mumbled Zoo Baby. His wide face closed into mine.

Shoshana nodded strongly: 'And they did not kiss because they were in love. This time the Jordanians will fight.' She suddenly turned upon me, looked quickly at the uncomfortable and bewildered Scheerer sitting opposite, and gathered our attention like a teacher explaining an awkward problem. 'Our large difficulty,' she said seriously, 'would be if the Jordanian and the Iraq troops in Jordan came across the middle of Israel to join up with the Egyptians from the other side.' I could see her full breasts hanging in the shirt. She turned and saw me looking at them and some anger flushed into her face. She raised her voice a little and it hardened, while she was continuing to look sideways at me. 'Tanks and soldiers and some Migs could do this.' She wriggled her finger on the dusty floor of the truck. 'You understand, this is Israel. Here is Jordan and the Egyptians would attack from here. If they have many forces coming across the desert from that side and this side, you understand, they would cut our small country in half.' She said 'small' in a pleading sort of way, directed immediately at Scheerer. He nodded with embarrassed agreement. Shoshana continued: 'They would remove our head from our belly. Tel Aviv and Haifa would be in one half and Jerusalem, Beersheba and this desert would be in the other. We would be apart. It would be hilarious.'

'Hilarious?' I said.

She coloured. 'No, no. Not that word. That is laughing, is that so? Yes. Like last night. It is some other word of English. But it would be bad for Israel.'

Zoo Baby grunted. 'They would not do it. The Arabs are bad at moving forward. Always I have seen them move the other way.'

Scheerer muttered in his poor English: 'In der war I vaz of der band of Seventh Panzers. It was bad. They made me play the drum. Me, Herbert Scheerer, I play the drum!'

'It is good to play the drum,' said Zoo Baby defensively. Scheerer glanced at him guiltily.

'Not der Army drum,' said Scheerer mending the slight. 'There is no good noise in it. Bang, bang bang.' He did it very Germanically and resoundingly and we had begun to laugh when his bangs were shattered by a line of terrifying real bangs that travelled alongside the truck throwing it up like a bucking horse, slewing it around, and sending rock and sand pummelling against its sides. The huge explosions ran with us.

Only after the attack did I hear the aeroplanes, a double roar across the roof of the truck. We were rolling and righting again with everyone pawing about on the floor and

103

shouting. I found myself holding Shoshana against the metal as though I feared she might in some way attempt immediate retaliation. Above the Hebrew shouts I remember hearing the hoarse Irish of O'Sullivan from the front. Somehow I was looking at the interior of the canvas roof and, quickly, wondering if Dov was still up there.

The truck squared itself and began skidding along the brittle road, tearing into something with a splitting of glass at the front, and then jarring and stopping heavily. Dov's head, inverted again, comical had it not been for the blood all over his face, appeared from the roof. We were crawling like reptiles in a tank. Zoo Baby was lying across my left arm and the crash had left my face against the fatty softness of the top of Shoshana's legs.

Dov's mouth opened, gulping breath. A thread of blood ran from his nose and strained through his thick moustache. '*Hachutza!*' he cried out at last. '*Hachutza!*' It seemed his eyes caught me. 'Out! Out!' he repeated. 'They are coming back, the bastards.'

Zoo Baby stumbled to his knees like a small and sleepy elephant and made to crawl to the tailboard of the truck. He had a blue and red gash over his ear. I looked at the canvas roof again for some reason looking for bullet holes. Everyone was moving now. I kissed the inside of Shoshana's thigh. There was a rattling at the tailboard and O'Sullivan was there pulling at the chains and ushering us out like the superintendent of a Catholic Sunday school.

He was watching the sky though. 'Come on then, my boys,' he said quickly, without excitement. 'Let's get out. This vehicle is not fit for the road.'

I could hear the jet planes returning, breaking their backs to turn over in the hot sky and come at us again. 'Egyptians,' said Shoshana. She was standing next to me by the tailboard of the truck, calmly watching the angrily approaching planes. Scheerer was having some trouble in getting down from the tailboard. He was only middle-aged, not old, but he was very frightened. O'Sullivan and Zoo Baby were helping him, both watching the sky, and O'Sullivan was muttering about getting the silly old Hun to hurry up.

Dov appeared from the side of the truck nearest the red wall of rock into which it had crashed. He was composed now, looking like a soldier, holding his sub-machine-gun, and wiping the blood from his moustache in the same casual manner as another man might wipe away soup. He fixed himself at the corner of the truck, conveniently found a wedged position between the lurching back and a slab of rock, and brought his gun to his shoulder and the muzzle optimistically to the sky.

Everyone else was dispersing to the rocks. As I ran I could hear the nasty approach of the two jet fighters and above them the urgently hard voice of O'Sullivan ordering Dov away from the vicinity of the truck. Dov looked up from his gun position, nodded and ran clear of the stalled vehicle.

O'Sullivan slithered around a rock and fell at my side. Shoshana was crouched next to me, her eyes like hard eggs, looking up, and Zoo Baby had rolled against a rock only slightly bigger than himself a few yards farther away.

O'Sullivan said calmly: 'Blind. Now just fancy not hittin' a target the size of the truck the first time. My God, what *do* the Russians teach with them?'

The jets were on us now. They skimmed like low shadows across the rocks and boulders, their cannon shooting into the truck. It blew up abruptly spewing a big sheet of flame all around for an instant then settling down to burn rather sedately like a suburban bonfire. The second jet came in and fired into the rocks and the dry scrub shattering everything about with deafening explosions, choking the desert place with smoke and setting fire to little parcels of brown growth that had been clinging to the place for some salvation.

'Thank Jesus they don't stay too long,' muttered O'Sullivan looking up. 'They might be back in a minute, so keep your heads down.' I noticed he had his revolver in his hand. He ran away from us quickly among the rocks like a wild rabbit, counting people, moving them, and finally getting back to us. 'Here they are again,' he muttered. 'Comin' back for a last bite. In the old days they'd have had us, you know. One thing to be said for these Migs is they can't hang about over you for more than a couple o' seconds. Right, get down – now!'

The planes were widely separated this time. The first one came in murderously, in a great swan's neck of a dive, and dropped a canister which fell with a horrible, slow grace into the clear space between the rocks where we were crouched. I felt Shoshana's soft flesh tighten as it came down and we forced our bodies nearer the earth as O'Sullivan yelled to us to duck. The canister bounced metallically like a ball on a blunt rock and then rolled and bumped playfully into the clearing, eventually coming to a standstill only ten yards from where we lay. Nothing happened. It lay looking harmless and uncertain. I closed my eyes and pressed my face to the earth. I heard O'Sullivan pass a quick message to the Virgin. Shoshana emitted a brief eerie laugh.

'It didn't go off,' decided O'Sullivan after ten seconds.

'I noticed,' I said. I realized I was calm and elated.

'Here is the other,' said Shoshana. 'From the sun.'

The Egyptian jet rolled across us spraying the ground with cannon fire. I thought they might hit the canister sitting close behind us, but they didn't.

Dov and Zoo Baby were firing back at the plane, forlornly but with great application. Zoo Baby was coolly sitting back against a bright orange rock and firing his sub-machine-gun from the shoulder with the logic he used sitting behind his drums in the orchestra. He continued firing, throwing up a fierce din among the rocks, for an unnecessary time after the plane had made off. We saw both jets turning towards the walled mountains of Sinai.

The truck continued to burn making a noise strangely like a grizzling baby. O'Sullivan got us across the road away from the silent canister and then we saw Metzer sitting in a gully holding Herbert Scheerer's big German head in his soft Jewish hands. Haim Mendel, the leader of the orchestra, was sitting in a begging attitude on the other side. The famous conductor had been rolled in the dust. His clothes and his face were coated with red like thick pepper. Metzer had opened his shirt and was inadequately pushing a handkerchief into blood running from a wound in the German's stomach. Scheerer was alive and conscious and looked up at me placidly, his face coated like a clown's. His lips were swollen and when he moved them no sound came.

'Don't talk, sir,' said O'Sullivan. 'Say nothing for the present, if you please.' He sounded like a cautioning policeman. He motioned Metzer to take the blood-wet handkerchief from the wound, and had a look. The others came in towards us from the rocks. No one else had been hurt. Dov ran from his gully laughing. 'Ran away! Did you see?' He stopped talking and walking when he saw Scheerer. Then he came forward quickly. 'He is shot?' he said unnecessarily to Zoo Baby.

'A little shot,' confirmed Zoo Baby turning away from the blood and looking at the innocent sky.

When I looked at Scheerer again his face was set and his eyes rolled around at our faces above him. He reminded me of a man I once saw knocked down by a bus in Hammersmith. The man was staring around at all the onlookers as though urgently seeking a face he knew or someone who could answer a question. Scheerer looked like that.

O'Sullivan's face moved. He scratched at his nose in a completely Irish manner. 'A pity,' he said quietly looking down at the yawning wound in Scheerer's abdomen. 'My field dressing was in the pack and the pack won't be much good now because it's back in the lorry.' He looked directly at me. 'Would you have a clean handkerchief?' he asked. I took out one of my special silk handkerchiefs which I had made for my concert tails. God knows how it was in my pocket at that moment. I handed it to O'Sullivan who glanced at the quality and then pressed it into the cavity. I watched it turn crimson.

Clear of the rocks it was very hot and exposed. Each one of us kept glancing at the sky fearful that the Migs might return. But it remained stark and blue and vacant.

'I think we should move this gentleman into the shade,' said O'Sullivan. He glanced up at Zoo Baby who had moved so that his big shadow kept the sun from Scheerer.

Zoo Baby nodded in his rubbery manner, his face moving independent of the movement of his head. The Israeli bent ponderously and put his arms under Scheerer's narrow shoulders. O'Sullivan took the legs and Metzer, as though afraid the wounded man might break in the middle supported the small of his back. They moved, in step, already like a funeral procession, across the red, dusty ground and the harsh yellow sunlight, towards a bay in the rocks fifty yards away. I walked on one side and Shoshana walked on the other, both of us looking down at the face suddenly aged a hundred years. The eyes had closed, collapsed, now. The dust gave him the leathery look of an ancient animal. It was scaled over his eyelids and on the rounds of his lips. The lids shuddered a little as they carried him and then his mouth began to move, dryly, and I leaned forward for I thought he wanted to speak to me. But as I leaned, and as the three men carried Scheerer delicately towards the shady rocks, I realized that the German was singing.

With his last hopeless breaths he was croaking out a melancholy musical noise, a few la-la-la notes, and then a tum-de-dum. I tried to listen closely. The noise came brokenly through all the dust and the blood in his throat.

By the time we had reached the deeper shade Herbert Scheerer, distinguished conductor, had sung his tune and was dead. We buried him temporarily, a German casualty in a Jewish war.

After we had buried him, with O'Sullivan and myself standing over him, O'Sullivan saying a few Christian words, and the Jews, Shoshana, Metzer, Dov, Zoo Baby, Mendel and the other two musicians, standing properly a couple of paces back, we returned to the road and the burned truck.

We stood about it in the manner of children stranded at a picnic because of a flat tyre. Shoshana was pouting like a spoiled schoolgirl. Now that our own excitement and noise was over we could hear the guns firing in distant Sinai, the explosions rolling and rumbling among the desert hills.

'Every Israeli is fighting today,' fumed Shoshana, 'and we are fixed here like fools.'

'Haven't you had your war ration for this morning?' I asked her tersely. 'Isn't it enough what has happened?'

'We did nothing to *them*,' she replied with sullen logic. 'We must get back to Jerusalem.'

I felt a bit sick of her just then. 'We mustn't miss the football match,' I said bitterly to O'Sullivan. I leaned on him as an ally, although he did not respond. What the hell was an Irishman doing with the Israelis anyway? It was like putting a Negro among Eskimos.

We hung raggedly about the hot, bent frame of the truck. It was still on fire down in its depths and little grunts and groans seeped from it. A front tyre exploded spectacularly making everyone dive for the road and then, embarrassed, rise with banal grins. The desert was large all about us, with the hot road winding and diminishing north and south.

'Usually,' said Metzer, 'there would be a truck or something else coming along the road before too much time. But maybe not today. Not with the war.'

O'Sullivan walked about the wreck with the morose air of a farmer who has seen his prize bull drop dead on the way to the cattle show. 'There's not much we can do about this,' he commented unnecessarily, kicking at a wheel rim with his police boot. 'I think it might be a good idea if we exploded that little bomb across the way.' He pointed to the Egyptian canister still lying ineptly in the opposite clearing.

'It would stop the local children playing with it,' I suggested. O'Sullivan looked at me, for the first time, in the odd way that the Irish sometimes look at the English.

'Good idea, Mister Hollings,' he agreed civilly. 'And if we blow it up it might attract some attention and get us out of here, don't you think?'

I was sorry, because I liked him. I merely nodded and caught Shoshana's cold eyes. Her English had not been abreast of what I had said. O'Sullivan waited, looking at me, as though seeking permission to get on with what he had planned. I looked over at the canister, round and black among the rocks.

'Everyone will withdraw in this direction,' he pointed to the far right, beyond where we had buried Scheerer. 'Behind the big wall of rocks. Then we'll explode this damned thing.'

109

He was the man in permanent uniform and nobody said anything. We moved up over the hard rising ground and arranged ourselves behind the parapet of red and yellow stones. From there the noise of the Sinai guns was more profound and Dov jolted me and pointed to a cloth of black smoke drifting over the hills of Egypt.

O'Sullivan came up last and we were strung in a line behind the rocks like ambushers. The Irishman gave a minor grin.

'If there's any of the spare-time soldiers would fancy his luck with his shooting...' he began. The canister was almost hidden from us at that height and position, perhaps a quarter of its black end projecting from a sheltering ledge of rock. O'Sullivan was about to add to his challenge when Zoo Baby half rose hydraulically from the knees and fired one, almost casual shot which exploded the canister. A shallow, white flash lit up the bright sunlight and the explosion cracked the air, and bounced about the broken desert. A rain of dust and stone fell down about us as we crouched. Everyone's fingers, except Zoo Baby's, were in their ears. I wiped the dust from my eyes and Shoshana was shaking her hair and laughing.

O'Sullivan said: 'If I'd been allowed to finish I was going to suggest that we pooled a bit o' money and made it a gamble. Your impetuosity, big fella, has cost you dear.'

We got up and walked down the slope to the road again. The force of the explosion, like insult to injury, had thrown the already disintegrating lorry all over the road and up on to the rock face. Where the canister had lain there was a black saucer cut out of the desert. O'Sullivan looked at the pieces of the lorry and said: 'There'll be no fixing that, now will there?'

Shoshana and Metzer called out simultaneously and pointed down the road we had travelled from the south. A tree of dust had appeared and was making towards us. We sat and waited, and then individually, as it occurred to each of us, we found some prudent cover in case the arriving vehicle was from the Arabs.

But four hundred yards away, when it was in the clear, we

110

could see what it was. Moving towards us at the top of its ponderous speed was the big amphibian from Eilat, the boat-truck that gave visitors a ride in the bay and into the desert. Someone was standing on its bow and waving to us.

O'Sullivan grunted. 'It seems,' he said sourly, 'only right and logical that a collection like this, English, Irish and Jews, could be picked up in the middle of a desert by a bloody ship.'

9

Clumsily the amphibian crawled up the track towards our waiting group. It had a broad snout and went about forty feet from nose to end. It was gaily painted in wide blue and white stripes which had always attracted attention during its recent life as a visitors' amenity in Eilat.

'Nicely decorated, you'll no doubt notice, in the Israeli national colours,' O'Sullivan pointed out. He was resigned and quiet. 'If those jets come back they'll know for sure it's not King Hussein out for a ride.'

The lurching vehicle came up the final slope of road and stopped just short of the skeleton of our truck. A Star of David flag was idling against a broomstick handle which had been fitted into a rupture in the amphibian's metal deck. A heavy and old machine gun was mounted amidships and two young Jewish soldiers crouched by it, touching it and adjusting it, like junior dressers arranging the garments of a revered actress. The barrel pointed at the sky.

The driver of the amphibian, seventeen, red-faced and with tight fair curls, strong, and stripped to the waist despite the sun, called over to O'Sullivan in Hebrew, pointing at the wreckage of our truck. The Irish border guard zoomed both hands through the air.

'Aeroplanes,' translated the young man enthusiastically in English. He had seen me and recognized me. I suppose the English was to impress me. 'It was aeroplanes, eh?'

'No,' said O'Sullivan quietly. 'Bloody carrier pigeons.' He walked forward. 'How far are you going anyway?' he asked.

'Maybe to Beersheba,' said the boy. 'Want a ride? Today it's free.' He grinned at me, wanting me to admire his English.

'Everyone up on the amphibian,' ordered O'Sullivan, wheeling about in the heavy dust. We all climbed over the hull of the ungainly thing and with a quivering engine cough it moved reluctantly up the desert road.

'I don't think much o' the camouflage,' commented O'Sullivan to the driver. 'What's your name?'

'Solen,' replied the boy. He smiled as though he was driving a new sports car on a lovely day.

'I'm *Segan Mefakeach* O'Sullivan,' said O'Sullivan. The exotic title again sounded strange from him. He moved over a few inches so the boy could see me. 'And this is Mr Hollings, the English concert pianist.'

I was surprised by his formality and the strange deference which came into his tone when he introduced me. 'I know Mr Hollings,' said Solen respectfully. 'I was at the concert. It was most fine.'

He whirled the big steering wheel and we took a slow corner like a great, stiff armadillo. 'The colours are not good for the desert,' he admitted returning to the matter of camouflage. 'They are good for the Gulf of Eilat, for the sea, but not good for the desert.'

'I should think not,' said O'Sullivan. 'This contraption can be spotted miles away.'

The young man looked hurt. 'Cont . . . contrap?' he asked. 'What is that? You mean it is not good?'

O'Sullivan said: 'Sure, the thing's all right. But I don't go a lot on the colours. The blue and white stripes, patriotic though they might be.'

'We *want* to be seen,' answered Solen patiently. 'We are out here waiting for Arab jets. Perhaps the ones which hit your truck. Who was killed?'

'Herr Scheerer,' I said. 'The conductor of the orchestra the other night.'

Solen shook his head in a strangely elderly fashion. 'It is bad to be killed in another man's fighting,' he said solemnly.

'How are you waiting for the jets?' I asked. Every time he turned the ungainly vehicle around another bend in the desert way the sweat oozed freshly from his thick face and big body.

'He means we're a decoy,' explained O'Sullivan. 'We're out here so that they'll attack us.'

'Jesus Christ,' I said.

'That's my sentiments,' said O'Sullivan. 'But it's a long walk to Beersheba and it's a hot day. Let's hope they don't notice our beautiful bright blue and white stripes in the middle of this red desert.'

I looked around. Shoshana and Dov were looking in detail at the old machine gun mounted behind us. Metzer and Zoo Baby were leaning against the vibrating hull of the amphibian, Metzer looking apprehensively at the sky and Zoo Baby as relaxed as a day-tripper. Mendel and the other musicians were squatting like a trio of monkeys at the rear arguing about music. They waved their hands, made rising and falling movements with their fingers and hummed and sang snatches.

'Surely we're not attracting Egyptian jets in the hope of shooting them down with that thing are we?' I asked nodding at the gun.

'It is possible,' said Solen seriously. 'But up in the sky also – somewhere – we have an Israeli jet fighter, a Mirage, which is waiting for Arabs to find us and attack us.'

'Only one?'

'One only,' he smiled. 'It is enough. The others are killing the Egyptian Air Force on the ground. The news is good from the war. We have had many victories this morning.'

'I can tell you two Egyptian jets they didn't get on the ground,' I grumbled.

'Ah,' he sighed happily. 'Some got away. From Luxor they came, those two. Perhaps they will find us.'

He sounded as though he had the entire conduct of operations of war completely in his seventeen-year-old grasp. He grinned at my consternation. That's how they all were.

'Every night for two weeks I have driven this road in this boat,' he said. 'Two big tank carriers, some other trucks and me in this. With kilometres of chains and other things making a noise. I know the road very well by now.'

'They've been pretending to be an armoured column,' explained O'Sullivan. 'Christ, the noise they made you'd have thought it was a Panzer Division. And the Arabs have been listening to it and concluded it was a big armoured movement to the gulf. So you can bet they've shifted some of their stuff down to the south to be ready for this phantom army.' He laughed quietly. 'You've got to go along with them, these Jews,' he said. 'They're a weird bloody bunch, but they do have ideas.'

'Like sending this thing out as a decoy,' I said. 'When you come to think about it, O'Sullivan, this isn't much of a life for an international concert artist, is it?'

He laughed. 'You should have stayed in Eilat,' he said. 'Though things might be very hot there by now.'

'Especially with a Jewish Army made up mostly of ghost noises,' I replied. 'My God, I could have been at the Winter Gardens Bournemouth this week.'

'Aye,' he agreed sagely. 'And we might all be paddlin' by the sea, or doing something else. But we're not, Mister Hollings. We're in the middle of a desert and a war, both of them bloody hot.'

Shoshana screamed, 'There!'

Her voice sounded girlish and excited. I knew it was the jets. I could hear them immediately but I couldn't see them.

'There!' Shoshana called again. She was pointing and the two exhilarated boys were swinging the wobbly machine gun about. I still couldn't see anything. The sky was full of midday glare.

'Do we jump out?' I asked O'Sullivan. I was surprised to find my tone weary, unemotional.

'You bet your sweet arse we jump out,' he said. He turned about and called: '*Hachutza! Hachutza!*' the word Dov had used before. Solen was still driving the amphibian at its full

114

ten knots. The two boys were swivelling the gun ambitiously towards the line of the approaching jets. I caught hold of Shoshana's arm and pulled her towards the side, but she shook herself free. We jumped independently. I struck the broken road heavily and rolled in the way they taught me in the British Army, which was not the right thing. It is fine in English mud but damaging among stones and outcrops of a painful desert. I felt my face cut and my lip split. I tumbled to my feet, frightened now, and began running for the cover of some elder rocks. Shoshana and Zoo Baby were scrambling away at an angle to me. I couldn't see the others.

I heard the old machine-gun fire before the planes used their cannon. It was obviously much too early, but the boys couldn't wait. Then the planes were on all of us, their cannon fire spitting ahead of them.

I was very afraid that time. Like some burrowing creature I kicked and wriggled into a narrow crevice, realized that it was too shallow and, in panic, tried to wriggle out again. But the first of the Migs was homing in on us then, very low, cannons clattering and the shells bouncing and bursting among the outcrops and the gullies. I cringed back into the rocks, hands beseechingly over my head, waiting for the dreadful second when I would die. I thought of them dropping another canister and this time it would explode.

The second Egyptian pilot held back behind the first, by about a minute, and then came screeching in firing as he descended. Even between the fire and the explosions I could hear shouts from those about me. The first jet had merely swung down and fired indiscriminately at the general area, but the second went for the blue and white striped amphibian, standing invitingly, blatant as a target in the red road. I realized this because none of the second salvo of cannon shells hit among the rocks where we were lying. Then I heard the amphibian blow up with a fearful noise and the plane wheeled away like some joyriding bird.

My head was buried, first by my hands and then by an avalanche of loose sand and grit thrown and disturbed by the explosions. I pushed this debris away and squirmed around so that I could see the vehicle. The body of the young man

115

who had driven it, Solen, was hanging over the snout, his naked back and his hanging head like a carcass ready for the hook. I could not see the two enthusiastic youths who had been behind the machine gun. The explosion had torn the metal plates of the strange truck and it was spread open like an ugly tin box. It was burning sedately, being worked over by the smaller pedestrian flames that follow an explosion and the first fierce fire.

I saw Zoo Baby, Dov and then O'Sullivan run from their cover towards the road. I looked about for Shoshana and saw her walking briskly in the same direction, holding her forearm and with thin blood running between her fingers. Scrambling up from my place oddly reminded me of being half buried in playing on some childhood beach, forgotten until then. My face was stiff with blood, not serious blood, merely gashes and scratches from my rolling, running and hiding.

Shoshana looked at me as I stood and I thought a small scornful expression came to her face as I, automatically, brushed myself down.

'Are you hurt?' I went close to her.

'A small thing,' she said continuing to walk towards the three men and the amphibian. Metzer was not there and I looked about for him. Two of the other three musicians were helping the third out into the open from a place where he had hidden. It was Haim Mendel, the doleful orchestra leader and reluctant air-warden. They moved towards us and he hung on to their shoulders as he walked between them.

'Let me see your arm,' I said to Shoshana.

'It is a small thing,' she repeated sullenly. 'Why do you want to look? Are you a doctor?'

I said nothing more to her. I felt my anger coursing through me; anger at her and at myself for being stuck here at all. Zoo Baby, Dov and O'Sullivan stood in a group, away from the burning amphibian like gardeners disposing of rubbish. Shoshana called something to them in Hebrew, but Zoo Baby without turning around made a hopeless sign with his hands.

'*Hem mechusalim,*' he said to her when we got there. Then to me. 'Finished. All finished.'

'Where was your wonderful Air Force?' I asked. 'Weren't they supposed to be up there to deal with the Migs? I thought that was the whole idea.' Then I said to myself sardonically, but only to myself because I did not want to elaborate on their failure, their hopelessness: 'The decoy, the hunter and the hunted.'

At that moment I could not help feeling how pathetic they were, these Jews. Standing in that deathly and isolated place, with O'Sullivan whispering, 'Shit. Shit. Shit,' to himself, I looked at the others, at their helplessness after their bombast, and I felt sorry for them. For the first time I thought, I felt certain, that they would all be wiped out by the end of the month. The Arab would accomplish what the Nazi had failed to do. Finish them.

Metzer had remained back, meeting the two men who were helping Mendel across the dusty place. The group stood for a moment in the sun while Metzer looked at Mendel's dragging leg. Then the three men stood around, discussing the leg, and eventually carried on towards us in a shambling echelon.

From the sky came the noise of jets again. This time it was a lofty noise, one plane fighting with another, very high. They trailed about the sky and I remembered how I, as a boy, used to watch battles like this from a field of gold stubble. Their whines floated down to us, and the coughing of their weapons.

They were very close to each other, twisting like interesting insects in a bright blue bottle. Their sounds varied. The whine sometimes built into a howl, and they howled up there in their immense bowl of battle. Then they fell low over the desert and it was easy to distinguish the Israeli Mirage from the Egyptian fighter, but when they drove up into the sky again they became indistinguishable insects once more. They were fighting at this top altitude when one burst into colours like one of those trick photographs showing the opening of a flower. First yellow then red blossoms and eventually a slender stem of smoke as the aircraft began to fall from its high place.

No one standing on the road said anything because it was

117

not possible to distinguish which plane was the victor. The three musicians and Metzer were with us now. We stood in a fixed group in the hot sun, fifty yards from the dead amphibian. It was like waiting for an important football result. Then the winning jet dropped behind the gracefully spiralling vanquished plane, following it down until they had both descended low over the distant burnished hills. Then it was the Mirage, curling in a victory roll, which came jubilantly over the rising ground to our right, only a hundred feet from the ground, flying across us in triumph. At the first sound of it every one of us crouched, but then, as its friendly shadow flew across us, we were on our feet again. The others cheered like people at a sports meeting. I looked up, grateful anyway, that we would not have to face more cannon fire, but then glanced again at the sadly burning amphibian and felt sick. I felt much more over the deaths of those youths than I had over poor old Scheerer. It was almost as though they had been persuaded and convinced of the joys of suicide.

'We seem to be running out of transport today,' I said to O'Sullivan.

'It's accident prone we are,' he agreed. 'Maybe there'll be an O'Connell Street bus along in a minute.'

'Did you see how our pilot shot down the Arab?' said Shoshana coming to my side. 'The Mirage was superior, is it not so?'

'Oh certainly,' I agreed. 'The Mirage was the best.' I nodded at the amphibian. 'Shame really that thing couldn't fly. They might have had more of a chance.'

She dropped her expression. Her face was covered with small cuts and bruises and Dov was tying some strips of Metzer's shirt around the flesh wound on her forearm. Mendel was receiving similar treatment for the minor wound in his calf. 'It is a war,' Shoshana shrugged. But she took her eyes away. 'We expect people to be killed.'

'They were very young,' I said. I wasn't going to dispute with her.

'Young people, babies, get killed in war,' she said.

I felt very angry with her. I wanted to tell her what a lot of shit this was. The whole terrible situation and the way they

118

talked about it as though it were some sort of pastime. But I did not. We stood together on the road, nine of us, and O'Sullivan said we ought to bury the three corpses if the fire burned through in time. I had not seen the bodies of the two youths on the machine gun and I did not want anything to do with them. I got the meaty cooking smell of Solen's body, but the flames were still all around and under the vehicle and it was no use taking more risks now.

We walked back to the shelter of the rocks. The sun was at its top now and there were only thin bands of shade. Nobody had anything to drink. For the first time it occurred to me that we could be left in the desert for days. I said this to Zoo Baby.

He shook his large head. 'No. No,' he said. 'The Mirage pilot. He will report. Somebody will come for us.'

'Just think,' I said to Shoshana. 'If the Egyptians and the Jordanians do their thing about cutting Israel in half – as you said they might – we shall be the sole defence force for this part of the Negev. That should make them think twice.'

She either let my humour pass or she did not understand it. Perhaps she could not be troubled to understand it. 'The most serious thing,' she said in her stern way, 'is not to know what is happening to our war. Being here is bad. If there was some way to contact Tel Aviv I would be able to send my report to my newspaper.'

'I can see it,' I said. 'Graphic stuff it would be. Girl reporter in desert battle. They'd give you a rise next week.'

'A rise? What is a rise?'

'An increase in your wages, dear,' muttered O'Sullivan. He looked in an annoyed way at me. 'You could do the report of how the great English pianist was attacked by Egyptian planes. Now *that* would be a fine one.'

'I only came for the publicity,' I said.

He laughed. 'All right,' he agreed, the sharpness gone. 'It's not your war. But it's hers. Try to understand, Mister Hollings, if she doesn't win she might just as well cut her throat. And that goes for all of them. But especially her. You understand?'

'The brutal soldiery,' I said. 'They're not always the best ambassadors.'

Suddenly the Irishman stood up. 'Here's a chopper,' he said. 'They've come to get us.'

The noisy chop-chop of the helicopter sliced through the heavy noon air and it came around the corner of the rocks, flying very low, like an inquisitive dragonfly on an afternoon foray.

It alighted delicately a hundred yards away, its rotors at first flailing the air and churning choking clouds of ochre dust from the desert floor. Then they slowed and died, hanging impotently above the machine like the broad, bladed leaves of a banana tree.

Before they had ceased swinging two crouching figures dropped out of the machine's dark belly. They ran across the sand to us, two pale young men in battledress, one with an officer's epaulettes and an untidily hanging revolver. Two weeks before, I supposed, they were clerking in the Leumi Bank in Haifa.

They stopped, called out in Hebrew as though a trifle uncertain of us, and the second of the pair cocked the catch of his Uzzi. O'Sullivan called back in his outlandish Irish-Hebrew, and Shoshana corrected what he had said, shouting harshly at the men. It is a strange language. In conversation it is liquid, poetic, like Italian. But shouted it becomes hard, hoarse, not far from Germanic. That is how Shoshana sounded then. Although she had been hostile to me all through that long, stifling morning, she pointed at me as she called a second time to the helicopter men.

'She's trading on your reputation,' muttered O'Sullivan with a smile. 'They're not anxious to take us to Jerusalem or even Beersheba because they say there's a war going on and they've got a lot to do. But the lady wants to get to Jerusalem to do her stuff for her paper so she's telling them how important and famous *you* are, and hoping that they'll take you. And if they take you they've got to take the rest of us.'

The two young men had walked back towards the machine. When they were almost at the hatch of the helicopter again the officer wheeled about and beckoned us. He climbed into the cocoon of the thing and we trooped after him. He had taken notice of Shoshana's strategy, because he called me on first and I climbed up into the machine, was guided along to the tail end and pushed firmly down to the floor. The others came after, each popping up from the hatch like miners emerging from a coal gallery.

We crouched in a bunch on the floor and Metzer began saying something to me when the engines turned the blades again and the frantic noise filled the close cabin. The hatch was kept open and the young officer knelt by it, looking at the red ground wheeling away as we flew. It veered spectacularly sideways and we fell against each other. I smiled at Shoshana and she smiled in return and nodded as though to thank me for the ride.

Once we were away from the enclosing cliffs of the Negev, up into the wide sky, the sound of the blades diminished a little. But conversation had to be shouted. The Israeli officer glanced at the minor wounds of Mendel and Shoshana and then turned and curled his finger at me. I moved towards the open hatch and he pointed to the brown horizon. I felt Shoshana moving and she crouched close beside me because she had guessed what the young man was showing me.

He was showing me the scene of battle, stretched across a great spread of the Sinai. It was miles away, but we were now at about two thousand feet and I could see. Smoke exploded in great distant puffs and then lazed across the sand dunes; there were bright buds of fire flowering against the yellow and the red of the land.

The young man shouted in Hebrew into the back of the helicopter. Then he turned and translated quietly for my benefit: 'We are winning the war already. This morning almost all of the Egyptian Air Force was destroyed before it could even take off from the earth, you understand. We caught them, how do you say in England, with their knickers down?'

I was getting fed up with this. 'If that is so,' I said, 'we had a nasty experience with a couple of bare-arsed flies this morning.'

'Flies?' he asked, not comprehending. Shoshana, not

understanding either, leaned forward to catch my words over the noise of the rotor blades.

O'Sullivan, who had moved up and was now looking out of the hatch to the distant battle, put his arm on mine. 'Forget it, Mister Hollings,' he said. 'The jokes aren't appreciated. You're just here through bad luck. Okay, that's understood and is fine. But you're in this mess with the rest of us just now. So even if it's not your war, if I were you I'd temporarily adopt it. When you get to Eastbourne or wherever it is, then you can raise your two fingers in this direction.'

Shoshana was doing her best to keep up with the conversation, but anything sly or idiomatic missed her. She shook her head. 'What is happening in Jerusalem?' she asked in English. 'What about the fighting there?'

'One hour ago there was no fighting,' said the young man. He looked at her obviously sharing her regret. 'The Jordanians have started nothing, so we cannot go into the Old City. Maybe they will later. Maybe we shall have luck.'

In ten minutes I saw Jerusalem again, yellow in the sunlight, gracing the hills, spreading into the long shadowed valleys; walls and towers and ramparts. The city of cities, so they say. The sun lay lovingly over it as though it were the favourite place on earth. The towers and domes cast shadows and the walls smaller shadows. As we dropped we heard gunfire from below and the young officer and Shoshana glanced at each other and smiled as though they had conceived and successfully carried out a conspiracy.

'The guns,' she said, again in English which I suppose could only have been for my benefit.

'I hear them,' he replied. He hung acrobatically over the hatch looking down on to the roofs of the streets. Pulling himself up he said: 'It looks very good down there today. It is a good day for a battle. Tomorrow, or perhaps upon the next day, we shall be at the Wailing Wall.'

10

The helicopter dawdled across Jerusalem, drifting west. There was hard firing in parts of the city below and smoke stood up like little grey trees on the wall and among the buildings. But we could see no men.

An orange-coloured puff, like a bright dandelion clock, appeared almost alongside the aircraft, making us rock drunkenly to one side. Then another formed quite slowly and beautifully at its side.

'They seem to be shooting at us,' I said, attempting to keep a traditional British calm in my voice, although God knows why.

'Unless these are the fireworks of victory,' smiled the young officer. 'Perhaps it is that we have already won and we celebrate!' He rocked back on his heels by the open hatch laughing, well pleased at his joke in English. He seemed disappointed that I only managed a brief and cold smile.

But the Arab gunfire had moved us on. We speeded now towards the west, to where the Jerusalem heights fell away to the Corridor through which Selma had driven me a few days earlier. I found myself searching for her house, marking it from the windmill which I had immediately picked up. But before I had sorted the house from all the others in the roads and alleys we were moving determinedly away from the city and towards the road to Tel Aviv.

The helicopter hung, then dropped like a large insect through some pines and into a clearing. It flapped away grumpily, bending the light trees with the force of its wind, until the pilot switched off the rotors. First the young officer climbed down and then helped Shoshana and myself to the ground. The others followed.

Under the trees, spread out like some concealed circus, was a formation of military vehicles, camouflaged tents, and caravans. Radio aerials stood up straighter and higher than the fine trunks of the conifers. There were sentries below the trees and other men moving about, bent and mysterious, through the woods.

The young officer from the helicopter said to us, as though addressing a group of tourists, which I suppose we were: 'We are near the command post of General Narkis, the Commander of the Central Front. I will tell someone I have brought you. Please stay here by our chopper because if you walk someone may shoot you. They are wanting to shoot people very badly today.'

'Preferably Arabs, but they're not particular,' I suggested as he moved off. The pilot was fussing around wiping the nose of his helicopter with a piece of rag as considerately as a patient mother tending a snotty child. We stood in a close group by the aircraft. I felt awkward, in the way a prisoner must feel awkward, standing about waiting for something to happen.

Shoshana was smiling and looking about her. Zoo Baby was wriggling in his sweated uniform. His eyes were closed up like a hippo's eyes. Dov considered the sky through the trees as though a military establishment was not to be spied upon and it would be cheating or presumptive to look. O'Sullivan and Metzer stood together with the two other musicians and the injured Mendel who was sitting unhappily on the ground.

From the dark tents our officer reappeared with a tall, thin, yet oddly military looking figure. There was no wind, hardly a breeze among these trees, but his wide Army shorts flapped like flags about his knees, as the man walked briskly to us.

'This is Captain Harris,' said our officer. 'He will speak with you.'

'I think perhaps under the trees,' suggested the new man in English with a fine Sandhurst accent. 'Bloody warm out here for a start and we don't want any damned aeroplanes prying on us do we? Come along.'

We went below the trees, Harris ushering us along fussily. We stood there, again like an awkward group of prisoners. O'Sullivan saluted and introduced himself first, bringing a mild raising of the officer's white eyebrows with his Irish accent, and then everyone else.

Harris looked around benignly. He had a ragged white moustache and a tight face. His military cap was pushed back of his fair hair and he kept scratching the exposed area. 'Christ knows what we're going to do with you people,' he said easily. 'We're likely to have a bash at Jerusalem in an hour or two, we're getting the tanks and things up from Ramla now, so we're all pretty busy here.'

Shoshana said: 'I want to go to Jerusalem. To the war.' She flapped her hands around inside her handbag like a woman looking for a bus ticket and brought out a pass in a perspex shield and some other documents. 'Correspondent,' she pointed to the pass firmly. 'I can go with the Army.'

He looked at her doubtfully. 'There are some newspaper people assembled down near the Mandelbaum Gate,' he said. 'Waiting for the balloon to go up, perhaps you could get some transport down there. Can't say I remember seeing any ladies there.'

I almost laughed when he said 'waiting for the balloon to go up'. He was so dated, so angular in every way that he could have been in one of the old films about our war. He checked that Mendel was not suffering from his wound. Then he considered Dov and Zoo Baby and a pleased expression broke on his thin face. 'You two fellows can go as escort for the young lady,' he said as though he had conceived a master tactic. 'That takes care of *you*. And you, sir, Mr Hollings, what are your plans?'

'For the duration?' I asked.

'For the duration,' he affirmed, acknowledging the cliché of the Forties.

'Well, I'd rather like to get back to London,' I said off-handedly.

'I expect you damn-well would, too. Well Lod is shut down for business, old man, as you might expect. I imagine BOAC have shifted their route through Beirut, but I can't get you there unless we advance a bit bloody quicker than I think we will. I think the best thing would be to get you to Tel Aviv. There's been a bit of odd shelling up there this morning, the Jordanian big guns from Kalkilya; and some silly bastard dropped a bomb on Natanya, obviously thinking it was Tel Aviv. But it was his last mistake.' He looked around at us. 'Right then,' he said, as though coming to a sudden decision. 'We'll try and rustle up some transport for you. It won't be much – but there's a war on you know!' He glanced at me again because of the expression. I nodded a smile.

'Mr Hollings, you will go along with the lady, er . . . Miss Levy . . . and with Mr Metzer and with these three gentlemen as escorts.' He indicated Dov, Zoo Baby and O'Sullivan. 'You can drop all five at the Mandelbaum Gate and then the driver will take you on to Tel Aviv. It will only be a jeep, but it is the very best we can do on a Monday.'

Metzer said: 'Because I am in the company of Mr Hollings, I have arranged his tour here, I should go to Tel Aviv with him.' He was looking very fat and worried that afternoon. He was very anxious to get out of Jerusalem.

Harris said: 'Good idea, too. You'll have to squeeze up in the jeep, but four will be getting out so it should be more comfortable for the rest of the way.'

The other two musicians were to remain at the command post with Mendel who was to have his leg wound treated. Harris gave a little chicken nod to each of us to check we understood, then turned his heel in the dust and strutted thinly away.

He called back over his shoulder: 'It might be half an hour before I can arrange anything. I'll get someone to fix you with food. You don't know when you'll be eating again, that's the bloody trouble with war.'

'He is British?' asked Shoshana doubtfully. 'He says strange words. What means "rustle up"?'

'It means he's going to obtain a jeep,' I said. 'He's British all right. Home Guard, I'd say, Sevenoaks, nineteen forty.'

'You can tell that sort an ocean away,' muttered O'Sullivan quietly. 'So we'll be saying goodbye to you, Mr Hollings. Off across the sea, are you.'

'As soon as I get something to cross it in,' I joked. At that moment I found myself looking first into the solemn face and then the full eyes of Shoshana. She was like she had been before the war. Her face had all the softness of the previous night and I remembered and felt her again, moving in love under the sheets of my bed in Eilat.

I suppose it was then at that moment that I let myself slip into love with her. When afterwards everyone thought I had gone off my head, my agent and my manager and all those others in England and in Europe, this was the time, I told them honestly, when it started. Her hand, now a gentle, small hand, moved out shyly to me, away from the others so they would not see. I moved mine two inches to meet her and they docked for a moment. '*Shalom*, Christopher,' she whispered. '*Shalom, shalom.*'

But it was not until an hour later, when the tanks from Ramla were lining up for the first Israeli push into Jordan, that I made the mad move. Now, today, I still cannot account for it. Nothing in my life until then had ever motivated me except that it was for my own good and benefit. No person, certainly no woman, had ever turned me from the path I had decided to make and take. No person had ever taken any real love from me or given it to me. But when we reached the road junction, the turning one way to the Mandelbaum Gate and the other the road back to rejoin the Tel Aviv highway; at that point, I decided to go with her. She and Dov and Zoo Baby and O'Sullivan had climbed from the jeep. They had shaken hands with me and with Metzer. We all laughed and Shoshana had pressed a wet face and then her wet lips to me, and I was left sitting in the jeep with Metzer and the driver. The four moved off like a little patrol towards a group of tanks hiding beneath some tamarisk trees, turning and waving cheerfully to me. Then I called to them and got from the jeep and ran across the sunlit road after them. I heard Metzer, in English, and the driver, in Hebrew, call out behind me and the four in the front shouted and told me to go back. But I didn't.

I ran down the sloping road to them like a schoolboy running towards his friends. God knows what I was thinking about. But I had done it and that was sufficient. I didn't care a bugger about the war or who was fighting or why. But I wanted to be with her. I could not leave her in Jerusalem.

'Forget something?' asked O'Sullivan wryly.

'Nothing. I merely thought it would be better to come along with you. I can't get out of the flaming country tonight anyway and I might as well be here than in Tel Aviv.'

Shoshana was staring at me. 'Christopher,' she said throatily. 'You must go. There will be fighting here in one hour.'

'They're shelling Tel Aviv,' I shrugged with new bravado. 'You heard Harris say so. Big guns from Kalkilya or somewhere. And they might move across the border any moment and cut the road or bombard it. I'll stay. I have a personal escort.' I nodded at the three odd soldiers, O'Sullivan, Dov and Zoo Baby. Then I said: 'Besides, I like Jerusalem.'

Metzer, his thick body turned around in the jeep as far as it would go, bawled something in Hebrew to Zoo Baby and then I heard him call angrily to Dov by name.

'He says you've got to go to Tel Aviv. You have not the insurance to get killed in a battle,' said Zoo Baby. 'Maybe I go tell him to fuck off. I have not liked this man very much.'

Dov interrupted, calling something to Metzer who was red with fury. The tank men, waiting for the big battle and peeping like calm mice from their armoured holes, watched the exchange with avid concern. Their heads went from our group to the jeep and back again, and then returned to us.

'We'll go,' decided Dov. 'Leave him to shout.' The five of us turned and ran down the road towards the Mandelbaum Gate. I half turned and saw Metzer apparently about to get out of the jeep. Then the artillery from the Jordan sector began shelling us. The explosions seemed to bounce up the road, blowing us sideways, leap-frogging among the tanks and the men. I felt Zoo Baby's huge protective arm over my head as we cowered in a ditch at the side of the road. It only lasted about a minute. When we looked up, with the air rolling with bitter smoke, two of the tanks were burning and there were soldiers lying dead a few yards away under the tamarisk trees.

The jeep had overturned and Metzer was lying on his back in the road about ten yards from it. I could see that the driver was trapped under the jeep. As we started back towards Metzer the vehicle blew up with the explosion of its petrol tank. It began to burn heavily.

There was a lot of shouting going on. Hoses were being brought up to the burning tanks and the prostrate men were being quickly carried off. An officer in the leading tank was shouting orders and the column began to move off noisily like some crocodile rudely disturbed.

Metzer was stretched out as though he were enjoying a nap. O'Sullivan touched him and then half turned him on to his side and grimaced at the great hole in his back. Some stretcher bearers lumbered to us and O'Sullivan gave them a small nod. Civilians apparently got priority because there were still some soldiers lying around. They picked up the dead man and put him on their litter. We continued down the road. I did not feel so badly about Metzer as I had done about Scheerer or Solen the young man in the amphibian, although I had known him since the moment I left the plane at Lod. But this had been a long day and there had been a lot of dying so far. And it was only late afternoon.

A military policeman farther down the road directed us to the house where the correspondents had assembled. Despite the shelling he was standing in the centre of the thoroughfare with that fireproof look of policemen everywhere. He was briskly directing three jeeps carrying long-nosed bazookas into a concealed turning, his hands flapping the signals. He paused when O'Sullivan approached him, smiled and pointed the direction.

The house had been previously fortified by the troops as part of the defences at the Mandelbaum Gate, which until that time had been the accepted crossing point between Jewish and Arab Jerusalem. Pilgrims and people with special passes used to go through that way from one country to another with the United Nations soldiers keeping a watch.

The house had not been used for ordinary living for a long time. We went into a cavernous, whitewashed downstairs room, empty except for a disabled table against the wall at one end. There were perhaps fifteen men in khaki Army fatigues in there and two other women wearing the same sort of clothes. Some of the men looked too old to be preparing to go into a fight. They had cameras and torches and a couple had portable typewriters. Since they were mostly Jews there was a lot of arguing going on, apparently about the distribution of some armbands with the word 'Press' in Hebrew, English, and prudently in Arabic. Several of the men and one of the women greeted Shoshana, but briefly and Shoshana said the other woman knew her but never spoke to her because of professional jealousy.

A squashed, fussy, Army major came through the crowd and came to us near the door. He spoke to Shoshana, whom he at once recognized, and then, having looked at me with some doubt, ushered both of us into a smaller room where a clean selection of fatigue uniforms was lying across a table, the jackets and the trousers joined and stretched out stiffly like steam-rollered men. The officer said something else in Hebrew and left us, closing the door.

Shoshana began to take off her clothes. 'We have come too late for the briefing,' she said, supporting herself with one hand on the table. I remained standing there, not moving, looking at her. She realized this and stopped with her trousers around her brown knees. Her white pants were a stretched triangle.

She bent towards me. 'Christopher, I love you, too,' she said kissing me. 'With all trueness, *mottek*.' She motioned towards the battledress dungarees. 'You must dress too,' she said. 'If you still want to be with me. I told the officer that you are a British journalist. I was afraid he would want to see your papers, but he trusts me.' She laughed. 'You are all over with earth and dust. You do not look like a piano player.'

'That is possibly because I am not a piano player,' I corrected a little huffily. 'I'm a concert pianist.'

'That is how I meant,' she smiled. I moved over and put

130

two fingers tenderly on the fatty rise of her bust. She put her fingers across mine and pressed them into her flesh watching me carefully while she did it. Then she pulled the battle fatigue jacket about her and buttoned it. I had some trouble with my buckles because the last time I did this it was with British infantry webbing. Eventually we were ready and we tied our 'Press' armbands like stewards preparing for a cross-country marathon. Then she kissed me and said: 'Good luck to us, Christopher.'

'Good luck to us, *mottek*,' I repeated. She smiled at the word. 'It means sweetness,' she said.

We walked out into the bare room. Half the men had gone. The place was shaking with the afternoon gunfire, plaster crumbled in small pieces from the wall. The fussy major approached us as we were joining O'Sullivan, Zoo Baby and Dov.

First he spoke in Hebrew and then stopped as Shoshana said something to him and changed to English for my benefit.

'As you have been delayed for the briefing,' he said carefully, 'I will again do it. The armoured column and the ground soldiers, the supporters, you understand . . . yes, the support troops . . . are moving into the positions for attacking. I show you.' There was a map spread on the leaning table and he took a ruler and traced a circle around the back of the Old City. He was sweating heavily in his uniform. 'We go both sides, like the classic German pincer attack of the last war,' he said. 'From here, where we are at the Mandelbaum and from farther north at Latrun we shall attack the high ground between Jerusalem and Ramallah where is the big radio station. We wish – for the reasons of our troops surrounded there – to get to the hospital at Mount Scopus, to cut the road – here – between Jerusalem and Ramallah, and to occupy all this area, the Mount of Olives, the Garden of Gethsemane, Augusta Victoria, and right down to Herod's Gate. It is through Herod's Gate that our paratroops will be breaking into the Old City.'

He paused. Some of the other journalists were going out of the low door now, waving nervous goodbyes to the few remaining. One man laughed and came back for the camera he had left behind.

The major returned to us: 'Difficulties there will be. We expect them. The Police School near the Ramallah Road junction. That will be one difficulty. The Arab Legion are there. You remember the Arab Legion of Glubb Pasha, sir?' He aimed the question directly at me.

'Not personally,' I said. 'Are they a good team?'

'Very good,' he answered missing, as they always did, the joke. 'That will be a bad place for casualties.'

'Latrun,' said the girl. 'That is a bad place also.'

He nodded. 'A bad place. Last time we left fourteen hundred dead in the fields there. The British gave also Latrun to the Arabs before they left.

'The area between here and Mount Scopus is mined and there are many ... holes ...' He hesitated and said something in Hebrew to Shoshana. It was Dov who translated. 'There are heavy mines and many trenches, bunkers and that sort of defence,' Dov said turning to me.

'Trenches, that is correct,' agreed the major. 'There will be much difficulty. Please do not move too much forward into the battle area. Telephones for the correspondents are in the farther room there. I shall be here in this position to help you. I shall be in this house all the time.' He smiled and said: 'Thank God.'

Dov asked him a question in Hebrew and received a laughing reply. Two telephones began ringing at once and the squat little major went towards the telephone room.

'First I must telephone to my office,' said Shoshana. 'I asked a man at the command post but he was very busy and it is possible did not do it. I will let them know I am in Jerusalem and they will be glad.'

Dov said to me as she walked away: 'You will have a travelling orchestra to accompany you. That is appropriate isn't it. We have asked where our Army units are located. It seems Zoo Baby should be at El Arish in the Gaza Strip and I should be in the Sinai.'

'Do you think they missed you?'

'It is possible,' he smiled gently. 'But it seems *we* shall miss very little.'

We crouched at that moment because a shell landed in the vicinity and swayed the entire house like a ship in a hurricane. We could hear the tank tracks clanking up the road towards the lane. That threatening, ominous clank. The firing increased immediately and the air of the room was clouded with dust and falling plaster.

Zoo Baby looked up apprehensively. He sniffed at the gritty air. 'Outside is okay,' he concluded. 'I'll fight them outside. But me, I don't want the house to bury me.'

'It would be a big house that buried you,' answered Dov. He was very calm.

Shoshana came back eventually. 'Two reporters and two cameramen are here somewhere in Jerusalem from my paper but they are glad I am here too,' she said. Then she added with sweet seriousness: 'But the editor said I must *not* get killed and I must *not* let you get killed, Christopher. That is his order.'

'Mind you obey the order,' I said.

She laughed spontaneously, because for once, she understood the joke, and gaily as though we were embarking on a fine treat. Dust continued to cascade from the ceiling and she shook it from her hair.

'We have good soldiers to protect us also,' she smiled patting Zoo Baby and Dov and smiling at the pensive O'Sullivan. 'No Arab will get us.'

The little major came forward with some infantry steel helmets which he distributed. He gave me mine last.

There were no others in the place now. They had all gone out to observe the start of the advance and the battle. I said to Shoshana: 'I'm surprised your officer gave me a hat at all. I don't think he likes the British.'

'Many of us do not,' she said indicating that the remark was completely logical. 'My father and my brothers have killed English soldiers. And we remember what took place at Latrun. That is a terrible place, a fortress on a flat hill, by a monastery. Our best soldiers died in that place in nineteen

133

forty-eight. We could not break the Arabs there. And Latrun was a present to the Arabs from the British.'

We moved towards the exit, going out into the sunshine battle. It was curiously like walking on to a concert platform with the lights and the haze. All the air was filled with dust and noise and filtered sun. There were some bright summer flowers at the door of the house, growing profusely, the dust of the battle already lying across their petals and their leaves. We could not see very much because we were deep in the lane leading from the house to the road where the tanks had been. But the air was choked and the banging of the guns made the ground and the walls shudder. Three jet fighters jumped across the small part of the sky visible to us, very low, passing along the length of the lane, then howling away.

'Jordanians,' said Dov.

'Hawker Hunters,' said O'Sullivan.

'British,' I said.

'Almost all the Jordanian Air Force is,' said Dov without rancour.

'We seem to be well represented all around,' I said. 'Your tanks are British aren't they?'

'Centurions,' nodded Dov. 'Very good tanks.'

We were at the entrance to the lane now, leading out to the main road. The bulky tanks were still trundling through the dust. We were in single file, O'Sullivan first, then Dov, then Shoshana, then me, and finally Zoo Baby. We turned the corner and walked towards Jordan. From there, through the heated haze, I could see that we were well in time for the battle. It was five-thirty in the afternoon. I stepped over two dead soldiers half lying against a wall and I wondered if at that moment at Caesarea, in the distant north, Selma, as promised, was driving her ball from the first grassy tee.

134

11

It was the time when the heat begins to diminish from the day in Jerusalem. It was frightening and strange going down that sloping street with tanks portioned out like a parade ahead of us, and quiet foot soldiers, walking steadily in front, behind us and beside us, moving to begin fighting the Arab Legionnaires. The leading tanks were embattled about half a mile away, where the ground began to rise again. They had entered Jordan and were several hundred yards beyond the border when they were delayed by the entrenched troops, and the hidden mines. I was not afraid, perhaps because Shoshana and the others showed no fear, only bemused by all the death happening about me. I could feel the sticky sweat and the dry dirt caked on my face like a mask. The steel helmet felt like an awkward basin. As I worked my face muscles I could feel the dried dirt cracking on my cheeks and forehead. Somehow my tongue was bleeding and I could taste the blood in my mouth. I wiped my hand across my lips and saw that it was streaked with orange. Only ten days before I had been playing to a polite and attentive audience at Cheltenham Spa.

An infantry officer jogged up the road, away from the advance, comically astride a portable motor-scooter. He was a big young man and it was his bulky battle kit, his Uzzi machine gun, and his lump of a helmet that made him look strange on the small vehicle. He saw our group of five and called in Hebrew, sweeping his arm to order us into a shallow enclave in the walls near the Mandelbaum Gate. We went into the space and immediately a platoon of staring troops, at the run, bayonets fixed, went by. They kept on running into Jordan and we could see them, where the road bore left, going through their own tanks and running on into the enemy. There was a terrible din; firing ahead, smoke, and then great flashing explosions that flung flame everywhere and tore huge holes in the view of the battle before us.

Shoshana said conversationally: 'Israeli officers never order "forward" as any other army. Always they say "*acharai*" which means "follow me".'

My eyes were streaming from a fat cloud of smoke that suddenly billowed up the street and as I tried to answer her I got it in my throat also. I spluttered and coughed. I tried to tell her that this little bit of claptrap propaganda is thrown at every stranger in Israel and it's time they stopped it. Why do they always have to justify themselves? In *every* bloody army the officer goes *first* whether the order is 'forward' or 'follow me'. Because if he doesn't go, neither do the men. But the Jews love to get trade from these white-lie clichés. That's the trouble with being both literate and businesslike. I did not tell her then because the smoke made me vomit and when I'd finished I couldn't be bothered to open the matter again.

Zoo Baby regarded me anxiously. I wiped the sick from my mouth and looked at him with watering eyes.

'Something maybe you ate,' he said solicitously.

'Like smoke,' I said.

His face beamed with the beginning of his laugh and when he reached its fulfilment point he let it fully go, causing the wry young soldiers to stare at him as they continued marching towards the battle.

'The British!' bellowed Zoo Baby. 'My God! The British! Always they keep their jaw up, yes?'

'No,' I said. 'Their chin. It's their chin they keep up.'

'Exactly so,' he conceded. He peeped out into the road. The immediate area ahead seemed quieter. The battle had advanced half a mile. He glanced at O'Sullivan. The Irishman nodded as though he were ordering a second drink and we moved ahead. There was a tank slewed across the road after about three hundred yards, one of its tracks broken like a garter. Some engineers were working on it. The tank crew were standing impatiently in the road.

136

'Now that's a hell of a time to have a puncture,' commented O'Sullivan. Nobody laughed so he said: 'The boys will be going hard for Mount Scopus.' We had sheltered behind the metal walls of the tank and O'Sullivan began watching ahead through a pair of binoculars decently passed to him by the idle tank captain. Shoshana, taking out a notebook the size of a stamp, began to interview the tank crew. I don't think she was a very good interviewer. When she came to England to write about me she seemed slow, yet fussy, in the technique. She wrote notes about the tank crew and they told her how the fighting had been just a few minutes before. Someone had raised an Israeli flag on both sides of the Mandelbaum Gate denoting the first conquest of the invasion. One of the tank men wanted to embrace Shoshana and refused to answer questions until he was accommodated. Shoshana called across to his tank captain who shouted sternly at the soldier, who then lowered his arms and began meekly to answer her inquiries. When she had finished, and when his captain was watching the horizon through the glasses retrieved from O'Sullivan, the soldier grabbed Shoshana and gave her a full squeeze around the breasts which apparently satisfied him. I suppose he thought he might get shot down within the hour.

'Why is Mount Scopus so important?' I asked Dov.

'Because we have soldiers besieged there, at the old Hebrew University,' he said.

'How did they get that far behind the Jordanians?'

'The United Nations escorted them,' he smiled. 'It is an arrangement, since the 1948 armistice. It is occupied by just over a hundred Israeli soldiers who are taken out every two weeks. They guard the old university and the books and such things.

'Every two weeks the Arabs let them go through with a United Nations escort. It is one of those strange things. Just an arrangement, just part of the game.'

'So they've got to be reached before the Arabs get in,' I said.

'There are so few of them that the quicker there is a link-up the better,' said Dov.

'Are they armed? Did the Arabs let them through with guns?'

Zoo Baby grinned and answered for Dov: 'They have a few little pop guns and other toys they have managed to smuggle. They will keep the Arabs away for a few moments or longer, maybe.'

We were able to leave the shelter of the tank now and go farther. The infantry had now passed us by. The street was curiously empty except for smoke and battle litter. The tank behind which we had crouched, its track repaired, came trundling after us, like an anxious pet left behind. It had gone fifty yards down the street when a small anti-personnel mine blew up under its tracks and it slewed about once more and shuddered violently into the shuttered window of an Arab shop. The shutters fell and an enormous avalanche of rice tumbled out into the road. The shopkeeper must have piled it in sacks behind his blinds for protection. From the back of the splintered wood emerged the hysterical Jordanian, leaping about in his robes and wailing, his fear of the Israelis overcome by the disaster to his rice.

The tank commander, like a rabbit appearing from a hat, came out of the turret and dismally climbed to the ground. The second track of the vehicle was now broken, split by the small mine, and was lying flat on the ground like a dried tongue. He pushed his goggles to his forehead and began to swear in Hebrew, hands on hips, red under his tank-man's helmet. The Jew and the Arab, each bemoaning his own particular disaster, suddenly became aware of each other, stared with a kind of hostile sympathy, and then both turned and began wailing again. The captain ordered his men from the tank and sent one of them running back for the engineering crew who were working on another vehicle two hundred yards up the rise of the road.

The Arab brought out his wife and his children and between them, using scoops and hands, they began to shift the mountain of rice back into the area of the shop. They were still engaged like this when the engineers began working once more on the tank. The two groups went about their occupations busily one not caring about the other, nor looking their way, while the war moved on another half a mile.

The smoke immediately about us was clearing; the explosions and the fighting were climbing the opposite hill and were halfway to the top. After a while the ears ceased to be bludgeoned by the din and I looked about and realized fully that I was in Jordan as part of an occupying force.

The shops were different, closer, crumbling. The signs were in strange scrawls and the street names were scrawled the same, with sober English translations beneath them. We inevitably leave something behind.

There were fires burning ahead but the street seemed now undisturbed except for ambulances and stretcher parties coming back through the distant curtained smoke. The Star of David was flying from the knobs and pinnacles of some of the higher buildings showing the extent of the Jewish advance as readily as small flags on a battle map.

The daylight was drifting from the hills. Cypresses stood like dark quills, and buildings on the distant mounds, those uncovered by smoke, looked fat, dull, white and complacent on the fringes of the battle.

Where the fighting continued the smoke rose and the fires glowed. In our street the activity was local, the Arab shopkeeper and the Israeli engineers about their separate tasks, but working so closely that the rice sweepers frequently got in the way of the track repairers and the track repairers in the way of the rice sweepers. Some Arab children came up the street astonishingly chasing a donkey which clobbered on determinedly through the rubble and thin smoke at a sort of downcast and patient pace. The tank captain, with the air of a man who can perceive nothing better to do, caught the donkey as it ran by and held it while the four ruffian children, hung in rags and alley dirt, held on to its tail and kicked it unmercifully around until they had it pointing in the return direction and moving down the cobbled street again. They ran along with it, shouting and beating it enthusiastically, until they vanished in the evening dimness and the curtained smoke.

Shoshana had watched the pantomime with us, unsmiling although everyone else laughed, especially when the tank captain caught the donkey. O'Sullivan was saying that he had often seen the same thing in Wexford. Shoshana turned on him and said incongruously: 'Why you laugh, I don't know. Arab children kicking a donkey. How funny!' Then childishly threatening: 'When we have won all this country – then you will laugh, Mister Border Guard. See how much bigger border you will have to guard then!'

She meant it and she said it so seriously, so idiotically, that we all laughed at her.

O'Sullivan said soothingly: 'If it is too much frontier we've got then maybe I'll borrow the donkey myself.'

It was very nearly dark over Jerusalem now, with the explosions, white, yellow, orange, red, blossoming like brief flowers on the slopes of battle. They bellowed like the fiercest thunder among the Judean Hills and the light of the conflict shone on the face of the darkened city, on its imperturbable walls and its aloof towers.

Major de Groucy, the fussy officer from the Press house, abruptly came bouncing down the street on a motor-scooter, skidded to a theatrical stop, and then handed a folded paper to Shoshana.

She read it and the major stood by his toy machine, tubby and important. He nodded to us benignly as though we were meeting on some leisurely walk.

'You got out for some fresh air then?' I said conversationally, but in the half-shout which we had all unconsciously adopted over the banging of the guns.

He missed the inference. 'There are much duties,' he said. 'We are winning everywhere in the war. Every Egyptian plane is destroyed, on the floor or in the air.'

I did not believe him then, although it turned out he was right. Some wounded were being brought up the road on stretchers to ambulances standing alongside some parking meters a little farther down. They seemed to be the same type of meter as they had in the Jewish sector, although I suppose the writing on them was bound to be different and the slot for the coin. I felt tempted to suggest that the major went down and gave his news to the dying, but I held off.

'Some English news I have also,' he said bowing to me. I

recalled that I was a supposed British correspondent, so I raised my chin in an interested attitude.

'We have destroyed many Hawker Hunters of the Jordanian Air Force,' he announced. 'Also the aeroplane of the British Air Attaché in Amman.' He looked smugly at me. 'Are you not going to write that down?' he asked me.

'My notebook is full,' I said. 'I'll try and remember it.'

'It was *destroyed*,' he repeated looking at me closely.

'Was the attaché in it at the time?'

'No, no. You do not comprehend. It was on the airport.' He waited. Shoshana stopped reading the square of paper and handed it to Zoo Baby. He and Dov read it together, muttering and gradually grinning, like two men checking a successful football coupon. The major had a last try: 'It was a . . .' he checked a list. 'Yes, a Devon aeroplane.'

'Good English name,' I said. 'Devon. We call it Glorious Devon.'

'It is no longer glorious. It is destroyed.'

'No, the place.' I sang for him, '*Devon, glorious Devon*'. Shoshana and the others looked at me quickly. I stopped. 'Cider apples, clotted cream, and that type of thing,' I added apologetically. 'And a prison.'

The major, understanding now, glared at me through the dusk. 'Jokes and jokes,' he muttered. Then with finality, 'The Devon aircraft was *destroyed*.' He turned his motor-scooter like an errand boy and went up the hilly street hurriedly, and with no lights. We heard a dreadful squeal through the dusk and a concentrated confusion, sounding even above the noise of the guns. Hebrew and other voices were raised and the motor-scooter engine was running wild.

We ran back into the dark and after two hundred yards perceived the motor-scooter lying on its side, the engine having now choked itself, but with the wheels still spinning. Major de Groucy was sitting flatly on the cobbled road, blustering and holding his right leg and left ribs, his arms thrown about himself as though he were hugging his own body. At a short distance the ragged donkey we had seen pursued by the Arab children was also sitting down, inspecting its right foreleg with much the same injured expression

141

as the Israeli major. It let out a small feeble bray and looked malevolently at de Groucy. I thought at the time that it might well burst into tears. In the shadows the Arab urchins were hiding with fear and laughter. Shoshana and Dov and Zoo Baby went forward to lift and comfort the major and O'Sullivan and I walked over and inspected the donkey, which obligingly held up its leg in the manner of someone making an insurance claim. Then it tumbled to its feet and jogged off towards its home in Jordan, or what had been Jordan until late that afternoon. O'Sullivan and I followed it for a couple of hundred yards and went behind a half-demolished Arab house to urinate and to laugh.

We waited for the return of Shoshana, Zoo Baby and Dov. They came back eventually jogging through the dark rubble. 'He is okay,' said Zoo Baby. 'He has gone back to the Press place.'

Dov was grinning: 'The donkey was a resistance terrorist,' he said.

'I think the incident was purely civil,' I returned. 'The first road accident in Israel-occupied Jordan. We saw history.'

Shoshana laughed too. I was surprised. 'How bad to crash with a donkey,' she said. Then she added: 'We have had great victories today. Already most of Sinai and Gaza is ours and we have finished all their aeroplanes.'

Zoo Baby said: 'And our tanks will soon be through the mines. This is the news we have.'

We went quickly through the leftovers of the battle. More wounded were being brought back now, the stretcher parties stumbling through the dark with the running orderlies and the hand-held plasma bottles beside some of them, the bottles held high as though in some ironic triumph. The ambulances were parked farther back, where the roads were clearer. Some of the men on the stretchers moved and had to be restrained, held down by the trotting orderlies, others lay patiently, and others lay dead.

The armoured column under Colonel Uri Ben-Ari had forced its snout deep into the Jordan positions to the immediate north of the Old City. The tanks, which had taken only four hours to reach the battle positions in Jerusalem from the base at Ramla, took another two hours to break through the mines and emplacements guarding the way to the dominating hills.

We met three journalists with an elderly Army officer and ran with them through the ground over which the battle had passed to the dining-room of a small hotel. A sign saying 'Savoy Hotel' hung desperately from one hook at the front. The garden was smothered under a hump of debris which had fallen from the upper floors of the hotel and there was a brave solitary pane of glass in what had been the windows of the dining-room. There was a smell of smoke about the place. Some of the tables were laid for dinner under a cloak of dust.

Pink flares hung over the steep ground, their gradual descent giving them long necks, like flamingoes. They lit the unremitting battle in patches, as did the light of the explosions, showing up suddenly tanks and men crawling over the stony slopes, fighting, falling and remaining felled. The noise was outrageous here. The air seemed solid with explosive sounds, but, strangely, the little sounds of battle could be heard, the whistles, the creaking of the tank tracks, the protests of strained engines, and even weak voices.

One of the journalists had obtained some cottonwool, and seeing all of us clutching our ears he considerately passed it around like someone distributing candyfloss. The nearest point of battle was about five or six hundred yards away, but within a moment it was only fifty feet. Almost casually an armoured troop carrier appeared outside the garden gate of the hotel and a dozen Jordanian soldiers jumped out. They had not seen us crouching behind the sill of the dining-room and were watching something approaching from our right. They turned into the garden and spread out in ambush positions immediately below us. I felt Shoshana, on one side of me, and Zoo Baby, on the other, both harden. No one moved, each of our faces, nine faces, five in our group and the elderly officer and the three journalists were turned on the backs of the Arab soldiers.

I wondered, almost idly, what they were doing there at all

since this was supposedly recently occupied Israeli territory. But I conceded that even the best invasions occasionally go at the seams.

The elderly officer, who would have been more at home, I fancy, in an outfitter's shop, slid along the floor towards O'Sullivan, Dov and Zoo Baby. Only they were armed. He would have liked to push the remainder of us back into the room, but he feared the movement would alarm the Arabs.

Inside I could feel big puffs of my breath gradually filling my body. For the first time since we arrived in Jerusalem I began to feel afraid. I had been afraid in the desert when the planes were attacking us, but that was an urgent fear, a terror. Since then, even when Metzer was killed as he left the jeep, there had been some sort of hard calmness within me. But now it was fear again. Not fear for my own death, although that was some part of it, but fear for this situation, its sharpness, its silence, its isolation from the main battle. We were crouching and they were crouching. They were exposed a few yards ahead of us. It was like a frozen cameo, an illustration in a boy's adventure book. My fear was for the entire event, for us and strangely, no less for the hapless Arabs. It did not seem fair.

They were observing something coming up the road. Their twitching showed their excitement and their anticipation. The elderly officer had relayed instructions by signs to the three armed men with us. Zoo Baby looked as set and ready as he would be while waiting to break into a Sibelius symphony with his rolling drums, Dov looked, as always, quiet and studious, and O'Sullivan had that strange gaunt expression of the Irish when they're about to be involved in a fight, whether in bar or battlefield.

Over the more distant noise we could now hear a slow vehicle platoon truck coming up the road. But it was an armoured scout car which came first. The officer, standing up in the turret, came into our view over the top of the half-demolished garden wall. We could see his head and face and neck, travelling slowly, looking about him. He could only have been twenty yards from the waiting Jordanians. The ambushers crouched lower in unison, then came up a little as though they were on individual springs. The officer in the middle of the group touched the man on his left with his finger. The soldier pulled a grenade and bit the pin away with his teeth.

It was now. The elderly officer crouching by our window let out the most awesome croak. *'Esh!'* and the four Uzzi sub-machine-guns immediately went off next to my ear. My God they made a row. They quivered in the hands of the men about me, the spent shells jumping about like grass-hoppers.

The man never threw the grenade. It ignited up in his hand and blew him to rags. Some of the dozen Arabs spun and fell, squirmed a bit, then rolled and were still. The officer was killed by the grenade explosion. Frantically the trapped Jor-danians turned to open fire at us, and the bullets bit into the ceiling and smashed the last pane of glass left in the window. The Arab soldiers were jumping about like children playing on a sand pile. I could see them through a small, convenient slice of missing bricks as I lay flat against the wood blocks of the dining-room floor. I found I had my arm across Shosh-ana's head.

One Arab was lying on his back, face enraged, firing at us between his outstretched knees. The fire coming from our windows was murderous, O'Sullivan, shooting with profes-sional coolness and Dov and Zoo Baby with all the rabid enthusiasm of gifted amateurs. The officer's Uzzi had become jammed and he cursed it and banged it on the floor with the tetchy expression of an urban man with some dependable household implement which has suddenly become unusable.

Then the Israelis began shooting at us from the road. The five or six remaining Arabs had charged over the wall to be quickly dealt with by the patrol from the platoon truck. Then the scout car turned its machine gun on us and three gren-ades burst nastily in the hotel's front garden. The elderly officer looked up with a hurt expression and then fell back, with an acrobatic back flip, a difficult manoeuvre for a man of his age, and lay dead with a Jewish bullet in his front. It was hideous in the room. It was full of a terrible banging.

They were plastering it from all sides with their guns. I could hear the scout car straining to get over the rubble of the wall to get a better shot at us. O'Sullivan and the others, suddenly impotent, were lying on the floor. O'Sullivan was swearing, saying 'stupid bastards, stupid bastards,' all the time, and Zoo Baby's big backside stuck into the air. There is nothing more pitiful than a fat man, exposed to death, trying to flatten himself against the ground.

It was Dov who saved us. Yelling in Hebrew he motioned the others to join in. I have rarely learned anything so quickly. '*Atsor! Yise'elin! Atsor! Yise'elin!*' They stopped and then it was Shoshana who got up and began screaming abuse at them. The officer from the scout car came over wearing an understandably worried expression and his men were grouped shamefacedly above the debris of the wall. Some of the wooden lathes from the building had caught fire in the garden, just smouldering and a small spitting flame, and on his way over to us the officer stamped on the burning and screwed his foot over it, as though that would do some good to partly compensate for the harm he had committed.

I thought Shoshana was going to attack the young man with her fists. It was the first time I had ever seen her displeased with anything Jewish. Zoo Baby, his face covered with black sweat, restrained her with one big hand. O'Sullivan stood up and faced the officer. The young man looked ashamed. When he saw the body in the Israeli uniform lying behind us, he put his hands over his eyes as though to block it out. Shoshana was hissing under her breath like an angered cat. She spat out some words in Hebrew at the young man but he merely turned his back on her and spoke to O'Sullivan and eventually Dov since O'Sullivan's Hebrew was not always adequate. He then checked the dead officer's identity discs and noted their information. Tearing a page from a notepad he wrote his own rank, name and number and handed it to O'Sullivan. It was like motorists exchanging details after an accident. The young officer remained very calm. He saluted the man he had killed, and then saluted O'Sullivan and the rest of us.

He then went back to his men, who watched him with

146

some misgiving, and they drove off the way they had come. O'Sullivan went over to look at the dead man. Two of the journalists had flesh wounds and Shoshana dressed them with the elderly officer's field dressing. I went over to look at the body. He seemed composed, the annoyance of the jammed gun had drifted from his face in death.

'Misfortune,' said O'Sullivan philosophically. 'I had an uncle once who was a footballer. Soccer international. And he put through his own goal when Eire was playing England and he never got over it.'

We turned abruptly as a movement disturbed the back of the room. A sickly-smiling Arab, a wasted little man in a long filthy robe, and wearing a fez, came around a door. He bore a tray of drinks; a polished tray and clean glasses, containing a variety of liquids, beer, scotch, arak, lime juice.

'Refreshments please,' he said in good English. He saw the dead man and stepped sedately around him. He offered the tray to Shoshana first and, after holding back, she took a lime juice. We all took a glass then, raised them to each other out of formal habit, and drank.

'Compliments of the Savoy Hotel, Jerusalem,' the Arab intoned. He collected the glasses from each of us when we had finished and padded away to the rear door again, stepping aside from the dead man as he went.

When he had gone, O'Sullivan grinned at me: 'There's a man who knows which side of the bread is the jam.'

'Perhaps he poisoned the lot,' I suggested.

Dov said: 'I doubt it. The Arab is well known for his hospitality.'

147

12

Late in the day, that long Monday, a brigade of Israeli paratroops who had been waiting at an airfield in the north of the country to fall on the Egyptians at El Arish in Gaza, were moved to the Jerusalem area. They were commanded by Colonel Morechai Gur who, at first, was told that only one battalion would be going to the city to fight, but later that all his men would be required.

We saw them at the Biblical Zoo when we went back into the Israeli sector at nine o' clock. We went from the wrecked hotel, retracing our path into the Jewish sector, in a returning Army truck. The two mildly wounded journalists and their colleague and the body of the elderly officer were eventually left at the Press centre although Major de Groucy was reluctant to accept responsibility for the body. O'Sullivan told him that he would send someone for the dead man, so the elderly officer was covered with an overall, and left on a table in a small space behind the telephone room.

Shoshana remained at the Press house to write and telephone the report for her newspaper. Major de Groucy was not fussing any longer but striding about, his arm, his leg and his ribs bandaged from his collision with the donkey. Some of the correspondents came in sick, dirty and tired from the battle, the death of it still in their eyes, saw he was hurt and patted him understandingly.

The major nudged me along to a typewriter at the end of the same littered table at which Shoshana was working. I sat down behind the machine and looked dumbly at it. I was conscious of de Groucy looking at me sideways. Shoshana glanced up, and smiled at me through her dusty face. Since I was required to behave as an English correspondent would behave, I pushed some paper into the roller and wrote

148

my feelings and impressions of the long day of travel and battle. I kept these notes, quite proudly, and I am using them now as I remember what happened in Jerusalem.

Shoshana when she had finished told the major that it was not necessary for me to use the cable facilities that night, since I worked for an influential weekly journal, and we found O'Sullivan, Dov and Zoo Baby outside in the lane with a newly acquired jeep.

The battle had become more subdued, as though it had tired itself out. By that time the Centurion tanks had overcome the last of the Jordanian strongpoints and were now working their way towards the Jerusalem-Ramallah road and Mount Scopus.

'Major de Groucy did not seem convinced about me,' I said to Shoshana as we climbed into the jeep. The night was warm and very dark with the poppings of the diminished battle going on to the north and east and louder rumbling to the south. Army vehicles were lumbering about in the darkened streets.

Shoshana laughed: 'He will say nothing. Only to us is it known that his wounds were from a donkey. All the others think it is from the Arabs and he would not like them to know.'

We all laughed. All the tension had gone from us now with the knowledge that we were behind the fighting and that we had survived through the deadly doings of the day. I ran my arm about Shoshana and felt that all her hardness had melted, that she was soft and tired and feminine again. She came to me, putting her head, her fine fair hair, on my shoulder and against my cheek. My hand moved and touched her breast through her sweaty shirt. Her face half turned to me and she touched me with her dry lips.

'Where are we going?' I asked.

Zoo Baby, who was driving, said: 'For some eating.'

Dov, beside him, added: 'At the zoo.'

I laughed because I thought it was a joke, but soon we went through a part of the Israeli sector which had been violently shelled by the Arabs that day, where people wandered in the lost way that survivors of a bombardment or a

149

raid wander, and the smoke still rolled from the rubble. It was there I saw a signpost in English, holed by a shrapnel but still readable in the dimmed headlights of the jeep. We waited by a cross-junction for the tank to go by, damaged and coughing like a consumptive, and I saw the signpost pointing to the right. It said: 'To the Biblical Zoo'.

We went through the little forest, the firm smell of the pine, the eucalyptus and the olive mixing with the wandering smoke that was everywhere in Jerusalem that night. Among the trees of the forest squatting like trogs and woodland gnomes were the paratroops who had come from the north and were waiting to go into the battle for the Old City. They sat quietly eating and drinking from their mess cans, stoic, their guns and their helmets on the ground. They were within the boundary of the zoo, sitting on the grass of the picnicking area and on the tree-shaded benches.

'Feeding time,' said O'Sullivan.

We drove on and then we heard the moans and roars of the animals coming through the dark. Dov said: 'The guns, maybe, have upset them.'

We pulled into an area near the pay-box at the entrance, left the jeep and walked into the noise of the zoo. I was unprepared. That day I thought I had seen every form of violent death. But this was different. The place was lit by dim flares and oil lamps. Two weeping men were carrying a dead ostrich on a wide stretcher. It lay more grotesque in death than any human, its ancient, wrinkled eyelids closed, its beak pleadingly half open, its great legs and feet crumbled like cables.

'Jesus,' I whispered. I felt myself grow sick. We stood and let the men with the ostrich go by. All around us caged animals were howling in the dimness.

'They bury their heads in the sand, of course,' said O'Sullivan nodding at the ostrich. 'That never was much of a way.'

We walked a few more paces. The zoo had been devastated. The cages and the trees were burst and wrecked. The animals which had survived were crying with fear and with the smell of blood.

'The main Arab shelling was in this area today,' said Dov soberly. 'It seems maybe we suffered some casualties.'

A giraffe, itself like a felled tree, lay in the ruins of its cage. There were birds lying about the place under the flares and lamps, their feathers grimed with the dirt of death. Four set-faced paratroopers marched by with a litter piled with the bodies of black, white and coloured birds. It looked like the rack at a butcher's shop before Christmas.

'Even the vultures,' said O'Sullivan sombrely.

We walked through the debris of the cages towards a clear area beyond some fig trees where another group of para-troops were squatting and eating apparently undisturbed by the unique devastation about them. Three foxes lay in their own blood at the bottom of their cage. On the cage, in Hebrew and underneath in English was, *'Take us the foxes, the little foxes, that spoil the vines'*.

Dov said: 'The song of Solomon, you will recall. The zoo was meant to be a collection of animals mentioned in the Bible, but it has grown, or it *had* grown until this.'

Zoo Baby and Shoshana had said nothing while we had been there. O'Sullivan pointed a finger at a torn and empty cage. *'As a roaring lion and a greedy bear, so is a wicked ruler over an . . . indigent people,'* he read with difficulty in the poor light. Then he spat and said: 'T'isn't much of a day to be going to the zoo.'

Shoshana stopped the two men who had carried the dead ostrich. They were returning with the stretcher. She asked them to sit for a moment and they sat wearily on the grass by the side of the zoo path. They wore their zoo attendants' uniforms which seemed strange among all the soldiers. The older one, a gentle, helpless sort of man in his sixties, spread his hands to Shoshana's questions and began to weep again as he answered her.

She glanced at me and asked him if he spoke English. He replied in Hebrew, but said the words, 'For the tourists.' He then wiped his tears with the flats of his hands, as a child smudges them away, and continued in good English.

'One hundred animals die,' he sobbed. 'All the time the

151

Arabs kill them. Bang, bang, bang. The lion, and the giraffe, the high one, the bear and the lion. . . .'

The other keeper, a younger man, grey in the face, put his arm on the old man's shoulder. The first keeper looked at me. 'Sir,' he said, 'we have loved these. In the war of 1948 we could not feed them by day because of the Arab snipers who shoot at us, you understand. We creep and crawl to feed them in the night.

'Then we put them to live at Mount Scopus, and the Arabs were around us. We took them from there, sir, in armoured cars, and buses, and all the monkeys in ambulances.'

The noise of the creatures and the movements of the soldiers continued around us. The keeper put his eyes into his hands, but then wiped them resolutely and got up from the grass. 'But some we save today. I show you, sir.'

We followed him to a compound with a high wall. The cages there were untouched and the animals were fretful but making no great noise. On a table beneath some shredded eucalyptus trees in one corner using an oil lamp for illumination, two women dressed the wounds of a patient monkey. It sat woefully while they bandaged its foreleg. In the cages immediately about them other small animals, and two child-like donkeys stood and watched the bright lamp and the unusual activity.

'All these have been a little wounded and will be living,' said the keeper. 'But most were dead or we had to kill ourselves because of their wounds. Now we have to collect the giraffe with a truck and the foxes and some others. We have a big hill of dead creatures, sir. . . A mountain.'

We could say nothing. When we were nearly clear of the wrecked cages and the torn trees, and into the untouched area of the little forest, away from the animal howling, where more paratroopers were feeding, Shoshana held my hand and said: 'You see, Christopher, what they do to the poor Israeli animals.'

Dov said to me: 'It is very interesting, the zoo. One day you should return and see it again. When everything is okay. When the animals were on Mount Scopus it was a lunatic situation. Maybe it could only happen here. The troops had

152

to be fed, but so did the monkeys. In the end they let all the harmless small animals – the ones that could survive by caring for themselves – they let them free and brought the rest back here, just as the old man said, in a convoy protected by the United Nations. The lions were brought down in an armoured car and the birds in double-decker buses. Most strange.'

The Army had a cookhouse established beneath the trees and we waited for ten minutes in a line with some of the fresh paratroops and some weary tank men who had come back from the battle with the Jordanian gun emplacements to the north of the Old City.

Zoo Baby was talking to one of the tank men, nodding his great head understandingly as he listened to the story. We collected our food in mess tins, a hot mass of meat and vegetables and went away under the trees to eat it. Dov was missing for a while and reappeared happily holding a bottle of red wine. He sat with us. Shoshana pushed a piece of meat on her fork under my nose. I bit at it as though we were enjoying a picnic. Dov said: 'The wine is not much, but just enough for five.'

I said: 'Last evening we were eating our dinner at Eilat. It's been a long twenty-four hours.'

'There is more,' said Zoo Baby. 'I talked to the men from the tanks. It was very bad they said because of the mines and the deep trenches. Men had to pick the mines from the ground before the tanks could go through.'

'There were no flails to fit to the tanks,' said O'Sullivan his face in his mess tin. 'The flail pulls the mines up before the tank goes over them, but they're all in the south. The tanks were all right, but it seems we were caught a bit short of flails. Sounds more like Ireland than Israel.'

Shoshana said, through her food: 'In Sinai and Gaza it is good. The Egyptians are being defeated and are running for the canal. Also in the south of Jerusalem the Government House, which was of the United Nations before today, is now taken by Israel from the Jordanians. We have crossed the road to Bethlehem but there is still much fighting there.'

I suddenly thought of Selma then and her coveted house in

Jordan, of the cypress trees and the strange little turret, and the postman with the red bicycle. I remembered watching it across the frontier through the binoculars and how proud of it she was.

'Was there much shelling about the windmill?' I asked casually. It would be strange I thought if the Arabs destroyed Selma's house in Israel and the Israelis her house in Jordan.

'At Yemin Moshe below Mount Zion,' said Dov. 'There was a big battle going on there. We went across to get Government House and Sur Bahir which was an Arab strongpoint. The windmill is useful. In the war before we used it as an observation point and there was much shelling there.'

'Don Quixote,' said Zoo Baby. 'This is what they called the battle. Yes, it was Don Quixote. Because of the windmill, you understand.'

I agreed that I understood. Again I wondered about Selma and if she had kept her word to play golf.

We returned to the jeep as they were lifting the dead giraffe on to the truck, using a block and tackle. It looked an awkward way to handle such a gentle creature. With its spread wooden legs the loading equipment itself looked like a giraffe. The old keeper was directing the loading and the paratroops were helping. The keeper's eyes were still streaming and his voice, as he called to the men, was thick as mud. He seemed very anxious that they should not drop the giraffe.

There was still fighting in the South, beyond the windmill, and some small-arms fire from the dark hills behind Gethsemane and the Mount of Olives. But the heavy Judean night had settled in with what I came to know later as its overpowering effect. It falls in summer upon everything like a hand, keeping it, containing it. It is a time for sleeping in Jerusalem, or for lying in helpless wakefulness. It is not good for fighting.

'There will be an attack on the Police School in a few hours,' said Shoshana. 'This I have been told also.'

'And you want to be there,' I said tiredly.

154

'Of course,' she said. 'But you may stay in your bed.'

'Where is bed?' I asked.

Dov answered: 'My brother has a house not far away, near the President Hotel. We will go there for a time. He will be with his Army unit, but maybe his wife is there. I tried to telephone but the telephone is not working too well in Jerusalem today.'

I found Shoshana lolling in sleep against my shoulder before we reached the house of Dov's brother. She was full against me, but light, like a child exhausted after a busy day. I woke her softly when Zoo Baby turned the jeep into a steep lane and stopped halfway down the slope. It was dark but quiet. The crickets were even active here, clicking in the walls and the hanging vines. The place was clean and clear for there had been little shelling in that area.

We went to the house, but there was no answer to the door. Dov walked around the enclosed garden to a window. He unfussily broke a pane of glass and opened the casement door. We walked into the deserted house.

'Breaking and entering,' I smiled at Dov. 'And your brother's house too.'

He shrugged. 'One more pane of glass won't make a lot of difference in Jerusalem today,' he said. He pulled all the shutters and put on one lamp. It was a small house, but very clean and sweet smelling. There were some children's books on a table in the corner. *Batman and Robin, Mickey Mouse* and *Yogi Bear*, all in Hebrew.

'How many children?' I asked.

'Three,' said Dov. 'Rachel has probably taken them to Ramat Gan, to her mother's house.'

Shoshana had gone to the bathroom to shower. Dov poured some arak for each of us and we sat and drank it. He said: 'When we have the Old City you must see the Garden of the Tomb. As a Christian it should very much interest you.'

'Why is that?' asked O'Sullivan. The remark had been addressed to me, but he came in quickly, as though anxious to be identified as a Christian also. Dov smiled because he realized this.

Zoo Baby said: 'It is without the City wall.' He said 'without' because of his unfinished English, but it sounded like the Sunday school hymn about a green hill far away. 'It is just into the Arab territory. There was fighting there today.'

'It is very convincing,' said Dov. 'I have seen it, though many years ago, during the last fighting in Jerusalem, and, as a Jew, it seems to me that it is more convincing as the resting place of Christ than the official place at the Church of the Holy Sepulchre.'

He was an extraordinary man, this Dov. We sat in dust and weariness, waiting to witness more dust and bloodshed, and yet he had time and enthusiasm to explore a small avenue of history. He poured some more arak all round. 'The garden is very quiet, just below an old Jewish cemetery on top of a rock that I think you will agree is shaped like a skull. Golgotha, the Place of the Skull. That's what they called Calvary, of course. Golgotha. There is a hill, a place like a skull, and known as a place of execution in ancient times. And within the garden there is a rock tomb, one which had a great stone in front of it at one time. You can still see the channels of the stone.'

Drawing with his finger in some arak which had spilt on the table he showed how Christ, bearing His cross down the Via Dolorosa, could have come to the place quite as easily as He could arrive at the spot where the Church of the Holy Sepulchre stands.

'It is simple,' he said as though explaining some battle logic. 'Christ turned *left*, not right, and came out of the gate and *up* to Calvary. The other way you go *down*. There is *no* rising hill.'

I could hear the shower running upstairs and Shoshana singing some military-sounding Israeli song. The guns were deadened from here. We sat and helped ourselves to more arak and listened to Dov. He went through his whole theory, how Christ coming out of the gate of the city met Simon of Cyrene, detailing the movements while I tried to remember the story forgotten since childhood. Then Dov described how at the Place of the Skull criminals were crucified or

156

thrown down to death on the rocks below. When I lived with Shoshana in Jaffa Road, Jerusalem after the Six Day War I got to know the rocks where they threw the ancient criminals very well because the Israelis built a bus station there.

Shoshana came down the stairs wearing a pink towelling bath robe belonging to Dov's sister. It was a good deal too big for her, but she had washed all the grime away and had tied her splendid fair hair back behind her neck. She came and sat down, her brown feet nosing out from beneath the hem of the garment and her neck and face looking clean and tanned. All four men sat looking at her for a moment, without saying anything, then Dov suggested that I should go and shower. Shoshana said she would make some coffee.

I went up and let the cooling water run over me like a river. I had a look at my hands. A great many pianists make a big thing about their hands, insure them for major sums and that sort of thing. My manager, Eric, always told me I did not worry enough about mine. If he could have seen them after one day of war he would not have been pleased. I doubted if an insurance policy on a pianist's hands would allow him to take part in a war anyway.

I had to put the same clothes on and I did not shave. My luggage had been left in the jeep which was destroyed when Metzer died. When I had jumped from it to run towards Shoshana and the others I had left the cases there. All my clothes, even my tails. I grinned when I thought about the improbability of my tails being blown up on a street corner in Jerusalem. But for the impulse of getting out then I would have been killed too. On the other hand the jeep had only waited because Metzer had been calling me back. Otherwise it would have been on its way with me beside the driver. It had only been there, in that deadly spot, because of me. I had not thought of it like that before.

I went downstairs and O'Sullivan went to the bathroom. When Shoshana bent to pour the coffee the front of the robe eased out and I could see the clean lumps of her breasts, brown and then the inner band of white. She looked up and saw me looking at her.

'They have fixed two searchlights on top of the Histadrut building,' said Dov. 'I heard at the zoo.'

'What's that?' I asked. 'The Histadrut . . .'

'Oh, what would you say it was? It's the sort of Association . . . no . . . the Federation, that is right . . . of Labour,' he said.

I smiled at Shoshana as she passed my coffee. 'Federation is a better word when it is connected with Labour,' I said. 'Association is a bit upper class. It's for people like antique dealers.'

'The difficulties of the English language,' shrugged Shoshana.

'What about Hebrew?' asked Dov. He looked at me: 'What do you think of a country where they called a scrambled egg "a confused egg"?'

'Or say the same thing for "hello" and "goodbye",' I said.

'*Shalom* means "peace" not any of those things,' said Shoshana huffily. 'It is like they say *ciao* in Italian. That is also for meeting and parting.'

'When will they use the searchlights?' I asked.

'For the School of Police,' said Zoo Baby. He was always glad to come in when the English did not become too quick for him. He was sitting by Shoshana and he looked an oddity, mountainous, grimed, sweated, but passive, alongside her cleanness. I could see the oily imprint of his sub-machine-gun on his palms. 'Tonight,' he said, 'in a few hours they will go for the school. It will be a bad battle there. They have the lights for the jet planes.'

Dov said: 'This is the particular thing about fighting in a city. It is so familiar. Even their side is familiar for we see it every day. It is not a war over many miles. It is just over a little space with the enemy country at the next block. In London it would be like fighting from Big Ben with the other army in Trafalgar Square, or in New York like shelling the lake in Central Park from the Plaza Hotel. In this sort of war you have no distance to travel.'

O'Sullivan had come down and was sitting on a bare wooden chair taking some coffee from Shoshana. Zoo Baby made his way up the stairs. O'Sullivan said: 'When the Irish pat-

158

riots were going to attack Dublin Castle in the 1916 Rising they went on a tramcar, forty at a time. And they all paid their fares.'

'They would,' I said.

Once the house was quiet I went to her. Zoo Baby was sleeping like a balloon on the other bed in the room I was given and I did not wake him. While I waited I almost drifted to sleep myself, but I kept myself conscious by watching flashes of the battle in the south of the city through the window and the fanned branches of a tree in the garden.

I knew she would lie awake for me because I touched her hand before we had left the room downstairs and she had gently pulled my middle finger out to its full length then sweetly closed her fingers around it. She was in a room belonging to the children. There was a Donald Duck on the outside of the white door with some Hebrew inscription underneath it. It looks strange to see Hebrew in that sort of context. It always looks in shape as though it should be preserved for religious, elevated things.

She had left the door only touching the jamb, so I did not have to turn the handle. I pushed it and went in to her.

In all the time since, I can never think about her without thinking of how she was when I saw her that moment.

She was lying full on her back, not asleep, on one of the children's small beds. There was a little nightlight, shaped like a lantern, burning on a table. The bed was against a wall and she was stretched, without her clothes, her hands behind her head, looking towards the pale, still flickering, light of a window. There were two other little beds in the shadowed room, toys on the shelves and big simple pictures on the wall. I could see, although the room was dim, a large painting of Popeye, a doll in a green dress, three wooden soldiers about a foot tall, Shoshana's breasts lying as quiet as the toys, her hair over the pillow flowing out over her arms; a baby's rocking-chair, a cuckoo clock, Shoshana's brown leg, her knee raised; the other leg, the nearest to me, flat like a plain lying below the high mountain of the first one. On a tray an assembly of model tanks and armoured cars, aeroplanes and ships of war. Shoshana's stomach looked flat and glistening in the same light.

As I came through the door she turned her head quietly to me and smiled. 'I am a child again,' she said.

'Oh, Christ,' I thought. 'Look at her. Just look at her sweet and naked there, lying among the toys.' Then I could again see her as she had been in the Negev that day looking at the bodies of the Israeli boys in the amphibian and hear her cold voice saying that all sorts of people die in war. I was clean but weary. All I wanted was to lie by her and feel her. The guns kept exploding, but they were to the south, towards Bethlehem. The sky flicked and occasionally flashed at the nursery window.

I closed the door cautiously behind me, then went to the little bed on which she lay. Beneath her she had a woollen rug, and it was rough against my skin. She moved over and I lay beside her knowing immediately the splendid touch of her beautiful skin, cool and warm at the same time, pliable, firm, painful but luxurious.

'Christopher, come to me,' she whispered. 'All day I have been so afraid.'

I could not believe her, but then, immediately, I did. She held me desperately, close to her, my nose and my wet mouth to her waiting breasts.

'What is that called?' she asked.

'What called, darling?'

'When you do that, like a small animal, pushing your nose.'

'Like this?'

'Yes, like this.'

'Nuzzling,' I said. 'Rabbits do it and moles and things.'

'Nuzzling is a beautiful English word,' she said. 'Nuzzling. It is about the nose and it sounds so soft.'

I put my nose to the cone of her nipple and began to work them together. All the time I could feel my tiredness seeping away from me, my strength growing; the tiredness did not go reluctantly for it would be back. But the temporary strength that comes to the body with desire was flowing within me now. I remember a schoolteacher telling me, her pupil, about some little glands which we have which give us extra energy in times of emergency, such as being chased by a bull. I suppose that these, or some other glands, work at times of love too. Something was waking me and making me.

Gently I moved above her. There was not much room on the child's bed. I realized how urgently she wanted me too. She was gasping and her face and her mouth were urging me on.

'Christopher,' she said suddenly and simply. 'We may die today.' And her hands went down to me, discovered me and drew me to her. She moved my point against her open underneath. 'Nuzzling,' she said. Her eyes were shut tight now. 'Nuzzling.' I needed to wrap myself around her and within her then, but I let her play us to and fro for a while until she stretched her flanks and coupled us with her hands. After that, despite our urgency, we loved quietly. There was none of the rhino play that we had enjoyed in the bed at Eilat the night before, that night now a year away in history. We made love as though we were dancing to the decorous melody of an old-fashioned music box. We took a long, long time. When we thought it was getting too much for us and we would have to climax we would lie, stiff at first but gradually relaxing, until the passion had been subdued, and we could safely continue on our journey.

While we rested in mid-love, in mid-stream as it were, we would lie, holding each other, our fingers and thumbs just touching the other's flesh in some comforting place. I turned my head to the wall and saw the three-foot-high wooden soldiers regarding us from their shelf with something approaching shock. Popeye considered me archly. I said to Shoshana: 'Popeye is watching us.'

She gave a giggle which I felt deep in her cavern. 'He looks like he winks,' she said.

'That eye,' I said. 'He looks like General Dayan.'

'Love me more, Christopher. Soon they will start again on this side of the city.'

We moved again. I tunnelled gently within her, both of us wide awake now, our senses on edge, but keeping, or trying

161

to keep anyway, to our slow and sleepy rhythm. But this time there was no stopping, no holding off and retreating to fight again. This time, we knew, it was our final run.

Our embrace tightened and our smooth movements became jerks until we were mad with it. Her teeth were in my neck and I was muttering and then hoarsely: 'It's here, my baby.'

'It's here, oh, it's here,' she cried, although her words were half choked back. 'Oh, my dear darling, I weep inside.'

We lay riding out the last moments like two boats tied together in a subsiding sea. I kissed her ear and her neck and felt my own neck where her teeth had entered. I could feel the small holes.

The toy planes and ships and army vehicles were on their tray within reach of my arm. I selected a neat tank with rubber tracks, examined it, and then put it on the shining surface of her belly.

'Come to the war,' I said. She smiled.

'It is always with us, Christopher.'

I moved the tank forward along her flesh and then, after glancing at her, rolled it on its rubber tracks up the nursery slopes of her breasts. The tracks clicked over easily for it was a well-constructed toy, made in England actually, and the tank tipped over the summit of her left breast, and I ran it slowly down into her valley and up the other slope. She watched it making its tracks in her sweat and then looked at me seriously.

'Soon,' she said. 'After Jerusalem our armies will attack the Syrians in the Golan Heights. Too long they have been killing Israelis in the Galilee.' I kissed her shoulder and returned the tank to its shelf.

Now the tiredness came back triumphantly, overtaking us like a conqueror who had prudently waited his turn. We lay exhausted in our wet arms, sore and heavy from what we had done. I could feel nothing but the weariness claiming me and the sloping pillow of her breast against my throat. She breathed with me, deeply, and then, when we were almost gone, stirred and protested briefly.

'Christopher,' she murmured. 'You must not make bad jokes about General Dayan and Popeye. General Dayan is our leader, remember.'

13

Within a half an hour of us sleeping after our lovemaking, the entire Israeli sector of Jerusalem came under heavy fire from the Arab artillery and mortars. The house shuddered and the picture of Popeye fell noisily from the wall. Shoshana sat up, naked in the bed, her bare breasts lit by the gun flashes. For a moment she looked as frightened and confused as the child in whose bed she lay would have been. I tumbled to the floor and sat there stupidly naked, blinking at the massive flashes outside the window.

I stood up and kissed Shoshana to calm her, but she was immediately well in control of herself. She swivelled her fine legs from the bed and returned the kiss hurriedly. In my mind I could still hear her saying, 'Christopher, we may die today,' but she was now brisk and businesslike. I left her and hurried to the next room where Zoo Baby was sitting on the edge of his bed scratching himself industriously.

'Toilet,' I said as I went into the room. 'It caught me in the lavatory.'

'Sure, sure,' he smiled. 'The Arabs always make difficulties.'

I began to dress. A shell landed very near the house, the blast nudging it, and I heard some of the windows fall in. I made for the door thinking it might be Shoshana's room, but when I reached the passage outside she was there, dressed, and talking patiently to Dov. They went down the stairs and Zoo Baby and I followed. O'Sullivan who had slept on the couch had made a pot of coffee and waved tiredly at the pot for us. It was one o'clock.

'You British had all this in the war, eh?' said Zoo Baby drinking his coffee. 'You sat under the stairways, eh?'

'When there was nowhere else,' I said. 'Sometimes it was warmer and drier than the air-raid shelter.' I was trying to be steady, to talk with the voice of one who had been brought up under bombardment. The difference was that I was now adult and knew exactly what it was about, and that these were twenty-five-pounder shells coming from half a mile away and not random droppings of a German aeroplane anxious to get home.

Dov said: 'I think maybe it would be a good idea to move into the forward area, where we were this afternoon. At least we don't get shelled there. That's too near the nose of this business for either side to shell.'

Shoshana looked fresh and placid. 'There will be an attack on the Police School before many hours. I would like to be there to report it. Maybe we will go back to the Press house to see Major de Groucy, he who fights with donkeys.' She laughed. The shelling eased after about twenty minutes and we left the house and went out into the close night.

There was a bitter smell of smoke over the city. The guns in the south were battling again now. It was like a thunderstorm that had moved away. Our area was now free of shelling, though, and the darkness was riven with the sound of motor vehicles, voices, and the businesslike click of the unfeeling crickets. Some houses had been demolished at the end of the road and a bus with a red cross painted on its side was there waiting for the digging into the debris to bring results.

Zoo Baby stopped the jeep behind the bus. 'Maybe we have some time?' he said without turning around.

'I guess so,' said Dov. He looked at Shoshana. She wanted to go on. I could see that. She did not want to miss the attack on the Police School. But we were looking at her and she nodded curtly and said something in Hebrew.

'They don't seem to have a lot of labour here,' said O'Sullivan. 'This looks like a job for the Irish. We're very strong on clearin' rubble, you know.'

It was when we were walking towards the demolished houses that I began to think about my hands again. Tearing

164

into stone and brick and wood is not an occupation my manager would like to know about. He seemed far away now like almost everything else in the world.

Two women and three men were trying to move a great cake of concrete almost at the centre of the confusion. Smoke wisped up from some fire below. Dov called to the five people in Hebrew and they waved us to hurry. Dov said: 'They've already had half a dozen people from here and taken them away, but there's a whole family fixed down below somewhere.' He spoke to one of the bending men. Then to me: 'They're trying to get some heavy rescue equipment here, but the road is in a bad way from the shells.'

We were working then, Zoo Baby at the front, lifting, digging, cutting, striving through the mess, handing back lumps of masonry and wood, sweating, making a hole and then a tunnel. Eventually he called out something, sobbed it out through his huge sweat. There was not enough room for him to get into the aperture to whatever he had seen, but O'Sullivan went forward and he crawled down through the rescue hole.

O'Sullivan's lean form vanished into the hole Zoo Baby had made. We stood back as though expecting something terrible to be brought out but when he emerged he came carefully with a little girl in a tender, green cotton dress, limp in his arms, hair hanging like weed. She looked like the doll in the nursery I had left half an hour before.

'I don't think there's much left in this one,' said O'Sullivan looking at the child's face. I heard Shoshana make a quick whimpering sound and hurry after the Irishman as he took the hanging figure to the bus. I went with Shoshana and saw O'Sullivan lay the girl on the rear, long seat.

'Can I help you?' I asked O'Sullivan. 'Down the hole, I mean.'

'Well,' he returned conversationally as he stepped from the bus again. 'There's a great sagging piece of wood and plaster and suchlike hanging down over the rest of the people down there. I think Zoo Baby is too big because he'll bring the rest of the stuff down on me, and Dov is a trifle small and a trifle middle-aged. I wouldn't have asked you, unless you'd mentioned it. . .'

'Come on,' I said. We walked across the debris again. He descended into the hole first, motioning me to follow. Zoo Baby seeing that I was going down tugged away some plaster boards and planks of wood to make the hole wider.

'I'm well known for my big entrances,' I joked nervously to him. He laughed and so did Dov. I went into the choking hole, down several feet into the pile and O'Sullivan's hand came up from below and pointed to a sagging lump of debris hanging over a cave formed by a fluke involving several of the roof rafters which had caught and held together.

I put my back against the pregnant bulge, not pushing against it too heavily but trying to prevent it bursting. Even then it was like carrying five hundredweight of coal on my back. I pushed my arms out, as though I was crucified, and forced my shoulders, gently but strongly into the pile. O'Sullivan had a big torch and by turning my head his way I could see him crawling, an inch at a time towards two large boots sticking up dramatically and, in an odd leisurely way, like someone resting their feet in front of a fire. There were holes in the soles of both boots. Then O'Sullivan shifted to one side and I saw four people, a man, a woman and two more children pinned beneath the wreckage. One of the children, a girl about seven, was looking at O'Sullivan with a pathetic, fascinated anticipation, the sort of look she might have reserved for Father Christmas if she had not been a Jew. The mother had her eyes closed peacefully, as though asleep, although her dirty outstretched hand moved jerkily as though she were calling someone on. The second child, a boy in a cherry-red shirt, was unconscious and I could not see the man's face or head.

O'Sullivan was patiently working on the first child, moving pieces of timber and stone away from around her with the fine care of a chess player making moves. The girl was watching him and once she spoke to him casually and smiled at his reply. She reached out her hand towards her mother's twitching fingers, but was unable to reach them. She made

166

one hard effort but it brought dust and rubble cascading around her shoulders and O'Sullivan told her to be still and she was. He burrowed around her, his wiry back working about in the narrow passage and the difficult angles. Once he pulled firmly at a diagonal rafter and began a rain of rubble around his own head. He covered his neck with his hands and waitèd until it was finished. I could see the little girl's face and saw her smile through the black dust when O'Sullivan lifted his head after the fall. He worked quietly, patiently and quickly. I forced myself back against the bulge I was supporting and saw O'Sullivan drag the child away from the cave and begin pulling her up through the tunnel. She began to cry and O'Sullivan soothed her.

'You'd better move out, Mr Hollings,' he said as he inched towards me. 'I can't get through.'

'What about this stuff,' I asked. 'It might come down.'

'Stick your belly in then, because I'm coming past and I don't reckon there's a lot of room for the pair of us and this kid.' I pushed back and he took her through. I could hear her crying loudly out in the open air. Then he came back. He went right down into the heart of the debris again and moved his torch on to the other people down there. Then the bombardment restarted, the shells breaking into the ground and the wreckage under which we were crouched rocking and creaking. Cascades of small debris were running over my head and shoulders. I could hear Shoshana, then Dov, urging us to come out. But O'Sullivan did not reply to them.

'Can you hold it another minute?' he asked me.

I was breaking under the weight and choking with the chuting of the dust and the brittle debris about me. 'Yes,' I said. 'I'll hold it, I think. I feel like Atlas.'

He moved around down there like a lizard, his torch sweeping before him and he went from the now still mother to the father and then to the child. Another rending explosion sent the rubbish around us jumping and the little tunnel was thick with dust. I supposed we were six feet below the surface debris. I wondered how long it would take them to excavate us. My nose and my eyes were clogged and I could feel a great pile of dust sitting on my head. O'Sullivan crawled back.

'Fine, Mr Hollings,' he commented. 'Would you like to leave now because there's nothing anyone except God can do for those down there.'

'Dead?' I said.

'Aye. I had a look at them. And there'll be two more unless we're lucky.'

'You'd better go first,' I said.

'That's gallant of you,' said O'Sullivan.

'Gallantry has fuck all to do with it,' I said. 'If I let go we'll probably both be caught. Get out quick. I'm coming right after you.'

He went, bowing and moving quickly but economically like a man trying to duck out of a pub brawl. Once he was clear I made to go after him. But there were three swiftly successive explosions, probably mortar shells, and the whole sagging mass I was supporting heaved and yawned. It was killing me to hold it now. I was covered in dry muck and I could not see nor hardly breathe. But I held it until the shuddering had ceased. Then I let it go.

At first I took my support away gingerly, easily, and very fearfully, expecting it to immediately fall upon me. I wondered if this sort of stuff crushed you or merely suffocated you. But it held, precariously it held. There was a space, air, between my shoulders and the passage wall. I moved out like a thief, treading carefully up the tunnel, very afraid now, terrified unless the bombardment should come near again.

It was only a few feet but it seemed like miles. I had a funny prick of Godly conscience which told me if I had not made love to Shoshana, a married woman, a few hours before I might have more strength now. I suggested now that God should overlook it, and worked my way towards the sweet-smelling air at the top of the hole. I made it just in time. The yellow-flashing guns were going from both sides now, but it was three Israeli jet fighters which flung themselves across the border and flew very low over us which caused the entire tunnel to cave and collapse.

Zoo Baby patted me. Then Shoshana was about me, arms

168

about me, kissing my dirty neck, while Dov brushed the piles of concrete dust from my hair and from behind my ears. Zoo Baby said: 'Those planes fly too low. Maybe we should complain.'

The bus had gone with the two children to the hospital. Shoshana said she thought the first one had died, but they could not be certain because the Red Cross man who had arrived with the bus had been hit by a shell splinter and was dying himself. There was nobody else qualified to know for certain.

I shook myself free of some of the dirt. O'Sullivan was already brushed off and sitting sedately in the back of the jeep. 'I suppose that took you back?' he said amiably as Zoo Baby started the engine.

'Back to where?' I asked.

'Well, you know, the Blitz,' he smiled. He looked twenty years older than he had looked the night when I first met him.

'Not really,' I said. 'I lived in a village in the West Country and there wasn't much of a blitz. A couple of land mines in the fields, killing a horse and some sheep, and three bombs dropped by Germans in a hurry to get home. One landed in the churchyard and threw up a lot of people we'd thought we'd seen the last of.'

He smiled. 'Christ Almighty,' he said. 'You should have been Irish.'

'And end up in the Jewish Border Police?'

He leaned close, to whisper, but as though we now had some bond and he were anxious to correct some grave misunderstanding. 'I was in the Congo with the Irish Army, you know. And in Cyprus. An Irishman has to go a long way before he can find an official fight.'

'I thought the Irish Army was there to keep the peace,' I said.

'It's the same thing in the end,' he answered. His voice went lower. 'Before I got this job I offered my services to the Arabs but the buggers turned me down. So I rang up the Israeli Embassy and asked them. There's nothing personal in it for me.'

169

14

Arriving back at the Press house near the Mandelbaum Gate we discovered that half the big room had collapsed, the debris providing a convenient stage for the bouncy Major de Groucy. O'Sullivan said: 'Now doesn't he look fine and operatic up there with all the gunfire flashing behind him.' The correspondents, some of them fresh from Tel Aviv, others tired and bent from the strain of what they had seen and known, stood for a briefing under the ceiling of the remainder of the room, which had been temporarily secured by a couple of sinewy timbers. The major, in his bandages and with his martyred arm, stood on the rubble reading from a communiqué. He glanced up as we walked in and a little spasm of pain crossed his face, either his reaction to our arrival or part of his wounded-soldier act.

'These Jordanian donkeys are lethal,' I whispered to Shoshana. She smiled absently, but she was listening to de Groucy. Her love in the nursery and her full happiness when I managed to climb safely from the shelled house were now forgotten by her. Now she was cool and occupied again with the business of her war.

There were some American and European correspondents near the front and they asked that the details Major de Groucy had been giving should be repeated in English. He was pleased to demonstrate his lingual ability and with a small plaintive gasp and a courageous rubbing of his damaged ribs he began again, telling that more than three hundred Arab planes had been destroyed by the Israeli Air Force, something I still did not believe, and saying that the Egyptians in Sinai and Gaza were cracking under the pressure of the Jewish armoured thrust.

170

'We have had a good day of war,' he said modestly. 'Here in Jerusalem our tanks – they are British Centurions of course – have overcome great difficulties and are well within the Arab sector, moving both sides of the Old City. All Holy Places, Christian, Moslem, and, even Jewish, will be protected as far as possible. We hope to be at the Wailing Wall tomorrow. The Chief Military Rabbi, General Schlomo Goren, has been told by General Narkiss to prepare his trumpet.' This caused an appreciative stir among the journalists.

'Is that official – you intend to go on to Jericho, then?' asked a serious young American correspondent in a green uniform with 'Vietnam' written on a shirt flash. 'With the trumpet I mean.'

'The walls will tumble,' forecast Major de Groucy complacently.

'How bleeding Biblical,' I thought. My God, they annoyed me when they started acting up like this. Their piffling propaganda, their bristling over-confidence. You would have thought they had chosen God instead of him choosing them. I wish they had seen the two little girls we loaded into the bus half an hour before.

'What is happening now?' asked one of the new correspondents. 'Are your troops going over the wall into the Old City?'

The major shook his head solemnly. 'The next action? I would not be surprised if it is against the Police School. It is heavily guarded by the Arab Legion and we have a requirement to break through so that our forces can reach Mount Scopus and cut the Jerusalem to Ramallah road.'

When he said, 'We have a requirement,' I winced because one of the Vietnam Americans had used the phrase in his question and de Groucy had salvaged it immediately.

'One more question, Major,' said one of the Americans. 'Where did you get your wounds?'

There was a quick guilty glance at our group from de Groucy. He spread his hands and he shrugged. Then he smiled blatantly in our direction and laughed a brave but secretive laugh. 'It is nothing,' he shrugged. 'Shall we say

171

that I collided with an Arab donkey.' A bellow of laughter came from the correspondents and some of them wrote in their notebooks.

As we left the place one American, still shaking his head and chuckling' said to me: 'Collided with an Arab donkey! They sure are something, these people, don't you think?'

'Oh, I do,' I said. 'I really do.'

We went out into the night again. The guns were busy to north and south. Zoo Baby had remained outside with the jeep. He said he had been told that the paratroops we saw at the zoo had occupied some of the gradually rising ground in the Sheikh Jarah district not far from the Mandelbaum Gate, and that we could go to one of the forward observation posts, if Shoshana required it.

As she spoke two arms of light reached across the city on to the distant Arab area. 'The searchlights from the Histadrut,' said Dov. 'We will be attacking the Police School now.' Three low-bellied jet planes came from behind us almost immediately and curved like birds on to the point where the searchlights were fixed. They fired their cannons as they went in and then a second formation dropped from the hills and bomb flashes jumped among the white walls of the buildings.

'Let us watch,' said Shoshana. We followed her into the jeep. We felt we were an odd, renegade, exclusive gang, moving about the fringe of the battle. None of the other correspondents, even the women, had escorts and I was willing to wager that there were no other international, neutral, concert pianists involved in the battle for the city that night.

Zoo Baby drove up through the broken streets in the same direction as we had taken earlier in the day. We passed the Savoy Hotel and saw the robed proprietor, the man who had served us drinks, in the enclosed garden trying to clear some of the debris. Dov said: 'That Arab is a businessman. Today he clears up, tomorrow he cleans and polishes and maybe paints a little. The next day he will be serving *lokchen* soup and *gefuelltefische*.'

We drove for another half a mile, the conflict spilling over to our right. In the night-time flashes of the guns we could see the Israeli tanks nudging forward and the paratroops moving behind them. Zoo Baby manoeuvred the jeep over choppy pieces of road, and curled it around shell and bomb craters. At one point we came upon a donkey cropping the gritty grass at the roadside and we all laughed and howled for Major de Groucy. We were near the battle, but apparently safe from it. The fighting was growing in the area to one flank, but on the other the hills were quiet in the night.

'First, I think, this place,' said Zoo Baby. He said something to Dov in Hebrew and Dov nodded after looking at O'Sullivan. Dov turned to Shoshana, but spoke in English. 'It will be no good to get too close, because of the planes arriving to bomb the Police School. I think maybe we can see everything from here.'

'But *here*?' asked Shoshana doubtfully. 'It is not a good place for us.' She argued further in Hebrew, but eventually nodded doubtfully. Zoo Baby took the jeep through a narrow alley and stopped outside a wooden door. We went through the door and into a dark garden.

Dov said to me: 'I told you of this place. This is the Garden of the Tomb. This is where, so some say, Jesus was buried.' He pointed through the darkness. 'Over there, in the wall. That is the Tomb.' He walked on along a narrow path, me behind, the others following. The garden was thick with warmth and sharp with spicy smells; peaceful, hardly stirring, even though the war was only half a mile beyond its wall. We stepped carefully through the vines and the hanging flowers. Dov said: 'And beyond here, *there* – where you can see the dark rock – that is, so they say, Golgotha, Calvary, the place of crucifixion. From there we will watch the fighting.'

Shoshana, I now realized, had not wanted to go to the crest of the small rocky hill because it was a Jewish cemetery. We climbed a precarious set of steps cut into the side of the skull-shaped hill, and emerged above the city, looking out over the forehead of the rock.

O'Sullivan said: 'Not exactly the place I would choose to

watch a battle. Dear God, I thought religion did poorly enough in the Congo.'

I said: 'Does it worry you that much?'

'Well, shall we say I never fancied myself firing a machine gun from the Holy Father's balcony in Rome. And this is a damned sight worse, mister.' He crossed himself, sincerely if hurriedly. Shoshana was looking doubtfully at the Jewish tombstones standing up like bad teeth in the dark. 'It's not a good place,' she said to Dov. 'All these dead around.'

She spoke as though there had not been enough dead all the past hours. As though the recent dead, the ones we had known and the strangers, were nothing, but that these old dead lying on top of this bald hill were different and important to her.

Dov said: 'The searchlights have got the Police School again, see?'

We stood on the crown of rock and watched the two big searchlight beams pin the walls of the school. It was like watching a gigantic cinema performance. The battle was bitter down there, the streets and alleys leading to the Police School were bursting with the orange light of fires. The tanks and the paratroops were edging forward through the diffused light and the clogging smoke. Explosions rebounded from the sector, echoed heavily against the walls of the Old City on one side and, indistinctly, against the Judean mountains on the other.

There was some protection from the Old City wall afforded by a shoulder of rock between our observation point and the wall itself. I walked gingerly along the hard summit and wondered where the middle cross had been fixed. The rock curled almost at my feet and dropped down a hundred feet or more to the place where, afterwards, they built the bus station.

The big noises of the heavier guns and the tanks now ceased and from the distance there came the playful crackle of the rifles and sub-machine-guns, the hollow cough of grenades. Small lights kept jumping up from the streets like the setting off of minor fireworks. More adult explosions were throwing sparks and flames to the Arab rooftops. All

174

the fighting was confined in the holes and hideaways of the narrow streets. Then the Israeli jets would return and the long eyes of the searchlights would pick out the Police School. The advancing paratroopers would wait until the bombs and the cannon shells had gone into the walls of the school, and then rise and go forward again.

'Street fighting,' said O'Sullivan. 'And God knows, there's no place that has streets like this. They're more like tunnels. It will take them hours to get through to the walls of that bloody school.' He sat down heavily and patted the rock by his backside. 'Now, just imagine, this might be the very place of the crucifixion of Our Lord,' he murmured.

For another hour we watched. We could see the advance of the attacking troops by the progress of the fires and the firing. Just before the major attack on the Police School itself the Histadrut searchlights swung over the entire range of the smoking battlefield, running like white ghosts through a destroyed country, and finally, inevitably settled again on the walls they had left. Then the fighters came back, wheeling freely over the Arab slopes of Jerusalem, and firing their belching weapons at the emplacements of the legionnaires. There were fires growing within the school now and the walls were like Swiss cheese. We had one pair of field glasses – O'Sullivan's – between us, and we took them in turns.

Through the glasses I saw the first Jews go in through the rubble of the school, scampering like spiders through the breaches. Yellow and orange flashes jerked into the sky from within the walls, the sharp sounds quickly following. Then everything quietened very suddenly. The searchlights yawned lazily, and the smoke drifted across the city. There were little eruptions, disturbances, but widely spaced. The guns in the south of the city had also lapsed. For the first time since the battle began there was no great noise in Jerusalem. Standing there on Calvary I could hear the city groan and cough through its smoke.

At four o'clock the daylight began to seep back, smudging the hills and gradually touching the roofs of the city. It

175

showed a hundred fires burning indolently among the ruins of Jerusalem's hem. Some paratroops returning with wounded from the battle of the Police School told Shoshana that forty of their men had been killed in the two hours of street fighting around the school and that more than a hundred dead Arab Legion soldiers had been counted. The lieutenant who told her said it with no great triumph over the conquest, nor over the deaths of his enemies, nor even emotion over the killing of his own friends. He merely reported it, level-voiced, and said that the Israelis were now pushing on to the American Colony and expected to capture the Ambassador Hotel before breakfast. He looked very tired and glad to drive his jeep away from the fighting.

We remained at Golgotha until the daylight strengthened. The smoke was drifting from its many roots on the battlefield. Deep grey in the pale grey dawn it had an air of hopeless resignation about it that had nothing to do with the brilliant excitement of battle, nor the joy of conquest.

The fighting was resumed to the north-east among the white box buildings and slender cypresses of the American Colony. Long puffs of smoke like trees themselves were standing up in the early daylight among the cypresses. The guns flashed paler in the growing day.

Zoo Baby had gone back with the jeep to fetch some coffee and food. Dov and O'Sullivan remained on the forehead of rock watching the movements of the armies across the spread of city and lion-coloured hill. Shoshana touched my hand and we walked down from the steep, mysterious rock, and into the sheltered garden. Now, in the sombre light, before the sun, I could see its simplicity and sense its peace. The paths were narrow, stepped and winding, hung with tendrils and flowers. In the far wall of rock was the stark open doorway of the Tomb where they say they laid Christ. We walked that way and I saw the saucer cut in the rock worn there in ancient days by a massive cheese of a stone.

I looked in through the door, into the two chambers. Then I stepped in and Shoshana followed me. The low roof made me bend. There was an iron grille in there and stone beds, places for the dead of some far age. I touched the stone with my fingers. Some of the dust came off. It was close and uneasy for me, so I turned and touched Shoshana and we went out into the calm garden.

'Do you believe, Christopher?' she asked. She jumped lightly like a girl into the depression of an old wine press. She sat on the stones forming its side and looked at her marked and dirty face in a pocket mirror.

'Not much,' I admitted. I climbed down and sat beside her. Abruptly the sun cleared the Judean Hills and flashed against the golden dome of the Temple of the Rock in the Old City, and then with brilliant arrogance lit the other domes and towers, and gave to the walls warmth and majestic fullness.

'How do you give an answer like that?' she asked. She took my hand and laid it on her lap. I could feel the softness of her legs under the coarseness of the fatigue trousers. 'Not much.'

'I don't think about it,' I said. 'I haven't come to any conclusions.'

'But you are a Christian?'

'In name,' I replied. 'In not much else.'

'Think,' she said. 'It is possible that this is the place where something special and sacred happened. Do you not feel anything?'

I smiled at her. 'A bit chilly,' I said.

She laughed. 'How much better it would be for you if you *did* believe, Christopher. Then this would be so much more for you, for your spirit.'

I leaned and kissed her. 'I wish it were like that,' I said.

Shoshana made a face. 'It is more difficult being a Jew,' she said. 'At least the one that the Christians worship was in recent times – only two thousand years. When you consider our people, Moses and Aaron and David, they are all much further away, and God is more distant in history than that. It is more difficult than your faith.'

'Do you believe?' I retaliated.

She shrugged. 'The whole State is built upon religion, so it is difficult not to touch it. But I do not go to the synagogue, nor do many of my friends. One day at a time in Israel is

c.w.—9   177

sufficient. We take care of that, making sure we use every bit of it. Because there may be no more in stock. That is our religion now.'

I said: 'Aren't you worried about your husband? He has been flying hasn't he?'

'I think of him,' she said. 'But I am not afraid for him. He is a soldier in the same manner as all these others. I am sure he does not fear for me.'

She seemed to lose interest in the conversation. The rumble and roll of the battle was more profound now from the American Colony and the first full sunlight of the day was tinged with dust and wandering smoke. A military ambulance was stalled in the lane below and I could hear the driver shouting.

'Will they not miss you in England?' Shoshana said, as though the thought had just occurred to her. 'Are you not supposed to be playing your piano somewhere?'

I grinned. 'I have a lot more to do than sit here in Jerusalem, in the middle of a war, if that's what you mean. I am supposed to be playing my piano, as you put it, at Bradford next week.'

'Is that a nice city?' she asked innocently. Her whole body was relaxed now against a wall of stones and flowers. I could see how weary she was.

'It's peaceful,' I said.

'That is a good thing, I suppose,' she said, 'to be peaceful.'

15

Zoo Baby returned with the coffee and was followed by another jeep driven by one of the American correspondents in green fatigues with the 'Vietnam' flash. Two of his friends were killed later that day riding in the leading tank of an armoured column when the Israelis had ordered all correspondents should travel in one of the vehicles towards the rear of the advance. They would not listen.

The American was moonfaced and overweight. His hair was falling out but he had the innocent cheerfulness of a boy. In the cool sunlight his face had a yellow tinge. He should logically have been chewing gum but he was not. He had come back with Zoo Baby because he fancied Shoshana and knew that Zoo Baby was with her.

'Joe Cumberland, Worldwide Wire Service,' he introduced himself when we had all gone down to the jeep and were drinking the coffee that Zoo Baby had brought. We were in the alley, deep and protective as a trench. The fighting was still growling to the north.

'We got the Ambassador Hotel,' said Cumberland assertively. 'And the Holy Land Hotel, and the Tomb of Saints.' He made it sound like a game of Monopoly.

'I just caught it on the radio reports to the command centre,' he grinned. He had a big amiable front tooth cut away at an angle like a cheese. 'I'm going up to get a load of this ambush. Are you coming, miss?'

He was looking with frank juvenile lust at Shoshana. 'There is an ambush?' she asked.

'Sure,' he said. 'The Israelis are going to ambush the Jordanian tanks.'

'We didn't expect it to be the Sioux and the US Cavalry,' I said. I am occasionally jealous and it shows.

Cumberland nodded without annoyance at me. 'Still,' he said easily, 'you never know who you're going to meet in a war. That's what I always say. And I've been to plenty, sir.'

I hate Americans who call you 'Sir' too. 'Where have you been?' I said. 'In the wars, I mean.'

'Well Vietnam, of course.'

'Of course,' I said.

'And India and Pakistan. Congo, Aden and a few other little bitty ones. Worldwide always send Cumberland.' He grinned pleasantly and added, 'I guess they think Cumberland is expendable.' He glanced at me as though pleased at knowing that he had made the observation before I made it.

179

'The ambush,' said Shoshana. 'Where is it, Mr Cumberland? I would like to go.' She said it as though it were an opera. 'Is this possible?'

'Sure,' he said. 'Why not? Let's all go.' He pulled a neat map case towards him and with professional economy had it quickly and logically spread. Shoshana climbed into the jeep beside him and looked across his arm. I watched her hair roll down and touch his arm. I casually lifted the hair with three fingers and placed it carefully around the back of her neck. She paid no attention. Nor did Cumberland.

'Nobody's talking, naturally,' he said. 'But my guess is that the showdown will be here, at the crossroads of the Jerusalem-Ramallah road. General Ben-Ari's tanks will be all through with the American Colony by now. That is where they'll go and wait for the Arabs, who will also try to get there to ambush the Jews.' Then he added brightly: 'My guess is that the Jews will get there first.'

I could hardly stand seeing her leaning over him, so close, her breasts bulging within her shirt and the bulge touching his shoulder. I wondered how a man could have been a correspondent in the places he talked about and still be so white-faced.

He folded the map over and consulted a new strip of it. 'Up here,' he said. He seemed only to talk to Shoshana. 'There is a big house belonging to a nice guy who is a doctor. I was here last year and I met him and went to the house.'

'But he is a Jordanian, this doctor?' said Shoshana. Her head and her breasts came up from his shoulder. 'This is what you mean?'

'Sure,' replied Cumberland agreeably. 'He's a specialist in rheumatic complaints. There's a lot of rheumatic fever in Jerusalem, you know. He told me. It's the changes in the temperature at different times of the year. Anyway, the whole of the area down here and then up to the Ambassador Hotel is now in Israeli hands, so we should be able to get high up above the junction of the Ramallah road with the Jerusalem road, and get a great view of what goes.'

'We will go,' announced Shoshana, immediately swallowing her prejudice. 'I will come with you in this jeep.' She looked at me and smiled at my uncertainty. 'And Christopher will ride with us too.'

'Get aboard, Chris,' said Cumberland. O'Sullivan, Dov and Zoo Baby who had stood watching this strange breed of uniformed man, went off to the other vehicle. We started down the alley, until we were almost upon the wall of the Old City. There was a distance of about a hundred yards when we were exposed to the Arab troops on the wall and a quick but harmless stream of machine-gun fire flew after us decapitating some tall crimson flowers topping a bank above us.

'Bad boys,' commented Cumberland, driving quickly and calmly.

We had all ducked, doubled up in the jeep, with the firing. As we turned north and were no longer visible from the wall, we straightened. Shoshana said: 'Today or tomorrow the Israelis will be on the wall.'

'That's a good bet,' agreed Cumberland. 'It looks like the whole thing is going your way. You'll have it cleaned up by the Sabbath, I guess.'

'You heard on the radio about Sinai?' she asked.

'Sure, the Egyptians have been tough,' he said. 'But they've been turned around and it looks like they're going to have to swim home.'

She laughed. 'We will send our Navy for them,' she said. I put my fingers over my eyes; my eyes aching with tiredness and smoke. The streets we were now travelling had seen the advance of the tanks and the paratroopers. The fighting had gnawed its way through the buildings, leaving great holes and bites. The debris looked as though it had been spat from some huge mouth. Some Arabs were already emerging, stumbling about and looking with strange eyes at familiar things changed so quickly. They made no fuss nor noise, but walked about viewing the damage with the outward serenity of visitors to some ruined civilization of long ago. We reached a wider space, which had been a square. Here the house fighting must have been savage because the houses had fallen all around; the dead soldiers, Israeli and Arab, were being cleared from the area. In the square were two lorries loaded with Jordanian prisoners, crammed and sullen, standing without their trousers. Their trousers were piled like a bundle waiting for a laundry on the rubble of what had been some kind of fountain in the middle of the square. Water still sprang hopefully among the fallen masonry.

I could hear Zoo Baby laughing at the Arabs without their trousers, but Shoshana looked away from them. They stared down at her when we had to pull up to let one of the prisoner lorries move through, looking down into the jeep, a small interest suddenly lighting their empty faces. Shoshana looked away from them but some Arab women with children and goats running about them, walked towards the jeep from the other direction and stood ten paces away staring at Shoshana.

She looked back angrily at them, as though she were the prisoner, and then returned suddenly to the captive soldiers. One of the Arabs was urinating over the side of the truck, his tool big and hanging, his expression bored. His urine hit the dry stones of the square noisily. 'Cannot we move?' Shoshana asked Cumberland. 'I don't like them. I can't stand to see them looking.'

'I would say that you're not the Personality of the Year with them,' answered Cumberland, reasonably. 'We all have our prejudices, I guess. And they've got theirs. They don't like the Israelis. And they ain't going to like you any better from now. You can tell that.'

We moved forward as soon as the truck had cleared from our path. Shoshana kept her head dropped forward from then on. She would not look up, but remained sullenly gazing at the floor of the jeep. We turned through the rubbled street and then began moving uphill until we were facing the growing hills and the amber city began to fall away behind us. There were some rich houses crowning the elevated ground and Cumberland immediately turned into one courtyard and brought the jeep to a stop.

A bomb or a shell had demolished the right-hand wing of the long splendid house, giving it a spiked and tapering tail of white masonry. The fig trees in the courtyard were split and hanging in shreds like the hair of old crones. Glass, pieces of wood and stone were strewn about the circular courtyard path and outside the door of the house was a metal rocking-horse, its legs buckled, its expression sad. We walked towards the door. Cumberland pushed the horse as though anxious to see if it still worked. It rocked clumsily on its bent legs.

'Couple of kids,' he said as though that would explain everything. Shoshana was looking anxious and more uncertain than I would have thought possible for someone like her. I glanced at her, glad to see she was vulnerable. The horse, its metal burned black, its mane singed, was still rocking after Cumberland's push. Shoshana stopped it with her hands. We went into the house.

We were almost shot by three Israeli soldiers who came abruptly from the room to our left. They were nervous and Shoshana cried out to them in Hebrew as they raised their Uzzi machine guns. They had obviously just occupied the house and had been detailed to go out as sentries in the courtyard. They lowered their weapons and Shoshana spoke to them in swift Hebrew again. They directed her along the passage and then went out into the courtyard. I turned and watched them move towards the perimeter wall. One of them had set the horse rocking again.

Dov and the others had followed us into the house. It had a strange hollowed-out look about it. Some furniture and carpets were still in place, but there were chairs and tables and fine cabinets thrown against the walls of the long corridor. 'He was a wealthy doctor,' said Cumberland. 'He had some great stuff in this house.'

Inside a room overlooking a steep drop of ground was an Israeli observation post; an officer watching the gradual sunlight stretch its arms across the valley, two other soldiers kneeling as though in meditation by a radio set. The officer turned abruptly as we went into the room. He was round and red and he forgetfully kept the field glasses to his eyes as he turned about, dropping them to his chest with embarrassment when he realized what he had done. One of the disadvantages of having an army of civilians is that their occasional military unprofessionalism has to be overlooked.

Dov spoke to him in Hebrew and he was angry that we had arrived. He ill-temperedly motioned us towards a window in the adjoining room, muttering some annoyance which included the word 'Press', and we obediently trooped in there. Cumberland went back to speak to the officer with Dov as interpreter. We crouched at our window and watched the cascading valley, brown and amber, haphazard with white houses and green trees. It had already begun to take the increasing heat of the sun, and the dust which the night had settled was moving once more in little rocky pockets and crevices. Some goats grazed pessimistically about a hundred feet down, and beyond them the vacant roads, one to Jerusalem, the other reaching to Ramallah, touched.

Cumberland came back with Dov. 'He says that my friend Doctor Asbar has gone to hospital with some of the Israeli and Jordanian wounded, and his wife and children are away. Nobody was on the rocking-horse when it got hit.'

He looked at Shoshana and she shrugged and said: 'Take the glasses. The Israeli tanks are hidden down there. They got here first, you see.' She handed O'Sullivan's field glasses to him and he turned them in a steady circuit over the ground below the window. His pulpy belly was hanging over his trousers in a damp cocoon. His sparse hair was sticking to his neck like the fine hair of a baby sticks. He was now chewing gum with a round, slow, movement.

O'Sullivan and I sat against a wall. Dov and Zoo Baby were standing in the shadows by the window viewing the valley, but keeping out of sight as if they too were part of the ambush. Shoshana had retained the glasses and her attention was fixed on the junction three hundred feet below. Cumberland was licking a stub of pencil like a railway clerk and making anxious heavy notes in an untidy little book.

I closed my eyes for the weariness of the past twenty-four hours was gaining on me. The daytime warmth was crowding into the room and some flies and other insects were moving about in the thickening air. I felt a layer of sleep over me, forming as it forms on a summer beach or in a midday park in England. I thought of Eastbourne and the gardens.

I slept for about twenty minutes and then woke reluctantly with O'Sullivan's thin elbow in my side. I was running with sweat within my clothes now and my mouth was thick and lined. I half rolled to the window where the others were already bent and watching.

Although it was still early the hillside was reflecting the high summer heat. The roads below were now less distinct. They were vacant except for the mildly majestic figure of an Arab on a donkey with a smaller donkey in tow, trotting carelessly along the route which was, within minutes, to be the conflict ground.

The Israeli tanks were crouched among the houses, behind walls and beneath trees on either side of the slopes. I could hear the red-faced officer in the next room giving orders to the wireless crew and then their voices came in to us as they talked to the tank commanders in their ambush positions.

We waited and watched the Arab and his two donkeys leave the road and take a rough, steep path into the rising hills. The noise from Jerusalem had settled and then we were clearly able to hear the squeaking tracks of the Jordanian tanks as they moved up towards the crossroads. 'They come now,' said Shoshana.

'I thought maybe it was mice,' said Cumberland. I decided I liked him.

Whatever the tank has done to revolutionize warfare it has done nothing to make it any quieter. You could hear them approaching a mile off, squealing and clanking, and coughing like sick old men as they came. From our place we could not see them until almost the last moment, but their hideous noise preceded them, getting louder and louder in the sun-filled valley. Waiting at that window was nothing like being hidden behind the sill of the hotel dining-room the previous afternoon. There we were yards from the waiting Arab soldiers, but here it was lofty and remote and safe. All we had to do was watch.

It was very sad seeing it take place. Knowing that it was going to happen. At that point I still knew no deep rights or wrongs or even sympathies for one side or another. I was there only because of Shoshana. I had seen and felt the bad

185

breath of the battle and known, of course, that it involved me as much as every man around. But I had reacted to dead Jordanians equally as I had reacted to the little Jewish children they had brought through the tunnel from the wreckage of the house the night before. I was embarrassed for the prisoners deprived of their trousers and sorry for the elderly officer who had died by mistake in the hotel dining-room. But I still felt that I was outside it all. Like O'Sullivan and Cumberland I was there only by chance.

A Jordanian scout car, like a well-made little toy, came first into view, around a shoulder of yellowed rock. It had a mounted bazooka across its shoulder like an ungainly tree trunk. Two more little cars, neat and running abreast, followed it, and then the fat-bellied tanks, rolling like a cumbersome parade to the crossroads.

'He'll let the first bunch go through,' said Dov.

'He's watched his Red Indian films,' said Cumberland.

The Jewish commander let the Arab tanks come on, undisturbed and majestic, until they were astride the road junction.

Our radio was mute now. None of the Israeli tanks were making a sound. Then the Arab commanders broke in over the wavelength and the soldiers in the next room smiled.

Dov said: 'The Arab tank captains believe they have reached the place first. They are congratulating themselves.'

Cumberland said: 'God, their intelligence service must be lousy. You'd think they would have been told.'

'They have been found wanting in a few directions these two days,' replied Dov. 'Their courage is good, but their intelligence and their leadership is not always so good. We sent infantry into this area first, before the tanks. They do not make a noise.'

I thought the Israelis would never shoot. They let the aching seconds go by and allowed the tanks to falter on. Then the Jewish commander's tank fired spitefully from a vineyard a hundred feet up the slope. The red tongue stuck out rudely and the shot knocked the turret half off the leading Jordanian. It hung open like a clumsily raised salmon tin, and it stopped, astonished, on the road and began to roar voracious flames. Immediately the other ambushing guns opened fire making the deep walled valley tremble and the sky suddenly become full of smoke and wheeling birds.

It was like watching the slaughter of buffalo. The Jordanians, caught and confused, swivelled and swerved on the road, screwing about like heavy trapped animals. One of the little scout cars had turned lithely and was firing brave and rapid bazooka shots into one of the ambush positions. But he was open and exposed on the road. A well-calculated shell from a Jewish tank seemed to burrow beneath the vehicle and then flung it high into the sky like some magic car of a child's fantasy. It tipped and slewed and blew up as it collided with the hillside.

The Israeli guns were going like massive hammers. The noise was assaulting us high above it, rattling the windows of the house and then shattering them. The soldiers in the next room were shouting into the radio set transmitting the instructions of the observation officer. I thought how strange it was that a tubby, beetroot-faced man, who was absent-minded into the bargain, could command and wreak such destruction.

Half a dozen Israeli jets came hawking in down the length of the valley but they were called off because of the closeness of the battle, and went away to the east without contributing. They spun off over Jordan jauntily knowing that they could fly unchallenged through the Arab sky.

The Israelis had caught the Arabs in a classic hold. Frantically the tanks in the rear of the column, those still sheltered from the main violence of the event, tried to back out. We could hear their tracks squealing even above the banging of the guns.

Those which were trapped were in a hopeless, escapeless net, a traffic jam with death. Fifteen were standing burning within a quarter of an hour, spitting and spewing flame like a series of squat smelting boilers. Their crews lay dead on the road or cooking inside the metal walls. One of the scout cars had run away towards Jerusalem using its speed to get out of the trap. But hardly had it gone than two of the Jewish jets which had been lurking and awaiting such a situation went after it like hunters after a fleeing rabbit. There was a section of rising road, about a mile away, which we could see from the window and we saw the planes diving on the scout car far off and saw the bright orange explosion as they dealt with it.

Some of the Jordanian tanks managed to force their way through or away from the battle. But those that were caught sat on the road and burned quietly while the guns ceased and the smoke moved away from the valley and the two highways. The birds settled surprisingly quickly again in the trees and houses. Nobody went near the road. The Jewish tanks remained in their ambush positions and there was a lot of laughing noise over the radio in the adjoining room.

Shoshana got up and went in there with Cumberland and Dov. Cumberland had remained outwardly unmoved by what he had witnessed. He jotted notes with his annoyingly stubby pencil. Dov was looking tired and carried his sub-machine-gun as though it were a dire burden. They talked to the observation officer who was now in high spirits, and then went over to the two soldiers manning the radio. After a few minutes they returned.

Shoshana whispered to me: 'Christopher, the road to Mount Scopus is ours again. We have just heard from the radio. We will go up there and I will show to you the most beautiful view in the world – our city of Jerusalem from this side.'

We took the jeep down the brittle hillside past a collection of dead goats, and to the road. Dov was driving now and he took it quickly past the tanks. There was a strong smell of cooking meat which I knew was the burned men trapped within the metal skins. The Israeli soldiers were probing about the gutted vehicles and even Shoshana was subdued as we went by them and headed along the beckoning road to the south.

'That, I imagine, is what they call the crucial engagement of the war,' I said to Dov. Cumberland had returned to Jerusalem in his jeep to send his words to America. He had kissed Shoshana hurriedly on the cheek before he left and she had accepted the goodbye with no change of expression, merely wishing him *Shalom* and sending him on his journey.

'We have the Old City completely surrounded now,' said Dov. 'I think anyway. The Police School and the American Colony, the Mount of Olives, and Mount Scopus, and on the other side all the Government House area. The Arabs have lost out.'

He was wrong because there was still the Garden of Gethsemane. And we were going in that direction.

But first, on the road, we came across the Arab with his two donkeys. He jerked along, riding one, the other at the end of a rope, just as we had seen him go by the road junction three-quarters of an hour before. The animals had their heads cast down and so did the Arab. He jolted on his journey, seeing nothing, hearing nothing and knowing only what he wanted to know. The men who had died in the fierce fifteen minutes a few miles back had not touched his life. He was at cautious peace.

The road seemed untouched by the war. We could see the smoke rising like a hedge above and around the Old City walls. It mixed with the deep morning blue of the sky and wandered among the fresh green cypresses. There were goats and mangy dogs and other animals by the side of the road but no people.

Then we swung close to the wall, around the sharp downward bend in the road, and immediately some concealed Arab machine guns near the shrine at the entrance to the Garden of Gethsemane opened fire. Dov suddenly turned the jeep off the road and ran up a red shale bank. It tipped almost on to its side and threw us out to the rough ground, but at the same moment made a shield between us and the ambush.

But they were not shooting at us. They had caught an Israeli infantry section in an elbow in the road and were lacing them with rapid fire. The Jewish soldiers were trying to get across the road out of the line of fire, but they could not do it. Zoo Baby and Dov and O'Sullivan were immediately up on the side of the jeep shooting towards the entrenched Jordanians.

189

Five of the Israeli soldiers were killed within two paces of each other, unable to get out of the corner. I could hear Zoo Baby yelling at me to get my hair down, not my head, I remember, and I realized that the Arabs could see me from their position.

Then Shoshana did the thing I thought women only did in Russia or in films. I had nightmares about it for months after. The dead Israeli soldiers had moved her to a sudden screaming rage. She was crying out in Hebrew, so loud that it was audible over the gunfire.

It was a rage, a madness. She sprang up from beside me. I made to catch her ankle as she went but she kicked backwards throwing the gritty earth in my face. From behind the jeep she ran into the open and then around the side of a crumbling wall and an extension of the bank on which we were caught. A sixth Israeli had reached our side of the road only to be shot down as he got to the gutter. Concealed by the jutting bank from the Jordanian position Shoshana reached out and pulled him to her like a fisherman hauling in a catch. I kept yelling at her, but the Arabs were now spraying the bank above my head and along from the jeep with intense fire and Dov told me to lie flat where I was.

Behind the jeep and with the bank for partial protection we were reasonably shielded from the position. Zoo Baby and O'Sullivan were firing methodically at the ambushers, but the Arabs were well under cover. Dov scrambled along to try to reach a ledge just above Shoshana, but the machine guns kept cutting into the bank with such ferocity that he would have died before he had gone two yards. I begged him not to go.

Shoshana had hauled the dead infantryman into a shallow vertical crevice in the rock. She was very near the Arab position and above it. I could see her as I lay by the jeep, before I put my face to the earth in sheer terror and fright for her. I was shouting stupid swear words at her and crying and vowing I would kill everybody in sight if she was killed. I could not understand what she was trying to do with the dead soldier until I looked up fearfully again and I saw her with the grenade in her hand. She let the soldier drop un-

190

ceremoniously then and steadied herself to throw the grenade.

'The pin,' I gasped out loud to her, and then to Dov, who had heard me. 'Tell her about the pin.'

'She's been a soldier,' he yelled back. 'She's done it all.'

O'Sullivan was hit about this time. Only a nick in the shoulder, but he called out and then went on firing using language that would have shamed a pub at Cricklewood. Shoshana took the pin from the grenade, gauged the distance, and flung it beautifully. It waited and then blew up right inside the Arab position throwing earth and flame and smoke all about it. She killed three men with that little bomb. The Arabs stopped shooting and then began again, and then stopped for good as the three remaining men ran out under shelter and towards the covering vineyards of the Mount of Olives.

It stopped then with that awful suddenness of small battles. The guns ceased to hammer and the ears only remembered their din. There was some smoke, but that moved away with the minor breeze, leaving us behind the jeep looking across to the formation of dead men on the road and to Shoshana, trembling, yellow-faced, with her back to the rock, with the infantryman at her feet lying as though in sleep.

O'Sullivan was saying a catechism of soft swear words as he examined his shoulder. Zoo Baby, his eyes on Shoshana, silently handed a field dressing to O'Sullivan who accepted it just as mutely. Shoshana, as though she had done something which now frightened her, moved, hunched like a cripple, from her place, stepped uncertainly over the dead Israeli and came lamely towards us.

'Never do that again,' I said stupidly to her as I folded my arms about her. Dov smiled and tutted and Zoo Baby laughed his fine laugh and said: 'Which training camp?'

'At Hebron,' she replied with her face still in my shirt.

'They make you throw good, eh,' said Zoo Baby.

'And far,' she replied. Then she said quietly: 'Let us go to Mount Scopus. I want to see Jerusalem from there.'

The jeep was holed and useless now. But we took a lift

191

from an Israeli infantry truck that had just come from the mopping up in the northern sector of Jerusalem. The driver, a cheerful young Latvian Jew who kept telling us that his mother only bathed every Friday as she used to do in Riga, took us to the south side of the Old City.

Shoshana was told by a military policeman that the road to Mount Scopus was still not cleared. She argued that the radio had reported that Mount Scopus had been relieved and he told her to take no notice of the radio because if they were not Arabs up on the hills then he did not know why they were fighting so hard. Dov laughed quietly at Shoshana and Zoo Baby put his arm about her shoulder. She sulked. She was a strange girl.

The military policeman directed us down the cleared road to Government House where O'Sullivan could get his flesh wound properly dressed. Now that the danger had gone I only knew the great weariness that was on me. I had slept only minutes through the whole of the mad day and fiery night and into this next day. We left the truck and walked into Government House. The United Nations flag was lying rolled in a ball by the door.

O'Sullivan went to the dressing station, Shoshana was given a telephone to call her office in Tel Aviv and I stood with Zoo Baby and Dov washing away the dust with hot coffee. I could not be frightened any longer, nor did I care what happened to me in the future. All I wanted then was a niche, a hideaway, to sleep for a while until all the panto-mime was through. I could hear somebody calling, for some reason in English, that the tanks had reached Ramallah in the north and that Radio Ramallah was playing Jewish songs.

'The next move,' said Dov behind his coffee mug, 'will be the heights behind us, the Augusta Victoria area. Then the city will be surrounded.'

Zoo Baby said: 'Tomorrow we will pray at the Wailing Wall, you think?'

'Maybe tomorrow,' said Dov.

I was tired of them, their Wailing Wall, and their war. So I walked from the building into the hot sun and the disturbed dust. Feathers of surly smoke were hanging over the Mount of Olives and the sounds of the continuing conflict moved about the sacred hills. I was wondering where I could go to sleep for a while when I saw, through the trees below me, a house with cypresses in the garden, a neat white tower, and flying from a tower a brave Union Jack.

16

As I walked down the hill towards the house with its incongruous Union Jack I felt myself slumping with weariness. The battle in this part of the city was over and the people were beginning to move about the gaping streets. Jewish soldiers walked cautiously through the Arab places with that embarrassment peculiar to intruders. The Arabs kept their eyes down or their faces covered, except for the children who stood in little humps on the rubble and surveyed the conquerors with intense interest.

I went under torn trees, walked by military and civil vehicles hollowed and scarred by fire, and made detours around pyramids of debris. It seemed that the local population was attempting to occupy itself. One old man stood at the centre of a wrecked house hopefully but hopelessly sweeping with a broom.

When I was near Selma's house I looked across the valley to see if I could locate her other house in the Israeli sector. By working logically from the windmill at Yemin Moshe I fixed the general area but I was too fatigued to summon the concentration to pick out the single building among the other houses and the clustered trees.

Her Jordanian house was enclosed in its little garden, its small white turret giving it a minor regal distinction. The Union Jack that moved with sickly jerks in the small breeze was old and torn at the hems. There was a shell crater in the garden and the explosion had uprooted a family of tamarisk trees and thrown them against the windows of the house next door. All Selma's windows were smashed and against the portal of the open door was the ancient red racing bicycle which she had told me belonged to the postman.

I rang the bell politely and heard the muffled confusion that resulted within. The hall was two inches deep in battle dust and three apertures, like rough portholes, had been opened in the elegant wall to the right.

After a minute Selma herself came to the end of the passage, paused, and looked at me standing in the doorway.

'Did you get tired of the golf?' I asked.

'Sometimes you can't play alone very satisfactorily,' she said. She was holding on to the wall at her side and I could see she was crying. 'Oh, Christopher,' she said. 'I'm sorry about the mess the house is in.'

'Are you going to leave me at the door?' I asked.

She sniffed like a child. 'Please come in, darling. It's very strange but I thought somehow you would be here in Jerusalem.'

I walked towards her and she walked into my arms, lying tiredly against me. I could smell my mother's smell again. 'Yacob's dead,' she said. 'He was killed yesterday morning at El Arish.' She sniffed again. Her breasts were soft and pushed against me as though they needed me. 'He never knew about this house.'

'You did not want him to know, did you?' I said.

'No, it was better that he did not. He would have thought it treacherous.'

She motioned me into what had been a large and fine room. Now it was in chaos, laden with dust and piled with furniture, curtains, books and crockery. It looked like a stage-property department.

'I brought everything I could salvage in here,' she shrugged. 'My God, Christopher, I've been so bloody frightened.' She hung on to me again and she cried heavily. I lowered her on to a pile of rugs. 'No,' she said. 'We can sit more comfortably over there. Just move those pictures.'

We lifted the paintings from a beautiful kidney-shaped

settee and sat on its velvet. It felt firm under my aching backside.

'Why did you come back to Jerusalem?' she asked me.

'You may well ask. At the moment I'm supposed to be a war correspondent.'

'That girl,' she guessed unhappily. 'The one from the newspaper?'

'A woman's intuition,' I answered.

'Is it?'

'Yes, I'm with her,' I admitted. 'But, my God, I didn't think I'd get into the middle of things like this.'

'Look at your hands,' she said sadly taking them. 'How will you be able to play?'

'I won't,' I said. 'But I'm lucky to have hands. That's how I feel about it. I had decided to go to Tel Aviv, to try and get a plane out, and I changed my mind. Then the jeep I was to travel in got a direct hit from a shell from this side. That could have been me.'

'I am glad you are safe and I'm glad you are here,' she said still cradling my hands. 'I have been trying to shelter some of the people around here. They are down in the cellar.'

'The postman left his bike at the door,' I said. 'Why didn't you play golf, Selma?'

'You know it was just a joke,' she said. 'I was frightened as hell when it all happened. I had come back to Jerusalem and I couldn't get out again because of the military. So I stayed in the other house, in the basement, by myself. An Arab shell went straight into the bedroom. The one we were in. Then, when the fighting had passed I walked over here to this house. And look what's been done to this.'

'I thought that might happen,' I said. 'You got it from both sides. You shouldn't spread your assets so widely. You got across here without trouble?'

She smiled tiredly: 'I put a nice quiet dress on, picked up my handbag and simply walked through it all,' she said. 'You've never seen such a mess, but I could have been strolling down Bond Street for all anyone cared.'

'Jesus, I'm tired,' I said lolling full back against the settee. It was strange how at home I felt with her. She never worried me as Shoshana worried me. 'I've seen so many men killed in the past twenty-four hours.'

'That's wearying in itself,' she agreed sadly. 'Would you like a drink or some coffee? I can make some coffee. The drinks cabinet we would have to tunnel for.'

'Coffee is fine,' I agreed. 'Who have you got in the cellar?'

'Abdullah, the postman, two women from Hassan's house. You remember I told you about Hassan who used to let his goats feed in my garden. Poor old devil, God knows where he has gone.'

I sensed that she was hesitating. 'Anyone else?' I asked.

'How do you mean?'

'Well, anyone else in the cellar.'

'No. There is no one else there,' she said. 'I'll get the coffee.'

She made it on a small stove in the adjoining room. There was a hatch, with one of its side pieces broken so that it seemed like a large fractured picture frame.

'You saw my Union Jack,' she called.

'Only you could have put that thing up in the middle of a war between the Jews and the Arabs. It's a wonder it wasn't the Rising Sun.'

'I didn't have a Rising Sun,' she replied. 'I'm not patriotic, heaven knows, I've told you how I feel. But the Union Jack was handy.'

'A sort of flag of convenience,' I said.

'Quite. It was either that or the Greek flag. I told you, didn't I, that my mother and my stepfather used to fly them on their national days?'

'Yes, you did. But why put it up now? Were you hoping for some sort of immunity?'

'Something like that,' she admitted. I could hear her pouring the coffee. 'I had a mad thought that both sides might leave the house alone if that was flying above it.'

I looked about at the sad wreckage. 'Well, they didn't, did they,' I said. 'No respect these bloody little countries. I'm sorry about Yacob.'

'Yacob was run over by his own car,' she called. 'That was not very gallant, I'm afraid. They got stuck in a sand dune or something. Poor Yacob, to go like that on the first morning of a war would have upset him.'

'Wasn't your father run over in Birmingham during the Blitz. You told me that, didn't you?'

I heard her emit a small laugh. 'That's true. My relatives seem to make a habit of dying off rather unheroically.' She waited and then said clearly from the other room: 'Christopher, I *have* got some other people in the cellar.'

I was drifting towards sleep. 'I thought you had,' I said. She hurried into the room. Then she went back, brought the coffee in and set it down.

'I don't know what the hell to do,' she confessed. 'These Israelis can be nasty, believe me. I know them very well. If they found me harbouring these soldiers.'

'Soldiers?'

'Three soldiers. Two are just Arab Legionnaires, peasant boys, both wounded. Not much, just grazes really. But the third is a Colonel somebody. Apparently he's some sort of intelligence officer and he knows a lot about the defences inside the Old City. He is terrified that the Jews will get him and make him talk. So I said he could hide down there.'

Wearily I said: 'Selma, you're out of your mind. For Christ's sake why get yourself involved like this?'

Her eyes were full of tears. 'I don't know, Christopher,' she said. 'I like them, I suppose. The Arabs. They are the only people I have ever liked or cared about.'

For her that was saying a lot. I put my arm out to her. 'You really ought to have gone to Haywards Heath, June or not,' I said. 'In the same way, I ought to be playing Beethoven in Eastbourne or even Bradford. God alone knows what we are doing here. I have never seen so much death and known so little about the need for it.'

'Do you want to sleep a while?' she asked. I wondered about Shoshana. I had left a message for her that I would be at the Press centre near the Mandelbaum Gate at one o'clock that afternoon and I would wait there until she arrived. But I had to sleep. 'If there is a spare bed,' I said, 'I could do with a nap.'

She took my hand and we went into another room. There

197

was a hole in the roof opening out on to the splendid blue sky. It was a large bed, but with no linen or pillows. I pulled off my shoes and lay out on it luxuriously, feeling its soft but firm grip enfolding my tired body. Selma took her dress off and lay down beside me, her adult softness moulding into the bend in my chest and my raised legs. I was hardly aware of her. She had her back to me and I put my hands about her waist, to hold her, before I dropped to sleep.

Shoshana's young voice woke me from the deepest sleep in the afternoon, calling through the house after me. I found myself looking up from the deep bare bed to the great roof hole and the blue Jerusalem sky. From where I lay I could see the corner of the Union Jack on the flag mast flapping like a torn and Technicolored shirt tail.

Selma was not with me, but the place where she had slept was warm. She came into the room with the puzzled Shoshana.

Selma said: 'This young lady wishes to speak to Mr Hollings.'

'That's me,' I admitted, sitting up and trying to shrug the weariness away. I felt that what with the war and the women circumstances were becoming too involved.

'Why do you sleep here?' asked Shoshana glaring at me and then at Selma.

'I thought it was the British Embassy,' I said. 'Didn't you see the flag on the roof?'

'In Tel Aviv is the British Embassy,' said Shoshana. 'I see the flag so I think this is where you are.'

Her English which had become good and confident with me had now slipped in Selma's presence. 'It is three in the afternoon,' continued Shoshana. 'I have waited at the Press house.'

I stood up. 'Shoshana,' I said tiredly, 'this is Mrs Haydn. Selma, this is Shoshana Levy.' I wondered why I had called Selma Mrs Haydn and not called Shoshana Miss Levy, and thought it must have been something to do with seniority. 'Mrs Haydn's husband has just been killed at El Arish.'

Shoshana said: 'Whose army?'

'The Israeli Army, of course,' I said.

'He was run over by his own truck,' said Selma firmly as though wishing to get the matter straight from the start.

'What is the widow of an Israeli soldier doing in a Jordanian house?' asked Shoshana.

'Her interests are somewhat diffuse,' I said patiently. 'She is a British subject. Anyway this is Israeli territory now. She'll pay her rates to your lot.'

Shoshana looked confused: 'Please keep from the jokes, Christopher,' she said. 'Why do you sleep here?'

'Chiefly because I was bloody tired,' I said. 'I know Mrs Haydn and Mrs Haydn had this spare bed.'

'It is a very big bed,' said Shoshana suspiciously looking carefully at Selma's dress. It was uncreased because she had gone to sleep with me wearing her slip.

Shoshana said: 'Are you with me, Christopher? Mount Scopus is opened to us now. The Arabs, they fire on the road from the Old City but we can go up another way. The view is beautiful from there. Zoo Baby and the two others are at Government House.'

She said it almost pleadingly and I think that I could have gone with her then and the situation would have been saved. I asked her to wait while I washed my face. Her confidence returned and she smiled at Selma and looked at the hole in the roof and the wreckage within the house. 'It is a nice place you have here,' she smiled insincerely. Sometimes she would come out with some cliché like that learned from an American film.

'It was,' said Selma quietly.

'Married to an Israeli soldier and you have this house in Jordan,' mused Shoshana cunningly. 'It is most curious.' She was more sure of herself now because I was going with her.

'Curious things happen,' said Selma dully.

As if to bear out her words a curious thing did happen then in the form of Abdullah the Arab postman wheeling his crimson racing bicycle into the room. He was bent and apologetic, shuffling and heavy with dirt. He began to speak in lisping Arabic to Selma and then saw Shoshana.

199

They both screamed at once. I think Abdullah screamed the loudest. They backed away from each other as though they were rival monsters. Then Shoshana recovered and went forward like a tiger, her young strong hands going out towards the little Arab postman. He dropped his bicycle to the floor with a thin crash. Then he stepped back, backing away from Shoshana, and accidentally put his foot into the frame. He would not take his fearing eyes off the girl and he extricated his leg with difficulty and without looking.

'Arabs!' Shoshana shouted at me.

'One Arab,' I corrected.

'Traitor,' said Shoshana. 'This Mrs Haydn, she is a traitor.'

'Shoshana,' I said. 'This is not Colonel Nasser, it's a postman.'

'Traitor,' spat Shoshana at Selma.

'What a bonny girl you've got yourself, Christopher,' said Selma turning away.

At that moment one of the women who had been hiding in the cellar and one of the wounded Arab Legionnaires appeared. They were trying to tell Selma something and pointing towards the cellar door at the far end of the other room. Shoshana stared at the man as though he represented the entire Jordanian armed forces. Then she stepped quickly into the outside hall and looked at the open cellar door.

She swung angrily back into the room. 'Traitor!' she screamed at Selma.

'Tell your little Jewess to shut up, Christopher,' said Selma icily. Jewess, the most anti-Semitic word next to *Yid*, came out with slow emphasis.

'I would hit you!' Shoshana bawled at her. 'But I never hit women.' She turned on me. 'You stay in a house and they hide Arab soldiers. Why is this?'

'You forget,' I said quietly, sick of it all. 'I'm neutral and very tired. That's why I'm here. You can see this man is wounded. What harm can he do?'

Shoshana's eyes remained vivid. I remember her well at that moment, her belligerent body, her breasts thrust out, her face alight with indignation. The Arab soldier and the woman were again trying to say something to Selma and she was attempting to listen with exaggerated patience over the top of Shoshana's angry voice. Then the postman who had, in the midst of the scene, extricated his naked and under-nourished foot from the bicycle frame, emphasized what the other two Arabs were saying, using some sort of rigged language that Selma understood.

'Oh, God, no,' said Selma. She moved forward and pushed by Shoshana with a sudden arrogant, inborn authority. A shot sounded from the cellar towards which she was making. She stopped then, in mid-pace. A woman screamed down in the cellar and began to wail. Selma turned towards me, pushing Shoshana firmly aside with her forearm. But it was the Arab Legionnaire who went. He moved decisively from the room and went down into the cellar, his heavy boots sounding on the stone steps. Selma then moved forward to the cellar door and stood there looking tall and rather fine, her hand resting against the cool wall. Shoshana was staring at me. I looked at her and then looked away towards the cellar again.

We could hear the wailing woman coming up the stairs. She appeared with blood splashed on her face and her head-dress, her hands flailing about, her ragged body writhing. The Legionnaire who had gone down to the cellar returned with her and a second Arab soldier followed. I heard Shoshana gasp when she saw the second Arab. It was as though rats were emerging from the cellar.

She jerked suddenly and made to run towards the door. I caught her wrist and pulled her back. She turned and tried to pull away.

'Shoshana,' I said firmly. 'If you're not careful somebody else is going to get hurt. Stay here and be quiet.'

She stood squarely, still full of anger, like a restrained dog. Selma said: 'The officer has shot himself in the cellar. He did not want to fall into our . . . their . . . hands.'

'It is *good* they should shoot themselves,' rasped Shoshana. Her head jerked forward towards Selma. The Englishwoman stepped forward like a strict schoolteacher, a strong decisive step as though she had suddenly made up her mind about something. She brought up her flat hand in a wide loop and hit Shoshana across the side of her indignant face.

In a moment they were fighting. Shoshana went at her like an animal with long claws, while Selma stood upright hitting at her with alternate hands, bringing each blow up from hip level, head high, very superior and controlled, like an elegant cricketer attacking fast bowling.

I tried to get between them. I felt responsible. But as I attempted to push into the spitting fight I tripped over the lying bicycle and fell into its frame and oily wheels. I was like a bear in a trap, crouching on all fours trying to pull myself free while the two women screamed and fought.

'Traitor! Dirty traitor!'

'Jewess. Rotten little Jewess!'

'English filth!'

'Bloody Jewess!'

Still caught in the bicycle, I called out to them: 'Ladies, girls, please ... ladies ...'

The Arab woman stopped wailing for a moment when the fight began but immediately began again, and louder, her howlings rising above the breathless insults of the battling women. The two soldiers appeared to be moving around with half-helpless sidesteps, like the impotent crab-walk of a referee in a boxing ring. I could see their boots moving sideways across my vision even as I tried to get up from the bicycle. Then Abdullah, the postman, leaned punily across to try and help me. Either Selma or Shoshana or both struck him with their angry bodies as they fought. He shot spectacularly forward with a sort of subdued wail, landing across my shoulders and knocking me flat on top of the bicycle frame again. I could feel blood coming from my knee where the pedal had thrust itself. Lovers I have had in later times always thought that was where a bullet had taken a trench out of my flesh. I truthfully told them it was a battle injury.

I pushed Abdullah away from me, rolling him over on the floor. He lay panting and mewing like a mangy old cat. I carefully disentangled myself from the bicycle, oil and blood over my hands and legs and arms. Selma was hitting Shoshana crisply back towards the big bed. It caught Shoshana behind the knees and she tumbled back but caught Selma's loose hair with two hands as she fell and pulled the Englishwoman with her. They rolled on the bed like primitive gipsies, legs and thighs open, screaming and spitting. The Arab Legionnaires were standing and observing with unconcealed sensual expressions. I staggered towards the bed and once again tried to part the women. They were fighting with every ounce of their spite and anger and strength. Nails and teeth were attacking. A whole hank of Selma's hair was on the pillow, pulled out by the violent Shoshana.

'Ladies,' I moaned helplessly. 'For God's sake.' Then lamentably: 'Where are your manners?' One of them, Selma I think because it was a heavy blow rather than a sharp one, punched me in the ear and after that I dived like a life-saver in between them, using all my strength to lever them apart. I managed to make a channel between them by forcing my body through theirs. Then with my left hand across Selma's breasts and my right across Shoshana's I held them down. It took all my strength to keep them like that. They were both exhausted and that helped. Selma was crying angrily and Shoshana was spitting out violent little words in Hebrew.

I was lying, face down, panting, trying to work out what to do next when I heard O'Sullivan's voice. He had arrived at the door and surveyed the scene contained in the wrecked room. The great hole in the roof, the debris from the war, the fallen bicycle, two Arab soldiers, two Arab women, Abdullah the thin postman still flat on his back, and Christopher Hollings, renowned concert pianist, holding down two heaving women on a large untidy bed.

'Will you be wanting both of the ladies, Mister Hollings?' he inquired calmly.

'Have them, for God's sake,' I said getting up gratefully from the bed. Shoshana leaped up as though released by a spring and, at last feminine, ran weeping like a schoolgirl towards O'Sullivan. He put a fatherly arm about her. Selma sat on the bed trying to arrange her hair. I leaned over and gave her the piece that Shoshana had torn out. 'Thank you, Christopher,' she said evenly. 'I think perhaps you had better go.'

203

I went with O'Sullivan. As we returned into the open Shoshana put her arm into mine and gave an ashamed smile. 'That was a very interesting situation, I think,' said O'Sullivan. 'Very interesting indeed.'

'You should have taken a look in the basement,' I said. 'There was an Arab officer down there and he'd blown his brains out.'

'Deaths are four a penny in Jerusalem today,' he said. 'But it's not every morning of the week you find a couple of ladies havin' a scrap like that. It must be something you do to them, perhaps, Mister Hollings.'

'It's just that I like my women to have spirit,' I said.

17

We had some food and wine at Government House and then Dov brought another jeep around and we set out for Mount Scopus. Shoshana continued to hold on to my arm, as though I were some prized possession recently reclaimed. I wondered what Selma would do. O'Sullivan had said to me when Shoshana was not there: 'That woman has nothing to worry about. Just as long as she's got her passport issued by Her Britannic Majesty's Government, all they'll do is throw her out on her ear. And she'll probably be glad to go.'

'She can go to Haywards Heath,' I said. O'Sullivan nodded as though he immediately understood.

When we reached the climbing road to Mount Scopus, Shoshana said: 'General Dayan was on the top of Mount Scopus today. I think it is very good that the War Minister goes to see how the battle is happening.'

'I thought he was the Defence Minister,' I said.

She nodded vigorously. 'War Minister is better, I think. It is more fighting talk, you understand.'

'More aggressive,' I suggested.

'That is correct.'

'You're right, I suppose,' I shrugged. 'There hasn't been much defence from the Israelis in this little affair.'

'We have to fight outside our frontiers,' she said.

'You have said that before,' I pointed out.

'It is still true.'

The jeep snorted as it surmounted the hot, rough road. The afternoon sun was lying at its fullest, unrelentingly across the stony mountains. Behind our backs, on the minor hills about the Old City the battle still moved, but tiredly, spasmodically. The whole country seemed to tremble under the fierce heat of the day and the occasional growl of the guns.

Zoo Baby said: 'Ramallah is ours again. The radio said it. Then they played Israeli songs to show that they told the truth.'

'And Latrun,' said Dov. 'No resistance at Latrun.'

'It is good we have Latrun,' said Shoshana. 'God knows it was too bad there last time. My father has told me of the hundreds of dead lying in the fields and the vineyards below the monastery. This time it was easy. The Arabs ran away.'

'When did you start playing the piano, then?' O'Sullivan asked me.

'At three years,' I said. 'We had a pianola, you know one of those old-fashioned roller things.'

'I know them,' said O'Sullivan.

'And one day my mother deduced that I wasn't playing it by working the pedals because my feet wouldn't reach the pedals. It took months before she noticed. And she went screaming "Eureka" down the village street, and all the neighbours used to crowd into the parlour, and in the passage outside, and in the street, with the front window open, to hear me play.'

'Like some sort of Holy Miracle,' he said. 'The sort we have in Ireland with visions and blood pouring out of some urchin's hands. And everybody turns up from miles around to have a look.'

'Just the same. I was the local miracle. They gave me scholarships and all sorts of things, and in the end I got a

205

manager and a publicity agent and an image and the rest of it. I'm supposed to be playing at Eastbourne next week. Or is it Bradford?'

'It's Bradford,' interrupted Shoshana.

From the university and hospital buildings on the summit of Mount Scopus the clean blue star flew from every pinnacle.

'Sure,' said O'Sullivan. 'It looks like the summer camp of the Jewish Lads' Brigade.'

From the top we looked over the fine golden city and the ancient country. It was spread out on every side. The long view from the flank of Mount Scopus over the sun-browned earth to the great flat, shining pan of the Dead Sea; then, to the south the strongly rising Wilderness of the Bible and the old and new roads to Jericho and Bethlehem, the Mount of Contempt, the Church of the Ascension, the Tomb of the Prophets, the Tomb of Absalom, the Tomb of Zachariah, seven destroyed tanks, and the Panorama Hotel.

It was clear that apart from the height of Augusta Victoria most of the surrounding country was in Jewish hands. Curling smoke had replaced now the flash of explosions. Little fires were burning in a hundred places as though everyone was industriously clearing up. Only the stronghold of the Old City, pugnacious behind its thick walls and dominating towers, remained in Arab hands.

'Tomorrow,' Shoshana said. 'Tomorrow it will be ours. I promise you that.'

'Don't promise me,' I assured her.

'The only thing that will stop us taking the city will be a Ceasefire,' said Dov. 'If that happens Jerusalem could become an Arab island, just as this place, Mount Scopus, has been an Israeli island. That would be disaster.'

Zoo Baby wiped his wide, sweating forehead. He said: 'A Ceasefire? A finish?'

Dov shrugged. 'The Egyptians are beaten. Already they run like crying children to the United Nations. Maybe we win too quickly, but not win enough.'

We remained on Mount Scopus until it was dark, watching

the extravagant sunset burn the roofs of Jerusalem with its hot colours, seeing the redness eventually drain from the Judean Hills and leave them to the pale touch of the stars.

Zoo Baby drove us back to the house at the Mandelbaum Gate where we found Major de Groucy in a deep sleep on the table where, a few hours before, we had laid the cold body of the elderly officer. Some of the correspondents and the Press centre clerks were lying against the walls or on the bare tables, sleeping away their exhaustion. Crouched across a typewriter in one corner was one of the middle-aged American journalists. He had been weeping and he told us about the two Americans who had been killed in the fighting that day and whom he had known and worked with and liked. He was very tired and he tapped out his story with two reluctant fingers.

Shoshana spent half an hour on the telephone to Tel Aviv. We waited for her in the jeep and were squatting, talking, when Cumberland drove up with almost a teenage flourish, tooting the horn of his jeep to us.

'Had a good day?' he asked brightly as though we had been fishing.

'So, so,' I said. 'How about you?'

'Jesus,' he said. 'This is some war! Everything happens so fast, and so near. In Vietnam you sometimes have to poke along for two days before you get to any shooting. It's just a great big place. But this is so dinky. Everything happens right around the block from the cable office.' He waited a moment and we smiled at him politely. 'Where's the young lady?' he asked. 'Shoshana. She's okay isn't she?'

'Unless she's tripped over the telephone wire, or pulled Major de Groucy down on top of her, she's in good health,' I said. 'We're just waiting for her.'

'Are you going to the Babylon Hotel?' he asked.

'Why should we go there? asked Dov.

'It's a great hotel and it's just been taken over from the former management – you get me? All the Press boys are going there for rest and recreation. There's chow there too. And the rates are reasonable.'

So we went to the Babylon Hotel. Someone in the Tel

Aviv newspaper office had told Shoshana to go there to link up with her colleagues. She greeted Cumberland quietly as she came out of the door, and he was on the way in. Then she said to Zoo Baby: 'Let us go to the Babylon Hotel. It is good there.'

'So the word gets around,' said Dov.

It was to the south of the city, just off the Bethlehem road, in an island of fig and tamarisk trees. There was an ornamental pool in the front with three fountains continuing to jump. In the middle of the pool, burned to a skeleton, was a military motorcycle and sidecar. That day, in Jerusalem, it appeared to be nothing out of the ordinary.

Apart from a few untidy holes near the front porch the hotel had remained unscarred by the battle. It seemed to be full of wounded and tired men, but a cheerful thin Israeli officer sitting professionally behind the reception desk said that there were rooms available for us. The attack on the Old City, he predicted confidently, would not now take place until the morning and everyone would have time to be in their places.

'Before the war,' said Dov quietly to me, 'this man was the manager of the worst hotel in Haifa. High rates, low stand-ards.' He smiled: 'One thing about the Jews, we always have the man for the job. This hotel was one of the showpieces of the Jordan Tourist Board. Our friend here will soon make a difference.'

'You,' I said, 'are a realistic man.'

'I have no light about my head, if that is what you mean,' he laughed. 'Too many people, especially those who have written stories and novels about Israel, try to show us as a race of courageous saints. We are not. We are people like all the others on earth. Just people. If God chose us then he must have long ago regretted it.'

They gave me a room to myself, Shoshana having told the officer at the reception desk that I was an important person. I ran the bath and lay in it for half an hour. My hands were sore and torn, my face throbbed in the warm water from all its scratches and bruises, and the pathetic injury behind my knee inflicted by Abdullah's bicycle hurt more than all those

208

brought about by the rough days of the war. I called the officer at the reception desk and he brightly assured me that he could send a razor and a toothbrush to me immediately and he could arrange for some clean underclothes and green denims. 'Nothing is beyond Israel, Mr Hollings,' he laughed. 'Nothing.'

In the mirror I saw that the sun had scorched my face. My forearms were almost black. The razor arrived with a packet of blades and some shaving cream. There was also a toothbrush and toothpaste and the change of clothes. The green fatigues were only slightly big. With the consignment was a typewritten slip which said: 'With the Compliments of the Management of the Golda Meir Plaza Hotel, formerly the Babylon Hotel'.

I changed and went to Shoshana's room. She opened the door to my tap and I went in and sat on the bed while she finished dressing. She was wearing a white nylon slip that fitted her well. Her face and arms and legs were deep brown. I kissed her when I first went in holding her soft body hard against me.

She went back to doing her hair in front of the mirror. She moved it up, handfuls of fair hair, with graceful womanly movements.

'This Mrs Haydn,' she said conversationally. 'She is a strange woman, yes?'

I hesitated. 'Well, different,' I said.

'You have made love on a bed with her?'

'What sort of thing to say is that?'

She turned unhurriedly. I could see there was a bruise on her cheekbone where Selma had struck her. 'It is a question,' she said. 'Have you made love on the bed with her?'

'And if I had?'

'Not today was it?' she asked softly. 'Not after me?'

I walked to her and she turned back to the mirror. I ran my arms about her soft middle, feeling the carefully domed flesh of her stomach beneath the skin of nylon. I put my head against her head. 'Not after you,' I said.

'That is good.' She turned against me, closely, so that her fine breasts pressed into my chest. 'There is nothing more to

209

tell me.' We kissed and then she laughed. 'Oh, Christopher, was it not hilarious!'

'The fight?' I said.

'Yes, of course, the fight.' She giggled like a child. 'When you fell into the bicycle! It was so hilarious.'

'Look,' I said. 'Take a look at this.' I turned and undid my trousers, pulling them down so that she could see the injury behind my knee. I did a passable imitation of the bumptious Major de Groucy. 'Shall we say it was caused by an Arab bicycle pedal.' We fell on the bed together and embraced and slept quietly for a while in each other's arms. Then the telephone rang and I picked it up. 'The Golda Meir Plaza Hotel announces that dinner is served,' said the voice.

Dinner was by candlelight because the mains electricity was cut. All five of us arrived at the table like strangers, clean faces that shone, tidied hair, and clean clothes. O'Sullivan had been to the dressing station and had his flesh wound bandaged.

'It's not every Catholic can say he got shot outside the Garden of Gethsemane,' he said. 'Or that he saw a woman throw a grenade like some women would throw a flower vase.'

Shoshana said slowly: 'It is something we must not talk about. Now I am very afraid of what I did. Let us eat.'

They gave her a decoration for it a few weeks later. But she put it away in a drawer under her Israeli embroidery and I never saw it again.

We ate with fifty or sixty others, some soldiers, some civilians, some war correspondents. It was self-service from a long table served by Army cooks. There was a bottle of Jordanian red wine between every two people. Soon the men at the table began to sing.

Hebrew is a good language for singing songs. It moulds well with music. They sang their favourites, *Hava Nagilla*, and *Yeroshalaim* that was soon to be the anthem of all, but soon they softened and men began to sing the songs of their own, old countries. We sat and listened, for many had fine voices, as the Jewish folk-songs of half the world were sung.

There was a fat Pole and a thick Lithuanian, two Munich Germans, a funny man from New Jersey, and a Cochin Chinese Jew who sang a foul Oriental Jewish ballad with finger movements.

'One thing you can say about this firm,' O'Sullivan whispered to me. 'They've got branches every bloody where.'

The wine was drunk and a new, captured consignment brought into the candlelit cavern of a room to schoolboy cheers. Another bottle between every two people. Shoshana and three Israeli girl soldiers were the only women in the room. Shoshana laughed, with her head in her hands, when the Chinese Jew was singing his finger song.

A man with his face bandaged stood up at one of the far tables and shouted, comically muffled, through his dressings, pointing towards our table. His ragged words brought wild cheering from everywhere in the room and a thumping of fists and cutlery on the boards.

Those around me applauded and looked at me. I grinned foolishly. 'There's no piano,' I said.

'Any army which can win a war in a couple of days can obtain a piano in a couple of minutes,' said Dov. Zoo Baby got up massively from the table and made a loud demand in Hebrew. Then, like the head of a raiding party, he made for the door and half a dozen others followed him like daring undergraduates. They returned within the two minutes, half-pushing, half-carrying an ancient and graceful upright piano. I stood up and everyone shouted and cheered. Around me I quickly saw O'Sullivan's grin, Dov's laugh, and the delighted eyes of Shoshana.

They put the piano in the centre of the tables and Zoo Baby made great play of dusting off the keyboard and obtaining a chair. I sat down, for once completely lost in front of the instrument. Its yellowed teeth grimaced at me. It was an Arab piano and for a moment I wondered if it might be a booby trap. I made a joke of this, standing on the chair and looking into the interior making an exaggerated search for a bomb. They roared and applauded.

Then I sat again and began to play. I played quietly at first and they sat attentively and listened. Then they murmured

211

and hummed and I played while they sang their songs once more. That *Yeroshalaim* they sang again and again.

I thumped it out like a bar-room cornerman when they got to the rousing marching songs, and then I played in a lumbering rhythm while some of them performed their distant dances.

I shall always think of Zoo Baby that evening. They cleared a space on the floor for him and the big man danced alone in the light of the candles. It was a Balkan dance, remembered since childhood, a gentle, rustic dance at its start, progressing into a brilliant kicking rhythm, hands on hips, legs shooting out, face cascading with sweat. Like many big men he danced beautifully, with huge, light movements and great graceful curves. He hummed the pastoral melody and I easily followed him, and then led him. When the dance quickened he swung into the exciting movements, his large feet banging on the floor and his mouth hooting out the calls, the sweat covering him, and all the others in the room clapping the demanding time. He was a dance troupe all on his own. I don't know how he moved like that. He worked it into a fantastic crescendo, his boots flying like hooves, his arms finely balanced, his mouth now speechless. The climax came and he sprang up and whirled in a great flying leap, a jump of joy and exuberance, grotesquely misjudged, that sent him crashing into the nearest table. Men and crockery were flung aside. The table collapsed spectacularly and chairs splintered and broke. Zoo Baby sat in the debris, panting and sweating, his huge chest rising and dropping, his arms full out, his tree-trunk legs flung apart, and a great, mashed smile on his big face. Everybody laughed and cheered. Dear Zoo Baby.

Shoshana said: 'It was hilarious.'

'For once I think that's the right word,' I said.

'And you played the piano very fine, Christopher.'

'I should try it for a living,' I said. 'Instead of doing acrobatics into shell craters.'

Playing like that had hurt. My hands were puffed and bruised and lacerated from all the ill-treatment of the past days. Lying on the bed in her room they throbbed.

212

'You don't know what playing for your Army has cost me,' I said. She was lying beside me in her slip and she looked at me quickly. 'You joke again,' she said, relieved. 'Sometimes it is not possible to tell with you.' I showed her my hands. She took them in hers. 'They are supposed to be very soft. That is correct?' she said. 'They must be for your career.'

'I was never even allowed to wash up at home,' I said.

She looked worried. 'They are so damaged,' she said. 'Put them here for comfort.'

She parted her thighs and took my sore hands and placed them at the top of her legs next to the triangle of soft material and the softer flesh. Then she moved very slightly with a bellows movement, squeezing them and releasing them, and squeezing them again. Her hands were on the sides of my head and she was looking with her splendid eyes into my face.

'That is good for your hands?' she asked me seriously.

'I recommend it,' I answered.

We moved around in the bed. There was a single candle in a holder in the room, making our shadows like monsters. The guns were still grunting about Jerusalem, but the armies were, for the most part, resting, waiting for the daylight and the attack on the Old City. My face now rested luxuriously on the pillows of her legs. I was lying on my side, hard against the sheet, my head turned, my cheek and my ear cushioned by her left thigh and the hair on the top of my head against her patch of thick hair enclosed in the white nylon.

I ran my tongue along her leg, knowing her reaction in the tightening of her trunk and the squeezing of her hands that came down to touch my forehead. I could smell her and I remembered very briefly that Selma smelled like my mother.

My hands were a little higher than my head, gently rubbing her flanks, bringing her warmth together at one spot. I wanted to get right to her then so I said: 'These pants are getting wet. I think they had better come off.'

She whispered: 'Please take them from me. I don't like them to be wet.'

I did, rolling them into a tight ball in my fist and then

wiping around her thighs with them. She sat up and held her arms high as though surrendering. I quietly pulled her slip over her head. She had already taken off everything else and now she lay there, brown, with two white stripes across her body, her breasts a little swollen, their nipples sleepy. We lay down without fuss, kissing fully, and then she opened the scissors of her legs to let me in.

'Come to me, Christopher,' she said. 'Give to me.'

'Aaaaaaaaah!' I cried. And, 'Aaaaaaaah!'

My body suddenly bent like a bow, arching backwards and she let out a cry and tried to hold me. 'Christopher! Darling, what is wrong?'

'Aaaah, oh my God. Aaaaah. Jesus Christ, I've got such a pain in my back.'

'A pain in your back? You joke?'

It was like a serrated needle going through me, skewering my kidneys, drawing every nerve together in a knot. I rolled and rolled again. 'Dear Christ,' I muttered, tears of agony in my eyes. 'It's no joke. Oh no. Aaaaaah! Aaaaaah!'

'A doctor I will get,' she said reaching for the phone.

'No,' I gasped. 'No. Not here. This is your room.'

'This is Israel,' she said as though that were sufficient excuse. 'And it is war.'

Because it was war she could not get a doctor because they were either treating the wounded or resting. I lay bent with pain at the bottom of her bed for about ten minutes. Then it receded and half an hour later we slept peacefully together. In the circumstances I thought she was very kind and understanding.

214

18

Zoo Baby was killed about an hour after breakfast the following morning as the Israelis broke through at Herod's Gate and the St Stephen's Gate and began fighting along the muscular walls and the tangled streets and alleys of the Old City.

We had breakfast at the hotel and everyone had patted Zoo Baby and told him it was a marvellous dance he had performed the previous evening. Dov was telling me about the trains which had been running to Jerusalem from the north, skirting the Jordanian border by only a hundred yards. The Jews ran them empty until just before the attack on Jerusalem to lull the Arabs on that side. 'They are good trains,' said Dov in his quiet schoolmaster manner. 'The Germans gave us the rolling stock as part of their conscience. They have also sent us fifty thousand gas masks.'

At eight o'clock we left the hotel. It was a settled, guileless morning, with no sounds of battle. Two Arabs were tending the plants in the hotel garden and did not look up. The sky was clear and full of sunlight. But at eight-thirty an Israeli tank column went straight up the road from Mount Scopus to the heights of Augusta Victoria, firing as it went, while Jewish recoil-less guns and the hard paratroops attacked the thick walls of the Old City.

As we went towards the battle in the jeep with Zoo Baby driving, a skein of Israeli jets ran across the towers and flashing cupolas of the Old City and loosed their bombs on the Arab troops inside. From above the wall we could see the debris flying and the flames lending their brief brightness to the brilliance of the sun.

'Another day's work,' I said to O'Sullivan. 'Right on time.'

'And the last day, I expect,' he answered. 'Nothing will stop them today. They'll be at the Wailing Wall in a couple of hours.'

The recoil-less guns and the dipping planes were attacking the troops positioned on the wall and the crowded Arab quarter within. Everything was breaking out now. The tanks, fat and noisy, clambering up the hill behind us towards Augusta Victoria beyond the Mount of Olives, the guns and planes bombarding the Old City. In ten minutes the bombing and shelling stopped and in a strange, short, smoky quiet the paratroops attacked Herod's Gate, climbing the cliffs of the great walls, bursting through the gate. Then a clanking tank column came up the road towards the St Stephen's Gate. Two hundred yards before they reached it the tanks began firing nastily. There were explosions on the walls and solid squares of masonry tumbled and fell. The noise gathered and came to a crescendo in the warm morning.

We sat safely in the jeep on the outside slope of the city and watched. Shoshana was close to me. 'We will not harm the Holy Places,' she assured me as though I were some church dignitary. Then she said: 'How is your back today, Christopher?' I grinned with embarrassment. 'Nothing,' I said. 'It went like it came.'

She ran her firm hand across my shirt over my kidneys and said: 'I am glad there is no more pain. It was not hilarious, was it.'

'No it wasn't hilarious,' I agreed.

She was calm, but I could feel the excitement in her as she watched the prize city that was to be theirs before the end of the day. Dov and Zoo Baby sat sweating and watching, like spectators at some sporting event. Dov said: 'It is like the Roman days, eh? The attack on the walls of a defended city. This does not happen in modern war. It is like something from history.'

The tanks had got to the St Stephen's Gate, torn open by their gunfire and the leading tank was putting its inquisitive nose into the Old City.

'There are six gates,' said Dov unable to resist one of his lessons. 'Zion Gate, Jaffa Gate, Herod's Gate, Damascus

216

Gate and Dung Gate and that one down there the St Stephen's Gate.'

'There is a seventh,' said Zoo Baby. 'The Golden Gate.'

Dov looked at me. 'But it is sealed. By tradition it will not be opened until the Messiah enters the city.'

'Let's hope He doesn't come today,' said O'Sullivan quietly. 'I think there's enough excitement already.'

The paratroops were all along the walls now, running and crouching and firing into the alleys and streets down below. Another ten minutes and they were within the guts of the city. We saw a jeep go below us crowded with war correspondents, with Joe Cumberland driving. They were making for the St Stephen's Gate where now the Israeli tanks crawled in, one by one, like thieving cats. Zoo Baby drove after the jeep and we arrived outside the wall and waited until a military policeman said that we could go inside.

The battle had been fierce in some of the streets, but not prolonged. In the stepped alleys the Jewish troops were forcing their way through machine-gun emplacements and groups of snipers. But the advance was quick and incisive. We followed the Israeli soldiers until everyone was held up by a brave machine gun which was perched behind the Al Aksa mosque.

We had left the jeep and were creeping through the alleys with the other correspondents just ahead of us. The enclosed places were hazy with smoke and occasionally blocked with rubble. I helped Shoshana along, she wanted to run eagerly to be there when her soldiers reached the sacred objective, the Wailing Wall.

Then the machine gun at the mosque opened fire and two soldiers twenty yards ahead of the correspondents went to their knees as though they had dropped in sudden prayer. A megaphone began to shout orders in Hebrew that bounced and echoed about the little courts and arched ways. All the Arab shops and houses were shuttered. In some places the shutters were broken and wrecked. Across the alley just ahead of us ran some thick, red, Arab treacle from a smashed jar. As if there wasn't enough blood around.

217

Then the machine gun fired again, the bullets smashing into the old stone above our heads. We were lying against a wall. I felt trapped and frightened. Shoshana was lying against me on the inside and her face was rigid. 'Not now,' she whispered. 'God, not now.' The soldiers and the correspondents ahead were unable to move because of the machine gun. It fired again, with a terrific chatter, and gouged a channel out of the stonework ten feet up. The next burst was lower, cutting across the shutters of an Arab shop just ahead of us.

'They'll have us in a minute,' grunted Dov. We couldn't get out backwards because the area behind us was an open courtyard, fully exposed. Zoo Baby lumbered up and moved towards the smashed shutters ahead of us. He retreated and then lunged at the shutter with his meaty shoulder. It split and splintered and he fell forwards comically into the shop. His fat sweaty head poked cheerfully around the corner. 'Okay,' he called. 'Come in. The shop is open.'

We ran, doubled up and flung ourselves through the jagged opening he had made. We pressed ourselves against the near wall as the machine gun opened fire again, a few yards up the street.

'That was better than your dance, Zoo Baby,' said Shoshana, touching him. 'We will wait here until they are destroyed. I could not bear to be killed now that we almost have the city.'

We were in a barber's shop with three round, swivel chairs, big cracked mirrors and deep sinks. 'I'll have a haircut while we wait,' said O'Sullivan.

It was not long. The Arabs with the machine gun fired twice more and then there was a close, violent explosion, and a whistle sounded like a conclusion of a football match. They did not fire again. O'Sullivan said: 'That seems to have settled that.'

'We can go?' asked Shoshana. 'I want to be at the Wall.'

O'Sullivan cautioned her to wait. Then an Israeli officer bent to the size of a dwarf came with a funny mechanical run up the alley and called in to us in angry Hebrew.

Shoshana said: 'We cannot move yet. He says there are

still snipers. He is very angry because we are here. Especially a woman. Maybe he does not know this is Israel.'

Zoo Baby then sat in one of the tubby chairs before the barber's mirror. He swung himself easily and made fat faces at himself. I laughed and sat in the chair beside him.

As soon as I sat down I got the pain in my kidneys again. I cried out and my back arched up. They thought I had been shot, but before anyone could move towards me a line of sniper's bullets drilled down the mirror in front of Zoo Baby. The last one hit him behind the ear, killing him at once. It was a mad situation. My pain was so intense that it even overcame my horror of his killing. I howled and he was dead. Shoshana rushed to me, because she too thought I had been hit, but I waved a panicked hand towards Zoo Baby. 'Go to him,' I squealed. 'It's only my back.'

O'Sullivan, still not comprehending, pulled me to the floor of the shop. 'See to him, for God's sake,' I spluttered. 'I'm all right.' O'Sullivan went to Zoo Baby and he and Dov tugged the big, dead man to the floor. There was a blood mark and a black hole behind his ear, but there was not a lot of bleeding. Shoshana was hanging over him, weeping and rubbing his fat hands. As though that would do any good.

An hour later we went to the Wailing Wall. We went because that is where everyone was going. Other men had died on the way. We saw the bodies of five Arabs and three Israeli soldiers in the steep alleys as we went towards the Temple area. There was still some shooting, but not much. Jerusalem was in the happy hands of the Jews.

We reached an elevated place, overlooking the great stones of the wall. Fires still burned, and dust still came from the debris of the ancient surrounding buildings. But the sun was in the clear and unperturbed swallows were flying about the Wailing Wall. Below crowds of Israeli soldiers were weeping and kissing the stones and posting little pieces of paper containing prayers through its ancient cracks. Dov walked down there alone and I watched him go slowly to kiss the wall. The religion dictated that Shoshana could not go with him, but only watch.

O'Sullivan, starkly thin, stood with me witnessing it all, detached from it as I was. We did not understand. We had seen a glut of death.

I said to O'Sullivan: 'Well, it's a good wall, isn't it?'

'Oh yes,' he said, very Irish. 'It's a fine wall, right enough.'

It seems very long ago now. They took me with all the other war casualties to hospital at Ramat Gan, outside Tel Aviv. They said I had sand from the Negev Desert in my kidneys. I was the only one to be injured by sand in the entire six days of the war. It took a painful month to get it clear. Shoshana came to see me every day and when I left the hospital we went to live in Jerusalem in the dusty house in Jaffa Road.

We lasted seven months together and then she went away with an Israeli schoolteacher to live on a kibbutz right against the border with Jordan. Selma I saw riding with the handsome Arab mayor of a small town on the Israeli-occupied West Bank. They had a big American car and they were driving through what had always been the Israeli sector of Jerusalem, in the direction that would take them towards both her houses. I half called to her, but she did not see me.

My return to England was a glamorous event, dutifully drummed up by Philip, my agent and Eric, my manager. The heroic publicity was tremendous and all my concerts were sold out. But I had to keep doing recitals for Israeli charities.

About three weeks ago I was lying awake in Faith's bed when I heard again the notes that Herr Scheerer had hummed in his last living minutes in the hot desert. Someone in the dockland street was whistling them in the early hollow hours. I lay and laughed quietly to myself. Dear old Scheerer, the grand master of Wagner, had died humming the tune of *Two Lovely Black Eyes*.

God knows why.

Leslie Thomas
Stand Up Virgin Soldiers 75p

On the eve of their return to Blighty, Brigg and the other boozy,
browned-off reluctant heroes of National Service are sentenced to a
further six months in Panglia Barracks, Singapore . . . the latest hilarious
instalment of their misadventures.

Orange Wednesday £1.25

The interior-sprung mattress took the excitement out of sex for
Prudence. Prudence took the excitement out of Lieutenant Brunel
Hopkins. Then she told him of Orange Wednesday.

That Old Gang of Mine £1.25

Meet ODDS – the Ocean Drive Delinquent Society – a band of geriatric
drop-outs chasing excitement and danger in their twilight years in the
Florida sun. There's Ari the Greek, K-K-K-K-Katy the dancing queen,
Molly Mandy who supplies the gang's arms cache (and one and only
bullet), and ex-hood Sidewalk Joe.

Hot on their heels comes the baffled Salvatore, local police captain, and
bumbling private eye Zaharran. Never was organized crime so
disorganized.

'Hilarious' DAILY MIRROR

The Love Beach £1.50

Sometimes Isslyn Davies wrestled with his conscience, other times
with Bird, a lissom seventeen-year-old . . . Preparations for a Royal
Visit to the fabled South Sea island – a twilight colony ridden with
petty jealousies, social taboos and love affairs – bring problems for
everyone . . .

George MacDonald Fraser
Flashman £1.25

This fascinating first instalment of the Flashman Papers solves the mystery of what happened to Harry Flashman – that cad and bully from *Tom Brown's Schooldays* – after he was expelled from Rugby. Self-confessed rotter, liar, womanizer and coward, he relates to us his early career in Lord Cardigan's exclusive 11th Light Dragoons, his scandalous conduct in bed and battle and how he quite undeservedly became a hero of the British Empire.

Royal Flash £1.25

The second part of the now celebrated Flashman papers, that saga of triumphant dishonour, reveals how Sir Harry Flashman VC – arch-cad and lecher – is lured to Germany by an unscrupulous adventuress and utterly confuses the Schleswig-Holstein question.

Flash for Freedom £1.25

The third outrageous instalment of the immortal Flashman Papers, 1848–9, plunges our hero, all unwillingly, into the West African slave trade. Soon he is fleeing from Dahomey Amazons, outwitting the American Navy, helping abolitionists up the Mississippi and being rescued from slave catchers by Abraham Lincoln . . .

Flashman in the Great Game £1.25

The most decorated coward in her Majesty's service – ever ready to cock an elegant leg over princess or get-away horse as opportunity or self-preservation dictates – plumbs new depths of knavery in the Indian Mutiny . . . In and out of disguise, in and out of beds, prisons, sieges and battles, Flashy remains a fellow of infinite cunning and resource.

Tom Sharpe
The Great Pursuit £1.25

'Frensic . . . a snuff-taking, port-drinking literary agent . . . receives a
manuscript from an anonymous author's solicitor – "an odyssey of lust . . .
a filthy story with an even filthier style." Foreseeing huge profits in the
US, Frensic places the book with the Al Capone of American publishing,
Hutchmeyer, "the most illiterate publisher in the world" . . .'
LISTENER

'The funniest novelist writing today' THE TIMES

Wilt £1.25

'Henry Wilt works humbly at his Polytechnic dinning Eng. Lit. into the
unreceptive skulls of rude mechanicals, his nights in fantasies of
murdering his gargantuan, feather-brained wife, half-consummated
when he dumps a life-sized inflatable doll in a building site hole, and is
grilled by the police, his wife being missing, stranded on a mud bank
with a gruesome American dyke' GUARDIAN

'Superb farce' TRIBUNE

' . . . triumphs by a slicing wit' DAILY MIRROR

You can buy these and other Pan books from booksellers and
newsagents; or direct from the following address:
Pan Books, Sales Office, Cavaye Place, London SW10 9PG
Send purchase price plus 25p for the first book and 10p for
each additional book, to allow for postage and packing
Prices quoted are applicable in the UK

While every effort is made to keep prices low, it is sometimes
necessary to increase prices at short notice. Pan Books reserve
the right to show on covers and charge new retail prices which
may differ from those advertised in the text or elsewhere